HUNTED &
SEDUCED

SHELLEY MUNRO

MUNRO PRESS

Hunted & Seduced

Copyright © 2025 by Shelley Munro

Print ISBN: 978-1-99-106378-6
E-book ISBN: 978-0-473-34437-5

Editor: Mary Moran
Cover: Kim Killion, The Killion Group, Inc.

Munro Press, New Zealand.

First Munro Press electronic publication December 2015
First Munro Press print publication February 2025

DEDICATION

For Paul, my husband, partner in crime, and fellow adventurer.
Every day is a good day.

INTRODUCTION

Love at first sight...

When she arrives on the planet Viros, Gweneth Swithin takes one look at royal bodyguard Ellard Tetsu and her inner feline—the one she didn't know existed—falls for the silent, alpha shapeshifter. She's thrilled and excited at the way her half-feline side has made her existence known and trusts her instincts when it comes to Ellard. He *is* her mate, and maybe she can have it all...if only the stubborn male would stop running.

The heart wants what the heart wants...

Ellard can't understand why the young and beautiful Gweneth is interested in him when she could choose one of the many handsome or powerful males who reside in the city, one who is whole and not broken. Despite the attraction he feels, he makes himself scarce, but Gweneth has a plan to stake her claim and isn't above maneuvering behind the scenes in order to have a chance with Ellard.

A royal assignment, undertaken together, changes the stakes into an adventure that can make or break this fledgling relationship...if they manage to survive.

Warning: contains a headstrong virgin heroine and a handicapped hero, a ghost or two and alien villains. Mix and see the sparks fly.

CHAPTER 1

HOUSE OF THE CAT CASTLE, VIROS CITY, PLANET VIROS

Ellard Tetsu's nostrils flared, and a shudder zapped down his spine, each of his feline senses under assault. A sneeze built and built until it exploded free with cosmic force. He wiped his streaming eyes and stalked along the corridor linking the public reception area in the castle to the council meeting room, his blurry gaze sweeping every small alcove he passed in case it harbored a woman—one of the *Indy* crew.

One of the unpredictable females who seemed out to get him this cycle.

Flowers. Stinky flowers and a maze of chemicals followed him as close as a tail. He stunk, positively reeked of floral scent. No chance to change before the council meeting commenced. He'd already been running late due to a training snafu when those women had accosted him with perfume bottles. Grata! He lifted the hem of his tunic with his Stores—his artificial right arm—and promptly sneezed again.

Those women were a phrullin' menace and Gweneth Swithin...

For once, her beautiful and mischievous face remained absent and he scanned the alcove to his left, every instinct alive with suspicion. She wasn't hiding behind the feline statue. The fact should have relaxed him, but then he wondered where she was, what she was doing, and worse, who she was gifting with her presence.

His feline stirred beneath his skin, agitated at her absence while he—the man—was glad. She...no! He increased his pace and jogged the remaining distance to the House of the Cat council room.

The ornate timepiece, imported by the previous queen at great expense from the planet Tempo, rang out the cycle portion, the tiny jeweled figures within the dome jerking into a programmed dance. He burst into the council room and came to an appalled halt.

As he'd suspected, he arrived last. His brother and friends wore irritated expressions while the council members already sat around the large oval table. A variety of refreshments covered the surface, and the more efficient males had readied their personal comp pads to take notes. Light and heat poured through the floor-to-ceiling windows, and the stink of the perfume made his nose twitch in a familiar manner. A sneeze burst free before he could get out a greeting.

"Ah." Prince Jarlath, Ellard's closest friend, grimaced, his handsome face frozen as he attempted to breathe yet not smell the stench. "They sprayed you too."

Beside him, Lynx, the current king, and Shiloh, Ellard's brother, were bare-chested, their tunics dumped in a heap in the far corner of the room.

Ry Coppersmith, the tall and fit captain of the *Indefatigable* and a new addition to the Viros council, added his tunic to the pile of laundry. The feline shifter, formerly of the planet Ibrox, let out a snort that held a smidge of humor. "Stinks like an Ornum whorehouse. What were they thinking?"

Six council members sat around the cloth-covered oval table, their expressions ranging from irritated to distasteful. Ellard caught the beginnings of a smirk from a younger one.

Unable to stand the pungent flowery scent a sec longer, he whipped his tunic over his head and tossed it into the corner with the others. If he wasn't so irked with the women's prank, he might have celebrated how his Stores cybertronic arm moved so fluidly. After coping with one arm for portions of the last rotation, the Stores made him feel normal again. Most strangers never noticed his artificial limb, despite the lighter gold, which didn't quite match his natural skin tones.

"I'll ring someone to remove our tunics," the secretary, one of the six council members already seated, suggested. He rose and stalked to the newly installed com system, his back rigid in distaste. A sneeze burst from him as he stabbed the call button for a servant.

Ry opened every window and door but the stillness of the cycle and the balmy weather seemed to intensify the stench.

Shiloh edged closer to him, his nose wrinkling. "Phrull, they got you good. How is the arm? Apart from the slightly paler color, it blends well with the stump. I can't see much of a joint."

Ellard flexed his artificial arm, still amazed at the real sensation. Initially, he'd hesitated about going through with the operation because the medics told him it was a one-time thing. If something went wrong, the attachment method meant...no! The chances of failure or catastrophic loss were low. The medics had assured him of that. "Almost as workable as my other one. I'm doing the exercises the cybernetic man told me to complete each day. The worse thing is having to compensate with each shift since it doesn't transform. They've designed the arm so I can remove it before a shift. Almost knocked myself out the cycle before when I started my change before I remembered to detach the Stores. I thought Jarlath was gonna split his sides laughing."

"I heard." Lynx joined them and slung a casual arm around Shiloh's shoulders.

He stared for a sec, still amazed his brother was mated with the king of the House of the Cat and a woman—a commoner and a previous slave. Things were changing rapidly on Viros, and while some of the elders and a rebel faction of naysayers preached about tradition and maintaining the same course they'd always followed, Ellard thought life had improved. He had friends—loyal companions—but the new informality at the court was taking time to become used to—at least for the older felines. He numbered a prince, a king, a duke and a queen amongst his friends, and they insisted he call them by their names instead of their titles.

The previous queen—Jarlath and Lynx's mother—hated the changes so much she'd moved from the castle into an expensive home adjoining the castle grounds. She spent a lot of the rotation off-planet visiting friends since her mate had died. Yes, things were different now.

A brisk knock on the door heralded the arrival of a cheerful servant. He stepped into the room and promptly sneezed, the sound explosive and sudden, his spiky black hair and bright green eyes reminding Ellard of a ruffled cat. "Ah, what is that stench?"

"According to my mate, it is a designer perfume from Earth," Lynx said. "Please remove our tunics and take them to the laundry for washing."

"Of course, your highness. Do you require fresh tunics?"

"No, we'll collect them after our meeting." Lynx gestured everyone to their seats. "Thank you. Leave the door. We want the stench to disperse." He stalked to the head of the table and dropped onto a gel-seat.

Ellard took a seat beside Jarlath, a part of him still amazed they thought him worthy of inclusion in the planning sessions.

Lynx studied his comp pad and tapped a few buttons, a silent signal to commence. "Right, now that the spaceport is fully functional, we need to attract visitors. We must find a way to bring in people willing to spend currency on Viros."

One of the councilors tapped his pointed turquoise-painted fingernails on the tabletop, his stocky shoulders held perfectly straight. "We need a share of the cash that goes to the casinos on Gramite."

"Exactly." Lynx studied each of them in turn, his green gaze serious and intent. "Ideas. Anything. It doesn't matter how outlandish or how impossible they appear."

Ellard made the mistake of breathing through his nose. He snorted back a tickle and commenced breathing through his mouth. Once certain he wouldn't sneeze, he spoke. "Is the new hotel ready for guests?"

"Not yet," Shiloh said. "But we need to plan."

"The workers who have come in from other planets enjoy visiting the colored sands," the councilor Jarlath had placed in charge of tourism spoke up. "The problem we've had is that outsiders have heard of the war between us and the House of Cawdor. They worry they might find themselves in the middle of renewed violence. They don't want their children playing with ours in case our kittens shift and injure them."

Shiloh snorted his disbelief, arms folded across his beefy chest. "Our young never shift at that age."

"I told them that, but they refused to believe me," the councilor said. "I don't know how the rumors started."

Lynx sniffed his arm and grimaced. "What else? Any ideas?"

"The House of Cawdor is holding a gambling tournament soon. It's a pity we couldn't entice some of their clientele over here. It's a short hop." Shiloh steepled his fingers, his brow furrowed in thought.

A squeak from near his feet drew Ellard's attention, but he mentally shrugged when it ceased. The herd of women inhabiting the castle was making him jumpy. Gweneth and the others wouldn't dare interrupt the council meeting.

"Camryn informed me the hotel furnishings are ordered, and some of the shipments are arriving already." Ry tapped his fingers on the tabletop. "They're furnishing several of the rooms this cycle."

Ah, his question answered. Gweneth was busy this morn. One less thing to upset his equilibrium. He frowned, still not understanding why the woman stalked him. She was beautiful—a young shifter female with everything in her future. He was bodyguard to Prince Jarlath, nothing in the looks department, and to top that he'd lost an arm during the war. He had nothing to offer a woman like Gweneth.

Nothing.

He'd tried to tell her. He'd tried to ignore her, and now he resorted to skulking around the castle and fleeing the sec he caught a glimpse of her. After this perfume incident, he intended to dodge her friends too.

Ry leaned back, and his gel-seat strained to conform to his relaxed posture, creaking and groaning and popping. Finally, Ry straightened and the overworked gel-chair sighed. "What about running fitness and security courses? Our soldiers are well-regarded. Perhaps we could pass some of our skills on to others who require them. Run a training school for civilians."

Lynx noted the suggestion on his comp pad. "Anything else?"

"We're not used to doing this type of thing." A junior councilor tugged his black beard then reached for his goblet of cacjuice. Spots of the pale green juice spilled when he sneezed without warning. He wiped his nose in a fastidious manner, patted the splashes dry with a kerchief and continued. "It's a foreign concept."

"Maybe so." Shiloh scowled. "But we need to change and adapt. It's necessary to our survival."

The strange squeak sounded again, and Ellard cocked his head, attempting to locate the source.

"Maybe we should ask for suggestions from the people," Shiloh suggested.

Their oldest councilor—the last remaining from Jarlath and Lynx's father's era—gasped, his stern expression appalled. "Ask the people? We've never done that before. Who knows what idiocy they'd propose."

Another high squeak.

"What is that noise?" Ry asked. "Has Royal managed to get loose again?" The rare calibore—a type of ape with shaggy black fur, big fluffy ears, sharp teeth and a tail—had attached himself to Jannike during her abduction and transportation to Manx Two. He'd become a firm favorite with the castle residents and visitors.

"If the furry creature is here, the perfume isn't bothering him," the tourism councilor commented dryly.

"When he's not in the forest with Kelvin, he's with Jannike." Lynx bent to lift the cloth and peer under the table. "Ah! Not Royal."

A woman burst from beneath the table, right near Ellard. Big green eyes, sultry pink lips, a tiny black cat tattoo on her right cheek and black hair pulled into a tight hairstyle that confined and flattened the long, luxurious locks. Immediately he wanted to touch, to loosen her hair, and he found himself reaching out with his good hand before his brain jerked into gear.

"What the devil are you doing here?" He countered his initial instinct with anger. "This is a council meeting. Men only."

Shiloh smothered a grin and helped her to stand. His brother's humor poked at Ellard's bad mood, making it swell within his chest, and the touchy-feely stuff. He hated seeing another man touching her, and he loathed that he thought that way. What did he need with a woman? Faithless, treacherous creatures.

What had Mareeka called him? A monstrosity too ugly to view for any length of time.

The memory balanced some of the angst inside him, placed him on firmer footing. He had no need of a mate, and even if he were in the market, he wouldn't take one as young and desirable as Gweneth. Most of the young feline women kept their distance and treated him like a dangerous species. Gweneth didn't behave in the same manner, which confused him.

"That is a silly rule since it is obvious none of you have a brain." Her chin jutted upward in clear challenge.

"Silence," Ellard roared and leapt to his feet. "Ry should discipline you more often since you clearly don't know the correct manner to behave. A kitten is better disciplined."

The other males glanced at him in surprise.

"It's all right, Gweneth," Lynx said after a fraught silence. "Please tell us why you are interrupting our meeting."

"And why you decided to attend," Ellard added. A thought occurred and his eyes narrowed on her. "Were you responsible for the perfume saga?"

Her pink lips pressed together, and she averted her gaze, suddenly fascinated by the number of bare chests in the council room.

"Gweneth," he prompted.

"I wanted to know what you discussed at these meetings. You hold them often, yet don't seem to get much done."

"And you needed the perfume to confuse our feline senses, so we wouldn't detect your presence," Ry said.

Gweneth gave an audible gulp.

Ry folded his arms across his chest. "I'll take that as an affirmative."

"I have an idea," she burst out, glancing in Ellard's direction.

Excitement made her eyes glow like jewels, and she'd done something with the stuff the woman called cosmetics. The black edges around her eyes made them more prominent, more enticing.

Ellard groaned inwardly. He had to get his thoughts off Gweneth. He had to persuade his feline that Gweneth was bad, bad, bad for them. They'd end up hurt again. No, better to stay far away. "You'd better go and let us get back to our meeting."

"But my idea—"

Lynx held up a hand. "Let her talk. Tell us about your idea."

"All right." Gweneth plonked her pert bottom, encased in the blue trews that Camryn and the rest of the *Indy* crew called jeans, on Ellard's seat.

A snicker sounded to Ellard's right, and he turned to scowl at Jarlath. He bared his teeth and hissed a feline warning.

"Stop that." Gweneth's tone neared snippy. "I'm trying to talk here."

To Jarlath's credit, he ceased his laughter, but his lips continued to twitch.

"The floor is yours, Gweneth." Lynx, too, was trying not to laugh.

She took an audible breath and puffed it free. Ellard wanted to tell her to spit it out, so she could leave and his feline would cease his agitation. It was getting so bad, it felt as if his skin might split. He leaned against the wall, pretending a calmness he lacked, and glared at her pretty face.

His sexy green stare held feline frustration. Gweneth bit her lip, wanting to laugh as Jarlath had laughed. Not safe. She didn't want him to throttle her, but she did want him to look at her as an eligible mate.

While it was true there were more handsome men, some of whom had shown interest in her, something about the large, hulking presence of Ellard pushed her to explore what might be.

She drew in a breath, pushed it out and began to expound on her idea.

"I think we should organize a festival. We can use it to showcase the food and drinks native to Viros, but we should also invite all the neighboring planets to have a stall to display and sell their goods and produce. The festival could run for maybe seven cycles with concerts and shows. Maybe organize city tours and show off everything Viros has to offer." Whew! That perfume stunk with the sharp piquancy of a well-fed hell-horse. No wonder Kaya had donated it to the cause.

Ry tapped his chin in a thoughtful manner. "Not a bad idea."

"Why should we invite our neighbors when we're doing all the work?" the councilor with the painted nails demanded.

"Because if we work together, we'll have more to offer tourists." Gweneth started speaking faster with enthusiasm. "It will foster closer relations between you all, and if you invite them to take part, spreading the word will become easier. With more planets involved, it will give us a bigger reach. Also, if we host the festival, it will mean the visitors will spend currency, stay in our hotels, and use our spaceport. If it works, we could make this festival an annual fixture. In time, it will grow and extend our reach. You should get businesses to do proposals as to what services they can offer. Craftsmen and women can have stalls selling their wares. Charge the locals a smaller fee to have a stall. Put the currency raised back into rebuilding the city and for public facilities. If you get everyone involved, the enthusiasm generated will go a long way toward building bridges for past problems."

The king and his mate exchanged a glance, but Gweneth never relaxed until she saw them start to grin.

"That is an excellent idea, Gweneth," Shiloh said.

Lynx nodded. "Yes, I think that will work well and make us popular with our neighbors."

Pleased, Gweneth inhaled again to settle the nerves that buzzed around the pit of her stomach. She'd done it. Now to set the next bit of her plan in motion. She took another breath and sneezed. Ugh, perhaps they'd overdone the perfume. "I believe your best weather—the most settled times—occur soon. We should be ready. I believe the House of Cawdor have a big gambling tournament then. We need to organize our festival to coincide with that to increase our chances of more visitors."

"But that won't give us enough time," Jarlath said.

Gweneth shook her head and surreptitiously pressed a hand against her stomach to still her renewed anxiety. "It will if we split into teams and visit each of the neighbors as soon as possible."

"I can't travel at present," the secretary protested. "My mate is ill."

She ignored the interruption. "Ry, the *Indy* crew could pitch in and help. I'd welcome a chance to visit a neighboring planet."

"I approve of the idea. This is what we'll do." Lynx rattled off assignments for the councilors. "Report back on the morrow. We'll have a meeting each morn. Shiloh and I will consider which of our neighbors to approach and will announce further division of labor at our next meeting. I want you to all think about the local businesses and services that would want to avail themselves of the opportunity. Make a memo."

Everyone started to file from the meeting room, but Gweneth remained seated. Ellard strode out with Jarlath and she took the opportunity to ogle his backside. The male might not possess the pretty face of his brother or friends, but his body rated top marks. Not even his cybertronic arm disturbed her. She sighed as he disappeared. Such pretty and kind green eyes when he forgot to scowl. What she wouldn't give to see him smile at her.

"Gweneth?"

She started to find herself alone in the council room with Lynx and Shiloh.

"Was there something else?" Lynx asked.

"Yes," she blurted. "I want to be partnered with Ellard. I want to visit a neighboring planet with Ellard so I can get to know him better." Seduce him, actually, but she wouldn't confess that snippet to the king of Viros.

"I see." Lynx shared a speaking glance with Shiloh.

Shiloh—big like Ellard, but much prettier—fixed her with his gaze. "My brother is much older than you."

"Yes." She nodded in agreement. Her feline remained unconcerned about the age difference. Instead, she'd come alive the sec she'd glimpsed Ellard Tetsu, when she'd thought she'd remain in a humanoid form for the rest of her life. It hadn't mattered. Ry had told her so. Camryn and Mogens had backed up Ry's statement. She was important, no matter what form her body took, despite how little her father thought of her.

"You realize Ellard doesn't want a mate," Lynx said.

"Yes."

"Yet you want to visit another planet with him, even though he'll behave like a grouchy bear-sloth," Shiloh added.

She nodded. "I have no idea what a bear-sloth is, but yes, I still want to spend time with him." She hesitated and after a lengthy pause, went with her gut instinct. These were steady felines, honest and kind males, otherwise Jannike wouldn't have mated with them. "I think he is my mate, and I want him to stop his mental struggles and get used to the idea."

Shiloh scowled. "What makes you think he's your mate?"

"My feline came to life within me. She wriggles and writhes until I think my skin might burst. I've never shifted before, but the instant I saw him, I felt this. I can't shift since I'm half feline, but I want Ellard."

Lynx and Shiloh shared a glance. Probably speaking to each other via their minds. Jannike possessed the ability now, and she knew Ry and Camryn spoke via telepathy at times. As she watched them, Shiloh grinned and nodded then they focused on her.

"All right. We'll team you with Ellard," Lynx agreed.

"But take heed, Gweneth, you had better not toy with him. Be very sure because he has suffered enough in the past. I'd hate to see my brother hurt again," Shiloh warned, his eyes edging toward kitty-cat in the same way Ry's did when his emotions ran high.

"I won't. I promise. I've heard the gossip, and I would never hurt him. In my eyes, he is a hero."

Shiloh softened. "He is at that. You realize my brother is stubborn. He won't take your maneuvering well."

A snort burst from her, and she clapped her hand over her mouth in consternation. "I'm sorry."

"What were you thinking?" Lynx asked.

"That Ellard seems slow on the uptake. Flirting and feminine behavior isn't working."

"So you're taking things to the next level." Lynx's grin widened to toothy.

"That's my plan," she said primly.

"I think he is a lucky man." Shiloh laughed at Lynx's tetchy growl after his compliment. "We'll try to point my stubborn brother in the right direction. The rest is up to you."

Later that eve in the king's private apartments.

"Are you sure we're doing the right thing?" Lynx asked as he and Shiloh strode into the royal suite—a place of easy comfort where the three of them could cast off their royal status and duties and be themselves. They'd cleared out most of the furniture used by Lynx's parents, the former king and queen, and had gone for the minimalistic look they all favored after living in cramped conditions aboard spaceships.

"Problem?" Jannike, formerly from Manx Two and their mate and queen, handed them each a glass of apecot port. Her blonde hair hung down her back these days, longer and arranged in a messy braid. Her face and body were also rounder since she carried the royal heir, a fact that still amazed Lynx. They were going to be parents. Mind-blowing and a little scary.

"Gweneth." Shiloh summed up their discussion in the one word.

"Ah." Jannike poured herself a cajuice, activated a hover-table to rest her drink, then flopped onto the nearest gel-chair and propped up her feet on a sturdy yet priceless antique table from Septius.

Shiloh bent over to pat her rounded tummy. She batted his hands away.

Lynx chuckled as he sank onto a gel-seat opposite her and set his feet on the same sturdy table. Shiloh joined him, his mates' proximity pleasing his feline.

"Well, is that it?" Jannike fixed them both with an intimidating stare. "I'm the queen. You can't keep secrets from me. What has Gweneth done now?"

"She organized us all to get sprayed with perfume."

Jannike's lips twitched, and her shoulders moved in tiny, jerky increments.

"But you knew that," Shiloh said, cuddling into Lynx. "I'm wagering you helped with the spraying."

Her eyes glowed, her feline pushing to the surface. She stood and sauntered over to the gel-seat he and Shiloh sat on, squeezing between the two of them. "I might have. Tell me what happened with Gweneth."

"She asked us to pair her with Ellard," Shiloh answered.

"She came up with a brilliant idea to attract visitors. A festival that spotlights food, the arts and attractions here on Viros. In order to move on the idea, she suggested we visit neighboring planets in pairs to solicit other races and make it a combined effort."

Jannike leaned into Shiloh and smiled. "She wants to have some alone time with Ellard. A bold plan."

"It's a gamble," Shiloh agreed, his hand coming to rest on Jannike's stomach. "My brother is stubborn and edges toward inflexible about some things. He's decided to do without women."

Jannike gasped with exaggerated horror. "No sex at all?"

"I never alleged that," Shiloh said dryly. "I believe he visits the whorehouse on occasion."

Jannike tugged on Shiloh's ears. "I'd better not discover you and Lynx visiting the whorehouse." She paused and Lynx could practically see her thoughts whir. "In fact, I think I'll outlaw them. I'm the queen. I can do that, right?"

"No, you can't," Lynx said. "Some of the soldiers would revolt. But back to Gweneth. We told her we'd honor her request, although I'm not sure how to pitch it to Ellard."

"Make it impossible for him to say no," Jannike suggested. "You say others are going to visit neighboring planets? Send Ellard away to do something for you that will keep him out of the city while you arrange the rest of the visits. Keep one aside for Ellard and Gweneth, and once everyone else has left, pitch it to Ellard that Gweneth deserves a spot since it was her idea, but you're worried for her safety. Appeal to his chivalry and his bodyguard profession. Make it so he can't refuse."

Lynx shared a glance with Shiloh before turning his attention to Jannike. "That is plain sneaky."

She grinned. "Yep."

Shiloh brushed a lock of black hair away from his green eyes. "I think it will work. Let's do it. We'll make a list of suitable planets—those with peaceful inhabitants, and meantime, I think Ellard and Jarlath could go to the colored sands on the other side of Viros to check on suitable building sites. The perfect place to build another hotel."

Jannike sipped her cajuice. "Excellent. Now that we've organized Gweneth's love life, can we focus on our own?"

Lynx's office, House of the Cat castle

"No." Ellard bunched his hands to fists. Even his artificial

17

fingers flexed more than usual, such was his determination not to agree to the king's assignment. "Can't someone else go with Gweneth?" No way in this universe he was going anywhere with the bewitching woman. Bah! The idea of being alone with temptation... No. Just no.

Lynx sighed with exaggerated patience. "I've told you. We've already sent everyone else off in pairs. The dragon shapeshifters on Narenda were the last to reply. Originally, Gweneth wasn't going to go, but she has done so much of the organization. She deserves a trip to Narenda, but I can't send her alone. It's not safe. You're a capable bodyguard and the only trustworthy male free to undertake the task."

"My job is to watch Jarlath. I can't leave him," Ellard protested.

"Jarlath is going to help us with matters on this end." He gestured at the silent Shiloh standing at his side. "He and Keira are staying at the castle for the duration." Lynx looked as if he fought a smile. "He'll be quite safe with us. Besides, he's been training with Ry and Jannike. He's not the same pompous upper-class jibberjabber he was when Shiloh and I left Viros."

A smile curved Ellard's lips, despite his bad temper. True. These days Jarlath held responsibilities, a worthy man, and Keira, his mate, was perfect for him even though Ellard had thought otherwise at the onset of their relationship.

"So you'll do it," Shiloh said. "Good, that is one thing off our minds."

"What? No," Ellard snapped. "Gweneth is a troublemaker. And the clothes she wears..." His mind slipped to her tanned legs and her cleavage—the vision she'd appeared in the dress thing. Appalled at the direction of his thoughts, he shook his head. Hard.

Lynx grinned. "Jannike told us there is nothing wrong with the way she dresses. That's the way they dress on Earth."

"Jannike and Camryn never wear clothes like that," Ellard pointed out, his voice emerging clipped and disapproving. But his mind slipped to a memory without permission. One of Gweneth in a brief red thing at the swimming hole. Two pieces of fabric to screen her breasts and her...female parts. Never mind that the other women who'd arrived with Ry Coppersmith aboard the spaceship *Indefatigable* had worn similar apparel. Gweneth had made him stare. All those curves...

"Jannike wears Earth clothes sometimes," Shiloh said with approval.

Lynx chuckled. "She says she prefers clothes she can fight in, although now that she is expecting our first child she won't be able to train, and Camryn is almost ready to give birth."

"She looks as if she might pop," Ellard said.

Shiloh thumped him on the shoulder. "Don't tell her that."

"Back to Gweneth." Lynx scanned his comp pad. "We're short of transport. You'll have to take our ship."

"What?" Ellard realized he was gaping at his brother and Lynx. He snapped his mouth shut. "You never let anyone fly the *Gallant*."

Lynx thumbed to his next page of notes. "You'll need to leave on the morrow. Let us know this eve if you agree to take Gweneth with you, otherwise we'll have to choose a senior soldier."

"Who?" Ellard demanded, his fingers flexing again.

"Durant might be suitable," Shiloh suggested. "Or perhaps send Councilor Chewang. He's sensible and would make sure Gweneth stayed safe. He sounded keen when I mentioned the task to him earlier this morn."

"No!" Ellard snapped. "Durant is an idiot, and Chewang has so many females I've lost count. He'd seduce her. He'd hurt her."

"Chewang has a steady business. He comes from an excellent family. Gweneth might be the woman to capture his interest." Shiloh shared a quick glance with Lynx. "She bears the feline mark on her cheek, even though she can't shift. She would make any Virosian male a fine mate."

Phrull. He couldn't let Gweneth go to Narenda with either of those males. His shoulders slumped momentarily before he straightened. "All right, I'll do it. But Gweneth has to listen to me and not do anything stupid. She needs to follow my orders instantly with no argument."

Lynx nodded. "Of course. We've already spoken to her."

"I'll go and tell Chewang his presence isn't required," Shiloh said. "He'll be disappointed."

Ellard grunted and turned to Lynx once his brother disappeared. "All right. You'd better give me specifics of what you want me to do. At least that way, the assignment will get done correctly."

A sound came from the corner of the room, and Lynx coughed, clearing his throat. "Beg your pardon. I believe Jannike told us the Earth expression is a frog in my throat."

"What is a frog?"

"A creature that lives near water, ponds, and such."

Ellard grimaced, none the wiser. "This Earth place is weird. I can't understand the women half the time, and Ry and their pilot, Nanu, are just as bad."

Lynx grinned, his feline-green eyes glowing with a private thought.

Ellard decided not to ask about the cause of the humor. "Tell me what we need to do on Narenda and who we need to speak with."

He listened and nodded.

"I'll send the full details to the shipboard comp pad," Lynx said once he finished talking. "But those are the basics."

"I'll go and pack." Ellard left the king's office, his mind full of all he needed to do. It wouldn't be that bad. Most of his cycle would be consumed with piloting the ship and plotting the course. They'd speak with the dragon shapeshifters on Narenda, get their cooperation, and fly back to Viros. No problem.

CHAPTER 2

ON BOARD THE GALLANT SPACESHIP, HEADING FOR NARENDA

Gweneth slanted a glance at Ellard as their ship plunged into the darkness of space and the green-and-brown planet of Viros grew smaller. His stubborn jaw appeared hard enough to break her fist—should she decide to hit him, and the thought had crossed her mind. His pretty green eyes remained glued on the instrument panels. His conversation nil.

Her mouth firmed while her brain busily played the angles. Somehow, some way, she had to get him to talk. Something more and better than manly grunts. Flirtation, but nothing too overt. But that needed to come after he started conversing.

An entire cycle portion passed in silence, and she thought back to the advice she'd received from her friends, those who had become her family.

Ry had told her not to prattle at him too much because males didn't enjoy useless conversation.

Camryn had warned her not to let him bully her because that set a bad precedent.

Jannike had suggested taking him by surprise and tying him up until he succumbed.

Kaya had told her to get her hands on his cock, to pet it and stroke it, and he'd follow her around like a pet.

Nanu had suggested she strip off her clothes and proposed she practice with him.

And Mogens had told her to be herself and trust in fate because the clouds predicted beneficial news.

All excellent advice, but she still needed to get him to *see* her as a potential mate instead of a troublesome child, which meant getting him talking.

"Would it be all right if I put on some music?" she asked in desperation, the view gone since they'd long ago left the vicinity of Viros. The bridge of the *Gallant* was smaller than that of the *Indy,* with seating for two in front of the instruments—the minimal lights and guidance systems not much in the way of distraction—and the silent disapproval started to weigh on her chest and her conscience. She couldn't continue this nerve-racking silence for another cycle portion.

He shot her a suspicious glance. "What sort of music?"

"Would you like to hear some Earth music? I have lots of different types. You can choose. Please, the silence is driving me mad. If I can't play music, I'll start prattling, and I know you hate that," she ended in a rush.

They stared at each other for a long moment, but she couldn't read him. Her stomach twisted, and a frisson of awareness swept her, tiny whooshes of pleasure ghosting across her breasts and to her sex. She experienced the same enjoyment whenever she used her vibrator, so definitely sexual in nature.

Weird. Ellard bore little resemblance to the man of her dreams—the one she'd described to her Earth friend, Olivia. Yes, he was big and strong, but no one could call him handsome. Some might comment on his arm since his right one was artificial. He never spoke much, didn't initiate conversations, and wasn't outgoing. Yet no other male made her feel this way.

Only Ellard.

"We could listen to music," he conceded.

Yes! "I'll play some of everything. I have lots of different playlists."

He appeared baffled as he often did when she used Earth jargon. Never mind. She'd start and see what happened. "This is classic rock."

A gritty male voice started to sing about being back in black. Since Ellard refrained from comment and scanned the instruments before shifting to autopilot, she relaxed a fraction, let the song finish and change to another about champions. Music she'd come to love, and each time one of the familiar songs played memories flashed to the fore.

Memories of her on the *Indy*.

Memories of dancing and shared laughter.

Memories of family.

Her stomach bucked at the thought, but it was true. Her friends were more family to her than her father had ever been. After the running of the Dowry Derby, he'd handed her over to Ry and turned his back on her. Not once had he attempted to contact her. She took after her mother, and the resemblance counted as an unforgivable sin in his eyes.

Another portion of a cycle passed, less strained thanks to the music.

"Want something to eat?" She unfastened her security harness and stood, aware she'd start blubbering if she continued to think

23

SHELLEY MUNRO

of her father's rejection. Ellard wouldn't deal well with tears. She sensed it without proof.

He unfastened his own harness. "I want to research Narenda anyway. I knew of its existence but know little of the planet and its residents."

"I decided to send the link message to them at the last moment. Lynx and Shiloh suspected the leaders would ignore their invitation. They attempted to land once and were escorted away by fighter ships."

"What?" He sounded appalled. "Lynx never told me that. I thought this was an easy assignment."

No, no, no! She'd hate him to insist they turn around and travel back to Viros. "As I mentioned, they responded after everyone else had left. Lynx and Shiloh want to meet all our neighbors and have contact with them. It's safer that way. Lynx said something about know thine enemy. They are offering a hand of friendship by extending an invitation for us to visit. They're willing to listen. Besides, do you think Ry and Camryn would let me go to Narenda if they thought the assignment would place me in danger? Or Jannike?" She crossed her fingers and prayed her gabble reassured him. "No, they wouldn't. Nor would Lynx and Shiloh. Go on, admit it." She paused because prattling made her mouth dry. She swallowed and swallowed again after sneaking a glance at him.

She hoped this stern expression vanished in the bedroom because that would never do. A definite mood-killer. "I'll sort out something to eat."

She fled to the tiny galley without a backward peek, her heart pounding with a *boom-boom-boom,* loud enough to alert a feline there was something amiss. How would she ever get him to kiss her when he kept his distance? What would Olivia do? For almost another portion of a cycle, she dithered and considered the matter while she made sandwiches, taking her time to regain equilibrium.

Set the mood.

Flirtation.

Finally, after even more soul-searching, she plonked the sandwiches on a small float table and set it to deliver to the cockpit. Once it floated off, she picked up two tubes of a fruit drink—a type of citrus-flavored fruit, purple in color and one she'd never tried until landing on Viros.

"Here you go." She plonked into her seat in the cockpit. "I hope the sandwich is okay for you." She batted her eyelashes in her first attempt at flirtation.

"It's fine." He glanced at her and tilted his head to the side.

It was working. She added a smile and continued a slow and sexy blink.

His brows rose. "What is wrong with your eyes?"

A puff of breath escaped her and she cursed under her breath. Stupid man. "I'm flirting with you."

"Why?"

This time the swear words slipped free. "Fuck a duck."

"What?"

Honestly. Did she need to hit the man over the skull to make him understand? She opened her mouth and let her tongue slide out to moisten her lips. Not a calculated move, but holy heck, she'd attracted his attention. To test her conclusion, she repeated the action and his gaze followed the slow glide of her tongue like a pet on a leash.

She still needed to get him talking—a topic to help him relax and pass the flight. "How does it feel to shift to feline?"

He stared a fraction harder, his brow knitted together like an Earth dishrag. "What?"

"I've never shifted, and I want to know what to expect, should a miracle occur."

"You want to shift?"

"Of course I do. Why wouldn't I? Jannike and Camryn can shift. I bear the feline mark on my cheek, yet I've never shifted. Describe

25

SHELLEY MUNRO

it to me. Please. When did you start shifting? Was it scary?" *Oops, prattle alert.*

"Prince Jarlath and I shifted at thirteen rotations." His gaze softened, the green of his eyes lightening as his mind drifted into memories, the dish rag effect fading to smooth, tanned skin. His lips—so sensual they tempted her to touch—curved into the beginnings of a smile. "If you ask him, he'll tell you he shifted first. That's not true." He flashed her a genuine grin, and her breath stalled, her tube of fruit juice halting halfway to her mouth.

The spurt of humor made all the difference. It took his face from plain to arresting. Never handsome. No, her Ellard escaped handsome, but oh, he exhibited heart.

"So tell me the truth." Gweneth set her tube down and leaned closer, mesmerized by his expression.

"I shifted a min earlier than Jarlath. We'd made a deal a couple of rotations earlier to attempt a shift together the sec we felt our felines stir."

"Did you do that?"

"We did. Jarlath told me his skin itched, and he felt as if his chest might burst." Ellard chuckled. "I couldn't feel a thing, but I told Jarlath otherwise."

"You lied?"

"My pride was on the line."

She smiled, easily imagining the two young felines indulging in a case of one-upmanship. "What happened next?"

"We decided not to tell my father. He was in charge of training us. Lynx and Shiloh too."

"You all grew up together?" She couldn't help the note of wistfulness bleeding into her voice. She had grown up alone with Amme, her nanny, as a companion. Her father allowed none of the other children on the planet of Ornum to play with the governor's daughter, and then, once she'd matured and the feline tattoo formed on her cheek, her father permitted no one to see

26

her face either. She'd embarrassed him, and he couldn't bear to look at her. He'd ordered her to wear a full mask whenever she left the governor's mansion. He'd lost her respect at that stage, but stupidly, she still yearned for acceptance, a show of love.

"We did. It was always Jarlath and me against our two brothers, Shiloh and Lynx. Shiloh and I grew up knowing we'd act as bodyguards to the two princes."

"And Shiloh and Lynx ended up as mates. Did you and Jarlath ever—"

"No. Jarlath became smitten at the first meeting with Keira. After he met Keira, things changed. Our lives are different now."

"For the better?" Curiosity and interest ate at her. He'd never talked to her this way before—as if she was an adult. It was...pleasant.

"I didn't think so at the time," Ellard said. "I told Jarlath he should listen to his parents and marry someone from a respectable family, someone from the upper classes."

"He went his own way."

"Yes. He kept visiting Keira because he enjoyed the pies she baked. At least, that was his story. I knew otherwise and tried to tell him to use her and move on."

"He still refused to listen."

"Yes, and looking back, I can see their relationship works well. Life has improved at the castle and in the city."

"But it took a war to change things."

"Yes." Something—maybe pain—flickered across his face.

"Back to you and Jarlath shifting. What happened after you fibbed to Jarlath?"

"We went outside to the rear garden where my father used to conduct our training. Although my father had prepared us and told us what to expect and how to advance the shift, we were both nervous."

"And you still couldn't feel your feline?" This was pleasant. He'd been chatting for almost a full cycle portion without freezing her out.

"No."

"You put on a good front?"

"A what?"

"Jarlath believed you because you behaved with confidence."

Ellard nodded. "He doesn't suspect to this day. We disrobed and pictured our felines. I closed my eyes and pictured a black feline, concentrating so hard I wouldn't have known if the House of Cawdor launched an attack on the city. Then, all of a sudden, I felt my feline and the change rushed through me so fast I almost blanked out with the pain."

"Camryn told us her first shift hurt. Jannike can't remember because her shift occurred while she was half asleep."

"It gets easier with practice." Ellard paused to take a bite of his sandwich. "This is good."

"It's an Earth dish. I learned how to cook when we visited Earth."

He picked up his drink. "My shift burned like firehell. According to Jarlath his never hurt, but I still don't believe him."

"I think it would be worth it, even if it is painful."

"It is. The rush of extra sensory perception is amazing."

Gweneth glanced out the viewport and let out a horrified squeak. "What's that? Why aren't the sensors screaming?"

The deep black of space now writhed with streams of blood red. Chunks of rock or some other type of material hid within the streams of colorful vapor material. They started to pelt the body of the ship. *Rat-a-tat-tat. Rat-a-tat-tat.*

Ellard cursed, his hands racing over the controls to regain manual control. Belatedly, an alarm began to screech, and Gweneth gripped the arms of her seat as the ship began to shake. The engine chugged instead of purring. Alarming pauses in the clamor of the engine brought another flood of curses.

"Phrullin' heap of fodo crap."

"What is that stuff?"

"Space debris."

Gweneth froze, her gaze on the swirling mass of color outside the ship. "Where did it come from?"

"Maybe a crash or cargo dumped on purpose. Any number of sources. Known debris fields are marked on the star maps."

"But not this one?"

"No."

"What do you want me to do?"

"Strap in," he ordered as the ship began to buck. "These things are unpredictable. I've heard rumors of people creating them on purpose and designing them to disable ships."

"Space pirates?"

"Yes. Put on the harness."

Gweneth did as he asked, her eyes widening as the red dust thickened until it obscured vision. The entire ship shuddered and whined, dropping without warning. The pelt and shriek of objects striking the hull became a litany. *Bang. Bang. Bang. Thump.*

She dug her fingers into her thighs and bit her bottom lip to stem her anxiety. Ellard needed to concentrate. Her hysterics wouldn't help. The ship's warning siren continued, the strident whine louder than the cacophony of the storm outside.

"Shiloh told me the ship was serviced five cycles ago, and he took it for a test run."

"He did. Jannike went with him."

"The ship's not responding."

Gweneth scanned the instruments and saw the readings were wrong. She peered through the window port. She couldn't see much. An object the size of a hand struck the viewport, and she instinctively ducked. The entire time, the siren blared.

"Can't see a damn thing. You?"

"No...wait! Go to the left. The dust isn't as thick."

Ellard grunted, fighting the steering. "Controls are sluggish. Shiloh needs to sack their ship mechanics."

Another chunk flung against the viewport, a scatter of smaller items. Each time an object hurled against the viewport, she wondered if it would hold.

"Keep going left," she ordered.

Ellard grunted, forcing the directional stick left. The ship initially responded, and Gweneth's tension eased free with her breath. Then something struck the undercarriage. Something large since the entire ship groaned. Shuddered. The engine cut, the siren ceased, leaving nothing but an eerie silence punctuated by the strike of fragments. Flashes of light blazed across her retinas. She swallowed, fear writhing to life.

"Are we far from Narenda?"

"No idea. None of the instruments look right."

Gweneth reached for the communication panel and pushed a button. Static.

She glanced up to see another chunk heading straight for them. She stared at the shiny chunk, her pulse racing. Way too young to die.

Without warning, an explosion boomed around them. Another flash of retina-searing bright light blasted chunk. It veered away, clipping their ship and scooting them to the left.

A shriek escaped her, and she blushed at the girlie squeak. "Um, sorry. Took me by surprise."

Ellard attempted to restart the ship's engines. "Phrull it," He swore at the engine's cough—three loud barks—before dying again.

"What are we going to do?"

"Pray," Ellard snapped.

A steady *thud-thud-thud* shelled their ship's exterior, and Gweneth realized the truth. No need to spell it out. They'd die if one of the bigger chunks hit them in a vulnerable spot. Not even breathable suits would save them in the middle of this storm.

Ellard tried the engines, and once again, they spluttered.

Gweneth turned to the communication equipment. Her fingers raced over the keys. Nothing. No signal. It could be the interference from the storm. She'd learned a lot from Nanu, enough to help and maybe fix the problem. She unfastened her harness and slipped from her seat.

"What are you doing?" Ellard snapped without taking his gaze off the viewport.

"I'm going to try to work out what is wrong with the communication system. It's something more than our position. There should be some static and there isn't. Not a peep."

"Stay in your seat."

"Why? If a big enough piece hits us, we'll be history. Either way, I'll be dead." And she wouldn't go down without a fight. Ry and Camryn had taught her that. But first... She scooted closer to Ellard and kissed him dead on the lips. "In case we perish. I'd hate to die without having a kiss. Bad feline." She patted him on the cheek. "You could have kissed me back." While he gaped, she slid beneath a panel and peered into the dark innards.

"Phrull it. Get back in your seat," Ellard barked.

The ship shuddered. Gweneth waited until the jolts ceased and prized her fingers free of the handy handholds. In the dim light, she studied the wires and followed the mass to the terminals. Several appeared loose, which seemed weird, and a couple of others weren't attached anywhere. She popped back out from under the panel. A quick glance outside the viewport showed luck had turned their way, and they weren't in danger of hitting anything in the next few mins.

"You didn't kiss me back." With her heart thudding, she turned to him and planted her hands on her hips. "You owe me a kiss."

"More important things to do."

"Where is the toolbox? I think I can fix the navigation system.

Maybe the communication too."

"You?"

Gweneth sniffed. "I'm not just a pretty face."

She'd kissed him. She'd kissed him and demanded more. He backed away a fraction and focused. "No more kissing talk. See that big chunk over there." He gestured out the viewpoint window. "It's heading our way." He hauled out a toolbox. "Show me the loose wires."

"Ellard, I know how to do this. Nanu taught me. I've learned lots of stuff because the *Indy* crew take the time to educate me. I'm not one of your helpless upper-class shifters."

Ellard ignored her affronted tone and slid beneath the main control panel.

"Pompous oaf," she muttered.

A flash of amusement, unexpected, shot through him until he checked the wiring. Phrull it, she was right. Someone had tweaked the wiring, loosening some and tugging at others.

"Hand me the tease tool."

The correct tool—one for teasing delicate wires into place—landed in his hand secs later. She possessed knowledge of tools.

"Ellard," she said, an urgent note in her voice. "Please hurry."

Her tone told him she wasn't mucking around. "Why?"

"Big bit. Big, big piece coming our way."

The engine was most important. Even half-power might help them get farther out of the field. He followed the wires and reached with his artificial hand to set them back in the correct terminal, ready to tease them back in to place. The ship juddered, rocking and shaking, buffeted by the material in the debris field. He flexed his shiny fingers and cursed under his breath.

"Ellard, are you almost done? Can I try the engine yet?"

"Just a sec." He flexed his fingers and tried to insert a wire in the correct place. At the last moment, his fingers refused to work in the correct manner. He swore, stretched his fingers, and tried again. Phrull. The surgeon had told him to have patience.

"Ellard?"

Gweneth sounded panicky, and that decided him.

He swung out and led with honesty. "My hand isn't up to the job. You'll have to do it."

She never hesitated but squatted and squirmed under the panel, the teasing tool in hand. He heard her muttering to herself about damn wires and moronic idiots.

Ellard wasn't sure if she intended her words for him or not. He stood, his gaze zapping to the viewport. A huge chunk of debris headed directly for them.

"Try the starter," she called.

The engine turned over and coughed twice before dying.

Gweneth muttered, but he couldn't make out the words. "Again," she called.

Fuck a duck. With the debris looming even closer, Ellard prayed the engine worked even as he stole Gweneth's curse and made it his own. He fired it to life, his gut twisting in the beginnings of fear as the engine coughed like a sick cambeest. But to his relief, the engine kept running, and he sprang into his seat. His hand gripped the guidance thruster, forcing it to the left, his attention on the chunk. The view turned red and dark while the ship slowly edged to the side. Too slowly.

"I think I've sorted the communication system too. Holy heck," Gweneth muttered as she slid into the seat beside him and stared their situation in the face. "If we die and I miss my next kiss, I'm going to blame you."

"Do you think of anything else?"

"Not often. I have a plan," she said.

"Strap in."

To his relief, she buckled in and wrapped her fingers around the seat sides. "We're gonna crash."

Ellard appreciated her calm manner. Most women of his acquaintance would be in full hysterics by now.

The ship shifted and obeyed but so sluggish to his will, he wanted to curse again. "Turn, phrull it."

The debris chunk came closer, closer, closer.

It struck.

The impact threw him back in his seat, the safety harness jerking him upright. A pained grunt squeezed from him, but he kept his hand on the controls, fighting to shift the lethargic ship out of the debris field.

"Full collision, but the shell isn't compromised."

A second crash spun them around and a third shot them to the left.

"Shell is breached." Gweneth's fingers flew over the controls. "Breach localized in the cargo hold. Segmented doors locked down."

While he concentrated on steering the ship farther from danger, Gweneth calmly took care of the problems on board, and despite the crisis, he found himself admiring her gumption.

Grudgingly, the ship started to respond to his direction, and they edged farther from the field and in to the blackness of space.

His breath hissed out with relief, and he consciously relaxed his tight shoulders. "If we get out of this mess in one piece, I'll give you your kiss."

"It's worth more than one kiss," she said without glancing at him. "Storage hold also breached and contained. I want a kiss for each day we're away from Viros. Now all we need to do is discover how far off course we've gone."

Ellard spluttered, his gaze going to her and getting trapped in her cheeky grin. "I...that...that's inappropriate."

"It comes under the heading of flirtation." Her voice emerged prim yet businesslike. "I'm not requesting anything impossible or improper. No one else will know apart from us. It's not as if I'm asking for happy ever after. I suggest a kiss each day, and if you decide you need more, we'll renegotiate our deal."

Ellard found his mouth dropping open as he attempted to decipher the underlying subtext. Every word she spoke hovered close to outrageous. If he wanted more...

His feline took that moment to flex beneath his skin, and because his brain was processing the possibilities beyond kisses, his cock began to swell. No, no, phrull it no! Maybe he should have listened to Shiloh and Lynx and paid for a woman. But after Mareeka and Marjo, the twin chameleon lovers of their enemy, and the way they'd played him and stomped on both his heart and his pride, the idea of touching a woman with intimacy in mind...

He swallowed, hating the way she'd directed his thoughts to sex.

"Do you want me to fix the communications?"

"You can do that?"

"Yes."

No way could she manage that. The saboteur had yanked on the wires and damaged the terminals. No, it was beyond her capabilities. Grata, how far had they gone off course? They'd been in the debris field for a while.

"If I fix them, I expect a kiss each day and a favor—unspecified—that I can claim at a later date."

The fine hairs at the back of his neck prickled, and his feline stretched again—not uneasy but curious. It was his alarms—the male—that shrieked a warning. Give the woman a little ground and she stomped all over it and demanded more.

"Are we far enough out of the debris field to put the ship on autopilot? There isn't much room under there. I need someone to hand me tools."

"Give it another ten mins. I don't trust the autopilot."

"All right. I'll start on my own and do my best." Gweneth selected three different tools and slid under the panels until only her legs and knee-high black boots remained visible. While he stared at her shapely legs, his mind darted to thoughts of them unclothed, wrapped around his hips. He closed his eyes, swallowed, cursed his traitorous body.

No. He must focus on getting this job done, getting safely back to Viros, getting away from Gweneth.

He was no good for a woman and not one like Gweneth.

No, he must allow Gweneth to meet other males. Worthy males. Males of better appearance and station than him.

He concentrated on steering the ship from danger and studied the navigation aid in an attempt to pinpoint their location. As he feared, they'd gone way off course, and he had no idea of how far they'd deviated. The navigation equipment had seemed to function, but once he'd started the autopilot, they'd been heading off course.

His gaze drifted back to Gweneth and her sexy legs.

Yes, with other more suitable males in the picture, she'd forget him soon enough.

CHAPTER 3

This wasn't going to be as easy as she'd thought. Gweneth chewed on her bottom lip as she followed the wires from source to terminal. Ah, clever. The saboteur had rerouted several of the wires. Interrupted, she decided, which explained why they'd yanked some wiring free. They hadn't wanted to kill anyone, merely cause trouble, which made her frown. The way the saboteurs had rerouted the rest of the wiring reminded her of the training she'd received from Nanu and Kaya. Come to think of it... Yes, both her friends had disappeared for a time last eve. They wouldn't, would they?

She unscrewed the homing terminals, just as Nanu had shown her and reinserted them in the correct ones.

The ship's engines died when she removed another.

"What did you do?" A tetchy snarl.

She quickly screwed it back into the correct terminal. "Try it now." The wiring she'd affixed earlier was correct, and when Ellard tried the engine starter again, the engine purred to life.

"Yes!" Ellard shouted.

She slid out to retrieve the special tool for the communication wiring. "We shouldn't have a problem now. Is the navigational system working?"

Ellard appeared unconvinced, but he stabbed the overhead monitor, starting when it flicked to life. "Skillful job."

His surprise was evident, and she wrinkled her nose at him. "You lacked belief in my talents and capabilities. Grrrr to you! I expect those kisses. You owe me."

"You haven't fixed the communication equipment yet."

She rolled her eyes, selected her tool, and blew him a kiss. "No problem." She slid back under the panel and made quick work of the task now that she understood how to fix the problem. And she had her suspicions regarding the culprits. She would keep quiet at present but grata, she'd have words with Kaya and Nanu on her return to Viros. She and Ellard could've been killed. After one final check of the wiring for the other ship utilities, she pushed herself out and stood.

She slapped the dust off her backside, almost laughing out loud when she noticed she'd captured his attention. "Time for that kiss now. A real kiss," she added. "I expect more than a mere brush of lips or a peck. A real kiss is what we agreed on."

He stared at her, that scowl taking possession of his features again.

"I said I'm ready for my kiss now." While she should have experienced nerves, they remained absent. Instead, a sense of fun and excitement bubbled as Ellard eyed her as if she were a three-headed monster. The thought made her laugh. "I promise not to bite."

But she might later on, she decided. His tight butt or his muscular chest. That chest... She sighed. It contained hard dips and curves. What she wouldn't give to lick his torso, down over the indentations of his abs.

"This isn't a sound idea." The big male actually retreated.

If she said *boo*, would he break and run? Although tempted, she decided not to test her theory.

"You promised. I always keep my word, and I thought you were a man of honor."

He drew himself up tall. "I am," he snapped. "Very well. Let's get this over and done so we can get back to our mission."

He pounced so fast she never had a chance to release the squeak that rushed up her throat. His beefy arm—the good one—wrapped around her back, and he pulled her against his muscular body. He was so big, so strong. So masculine.

Gweneth pulled her tattered complacency around her and slipped her arms around his neck. He wore his black hair longer than Lynx and Shiloh, a bit scruffy as if he had little care for what others thought of him. Something to consider later.

Now that he held her in his arms, he hesitated, his bulky muscles tightening until she feared he'd renege on his promise.

Quick. She had to act.

Gweneth used her arms around his neck to lever herself up and stood on tiptoe to reduce the space between their lips. Their gazes connected and held, his open for a fleeting sec before he screened his emotions.

The big feline was nervous. She'd pushed past his comfort zone and wrong-footed him, and now he hesitated in his actions and thoughts. Although she hated to confuse him, perhaps an off-balance feline shifter would work in her favor. And, she had better make this a kiss to end all kisses. The best kiss he'd ever received.

No pressure.

She crushed her mouth to his, caught his quick gasp with her lips, and sank into the sensation of kissing the male her feline was directing her toward.

Soft. Warm. Decadent.

His lips were a beautiful shape, and she should know since she studied them often enough. Craving more, she opened her mouth and used her tongue to trace the sensual curves. He groaned and she used the sign to take the kiss deeper. Her tongue flickered past his lips, and she got her first taste. He tasted of the drink they'd consumed—tart and yet sweet.

His arm tightened around her, and a groan rumbled in his chest. The man—obviously slow on the uptake—started to participate and kiss her back. Instantly, her nipples pulled tight, and the physical contact seemed to seep into her pores. Her feline gave a lazy stretch beneath her skin, a sort of yawn as if waking fully from a long slumber.

Ellard pulled back a fraction and frowned at her. "What is that noise?"

Gweneth blinked. What—? Well, fuck a duck. The noise was coming from her. It sounded...it sounded like a feline purr. "It's me," she said with a trace of wonder, unable to believe her ears. "It's me. Ellard, please kiss me again. I think it's my feline. Maybe I can really shift instead of dreaming about the transformation."

For a sec, he fought an inner struggle, but she thought their earlier conversation—her prattling about feline shifting—might have helped him make his decision. He gave a curt nod and took her lips without hesitation. This time, he swept her under into a place where sensations ruled and good sense fell by the roadside. The first kiss was a pale imitation of the passion he unleashed on her now. He sipped and tasted. He tempted and seduced. He owned her with this kiss.

A small part of her was aware of him lifting her, pressing her against the control panel. She didn't care. He could do anything. She wrapped her legs around his hips and rocked against the hardness of his body. Both she and her feline sighed and purred, drawing every bit of pleasure from the contact.

A foreign sound invaded their bubble of passion, but she ignored it in favor of the kiss. Ellard seemed just as willing as her, and he continued to kiss and caress her past the bounds of the one kiss she'd demanded.

"A-hem! Ellard. Gweneth." The familiar voice of their king had them breaking apart and spinning around.

"Um, I think the communications are working again," she said in a weak voice.

"Where are you?" Lynx asked. "The Narenda delegation contacted us because you hadn't turned up as scheduled. Why?"

Shiloh winked at her. "I think it's easy to see why, my king."

Lynx snorted. "At the cost of this mission?"

Ellard pulled back but retained his hold until she stood on unsteady feet.

"We had some trouble. Someone sabotaged your ship. They rewired the controls and yanked others out. I put the ship on autopilot while we had a meal. We didn't realize we'd gone off course until we hit a debris field." Ellard reported the facts clearly and concisely.

"But the ship was fine. We had it serviced and did a test flight."

"Someone rewired it so the ship would function but go off course. Communications were down, and of course, the navigation took us in the wrong direction," Gweneth added.

"Ah, the true reason for the kiss." Shiloh smirked. "You're both celebrating the fact you're alive."

Ellard glowered at his brother but Gweneth winked once she knew Ellard couldn't see.

"It's lucky you could fix the problem. How is our ship?" Lynx asked.

"Gweneth fixed it," Ellard said. "My hand wasn't up to the delicate wiring. I need to practice more." His explanation emerged stiff and displayed a hint of mortification. "There is a crack in the cargo hold area, and we had to seal the lock doors. I'm hoping we can get it fixed on Narenda."

A glance showed a blaze of red in his cheeks.

"Good job, Gweneth," Lynx said.

"Nanu showed me some basic repairs. Ellard steered us out of the debris. We're a capable team. One person alone would have perished."

"What is your location? How far away are you?" Lynx asked.

"About half a cycle, I think," Ellard said. "Now that we're away from danger, I've reduced our speed. I didn't want to shake the ship apart. It's not handling as well."

"We'll be asking questions this end," Shiloh gritted out.

Lynx frowned. "We've had a series of isolated incidents in the city. Vandalism and such. Someone painted anti-royal graffiti on the new buildings. This might be connected. I'll contact the Narenda delegation and let them know why you're delayed."

"We'll attempt to contact them too," Ellard said. "Tell them we're coming from west-south sector."

Lynx gave a brisk nod. "That is off course. Try not to dally too long. Over and out."

The communication broke abruptly but not before she caught another sly wink from Shiloh.

"We'd better attempt communication," Ellard said in a stiff voice.

Gweneth nodded, irked when he avoided her gaze. "Of course." Her feline rumbled in disapproval as she calmly sat and fastened her safety harness. "We're representing Viros. This is an important mission." But they were safe and while her fingers tapped on the communication keys, her mind busily planned for the next stage in her Ellard offensive.

Ellard watched Gweneth from the corner of his eye as he guided the ship toward Narenda. She'd handled herself well in the crisis, and he still couldn't believe they'd escaped the debris field alive.

He loosened his grip on his knee, the prick of claws into his flesh doing little to still the clamor taking place within his body. That kiss.

Gweneth sat in her seat, her fingers flicking buttons as she attempted to reach someone on Narenda.

"Ah," she said, the sound carrying a wealth of satisfaction. "Narenda, please come in. This is the *Gallant* from Viros."

A face appeared on their communications screen. A dark and handsome man. Ellard disliked him immediately.

"*Gallant*, I read you, but I can't see you."

Gweneth popped under the panel, and he heard the rumble of her muttering along with a word that sounded suspiciously like "sexy beast", but no. He couldn't have heard right. Without warning, she emerged from beneath the panel, and he noticed a smear of grease on her cheek. It highlighted her high cheekbones and pouty lips.

Ellard muttered a curse and wrenched his gaze away from temptation. He failed to understand why this particular woman wormed under his skin and bothered him. That kiss... A shiver rippled through him as he recalled her soft curves pressing against his chest, her lips moving against his...

"Can you see me now?" Gweneth asked.

"I certainly can," the dark-haired man said. "I never realized our visitors included a woman."

"I'm Gweneth Swithin, and I'm traveling with Ellard Tetsu. I'm sorry we're late. Our ship suffered mechanical problems. They're fixed now, and I believe we should arrive on the morrow."

"Excellent," the man purred. "I am Gryffnn Drake, brother to the chieftain."

Ellard caught the narrowing of the man's gaze and the shift of his pupils. A dragon shifter. Ellard hated the way the male eyed Gweneth like his next dinner.

"We're looking forward to visiting your planet," Gweneth said in her melodic tones. "Will your chieftain still be available to meet with us?"

"Yes, of course. We welcome the chance to trade beyond our borders."

A feline snarl burst from Ellard, and his claws dug into his thigh. The dragon wanted to meet Gweneth. That was clear from his drool and his oozing sexuality.

"Problem?" Gryffnn asked, one dark brow arching.

"My pilot requires his dinner." Gweneth smiled sweetly at Gryffnn. "He gets cranky if his blood sugar is low."

Another growl escaped before he could contain his feline. The woman would drive him to madness, and his cat disliked this Gryffnn character and his flirtation with Gweneth.

"You had better make sure he eats then. My brother will interpret his growls as rudeness." Gryffnn's eyes shifted even farther to dragon. "I look forward to the morrow. Over and out."

Ellard growled without restraint as the male's visage blinked off the communications screen. "I dislike that man."

"Control yourself. We're not going to achieve our objective with you grunting and growling all over the place. This is important to me, Ellard. This is my idea, and I want my new home to prosper. Ry and Camryn, and the rest of the *Indy* crew feel the same. Most of us have never had a permanent home before, and we want to fit in."

Ellard stared at her impassioned face, and guilt slithered through him. She thought of her friends and of others—strangers—who would look down on her because she couldn't shift. He thought of himself.

"I'm sorry." He tried not to choke on the words. "My feline is rattled and unsettled because of the sabotage. You're right. This is an important mission. I promise I'll do my best to help you."

Gweneth gave a clipped nod and released her safety harness.

"Would you mind if I take the first rest break? I'll bring you something to eat before I retire."

"You don't have to wait on me."

"I know. I'm getting myself something to eat, and it will be no trouble to prepare food for you at the same time."

"Thank you." He turned back to the navigational equipment, scanning and rescanning the instruments even though he knew the ship was flying in the right direction now. Although the *Gallant* limped at half-pace after colliding with pieces of debris, he felt confident they would make their destination on the morrow. Whether he'd arrive with all his hair intact was another matter since he couldn't stop thinking about Gweneth and her kisses. Surely she wouldn't expect him to kiss her tomorrow?

His feline shoved a growl past his restraint, and Ellard groaned in sympathy. The woman had thrown him off balance and had his feline in a tempest.

Back at the castle, it had been easier to ignore her. But here...here on the *Gallant,* the tighter quarters offered no escape from her determination, her force-of-nature personality, her beauty.

"I brought soup." Gweneth appeared, following the silent float table that bore his meal. "I'll set my comp pad alarm for three parts of a cycle. You should have some rest too. I know how to fly the ship, and you're close if I have any difficulties."

Ellard nodded agreement since it beat arguing. His feline registered her retreat, listening until her footsteps entered the sleeping chamber. His shoulders slumped in relief. Anything to get her away from him, to give himself a chance to think, to regroup. Maybe he'd contact Jarlath and plead for advice. He didn't trust his thoughts or emotions anymore, not after Mareeka and Marjo.

Betrayal.

No. He couldn't compare this situation with Gweneth. She was young, not far into womanhood, and she didn't seek to overthrow the House of the Cat.

Ellard commed Jarlath and prayed his friend would answer. A sleepy Keira came on screen, her brown hair tousled, the cheeks of her pale green face flushed with a darker green, and her lips swollen. An equally disheveled Jarlath popped into view beside her, his chest bare.

Ellard groaned. "I'm sorry. I've interrupted. I'll call another time."

"It's all right," Keira said.

"What do you want?" Jarlath growled. His friend refrained from using the same niceties as his mate.

"I..." Ellard swallowed and wished he'd thought twice before contacting his friend.

Keira cocked her head, reminding him of her crow status with the birdlike movement. "Did you want to speak with Jarlath alone?"

"I did, but I've changed my mind," Ellard blurted when Keira started to back away. "I...I'm confused."

Jarlath and Keira stared at him, and why shouldn't they? He'd never admitted to anything like this before.

"Gweneth?" Keira asked with a smile that held a healthy serving of amusement.

"Yes! I kissed her, and I don't want to do that again." He rubbed his hands over his face and tried again. "I mean, I do, but I shouldn't."

"What does Gweneth say?" Keira asked.

At least she'd reined in her laughter. Jarlath didn't even try, his chuckle unrestrained.

"I'm glad I amuse you."

"Gweneth is a confident young woman. If she hated your kisses, she'd tell you so," Keira told him. "Has she refused?"

Ellard sighed. "She expects me to kiss her every day."

Keira's grin widened, her eyes sparkling in echo of the humor. "Then why do you have a problem?"

"Why would she want to kiss me? No one else does," he added miserably. *Talk about embarrassing. Difficult to admit the truth.* "I seldom compare well with the other single feline males."

"Not true," Jarlath barked. "You are worth double those useless nits."

"Jarlath, that isn't what Ellard means. He's worried about his appearance and the fact he has lost his arm."

"He's a hero," Jarlath said bluntly. "If Gweneth and the other women don't recognize that fact, then they are dense."

Keira's gaze took on a crow sharpness. "I doubt Gweneth is toying with you, Ellard. She is a beautiful woman."

"My point," he blurted. "Yet she made a bet with me, and now that she's won, she expects me to kiss her every day."

"Clever girl," Keira said. "She's managing you nicely."

"I don't want to be managed," Ellard snapped.

"You need to think about what you do want." Keira ignored his testy tone. "What about your feline? Does he want her?"

Ellard slumped. "Yes."

"Did your feline want Marjo and Mareeka?"

"I thought he did, but..." He shrugged in helplessness.

Keira sighed. "None of that was your fault, Ellard. You have a big heart. You're loyal and true to your friends. Would you like my advice?"

He nodded, each of his muscles tensing as he waited.

"Give Gweneth her kiss every day. Enjoy spending the cycles with her and being away from the prying eyes at the castle. Take each cycle one at a time instead of worrying about the future. Relax for once and think of yourself instead of duty to Jarlath and the other royals. Treat this assignment as a holiday away from your responsibilities. Do you understand what I'm suggesting?"

Give Gweneth her kiss every day.

He shuddered while his feline issued a purr.

"What if I want more than kisses?"

47

"Remember what I suggested about taking each cycle one at a time?"

"Yes," Ellard said.

Jarlath smiled at him, and this time, his grin lacked any joke-at-your-expense humor. This smile held approval, something pleasant and reassuring, and Ellard felt the tension in his shoulders shifting.

"Keira is right. One cycle at a time," Jarlath agreed. "Use this journey to get to know her, the things she likes and enjoys. Trust your feline to steer you in the right direction. What do you have to lose? At the very least, you'll make another friend."

Ellard nodded again. "Thank you."

He thought about their advice during his cycle portions alone. One cycle at a time. He could do that. Break his fears into manageable slices. A workable plan. His only plan. He just hoped it didn't come back to bite him in the arse.

Gweneth burst onto the bridge at a skip, her long black hair confined in a bouncy ponytail instead of one of her complicated twists that she piled on top of her head. It made her appear younger and mischievous.

Ellard swallowed, his stomach muscles quivering as his gaze shot to her pouty lips.

A float table sailed toward him and the control panel.

Gweneth plonked down in the seat beside him, glanced out the viewscreen and at the instruments before shifting her attention to him. "Do you want to have a snack before you go and rest? It's nice to share a meal."

He found himself nodding when he hadn't intended at all. "You're a witch," he grumbled.

She blinked. "No, I'm a feline. A failure of a feline, but a cat nevertheless."

"Before you and the rest of the *Indy* crew arrived on Viros, before and during the war with the House of Cawdor, many of our shifters lost their ability to shift. And without regular shifting our cats suffer. Some die."

Her white teeth caught that pouty lip and worried it. Ellard stared at her until the stirring of his feline warned of his idiocy. He shouldn't stare at her or encourage her because, despite what Jarlath and Keira thought, he was older and damaged. A young, beautiful shifter like Gweneth could have anyone she wanted, and he feared another joke at his expense.

Phrull.

He puffed out a hard breath, every muscle in his body tensing at the memory of how Marjo and Mareeka played him. Because of his mistakes, Jarlath had faced great danger, and he'd lost an arm.

"Ellard. *Ellard.*" Gweneth reached out to touch his artificial arm. He couldn't truly feel her touch, but the sensors built into the limb transmitted to his brain and told him he should. His cock started to fill.

"What?" he snapped.

"You were telling me about the shifters who couldn't transform. What happened?"

"The House of Cawdor managed to place an additive in the food supply, and that worked to stifle shifting. Some were lucky and never succumbed. My feline remained, but Jarlath's didn't. Until he met Keira, his feline was dying."

"He's all right now because I've seen him shift."

"Most recovered, but a few..." Ellard trailed off, the horror of a part of him dying even worse than losing his arm. Something to remember. Some of the Virosian citizens had it worse than him. Gweneth, for example, had never shifted, yet she embraced life and new experiences. He could learn something from a friendship with her. The thought, the decision, made a weight lift off his shoulders. "Thanks for the food."

She wrinkled her nose. "It's not much. I didn't bother stocking much since the voyage to Narenda shouldn't have taken this long.

You should take a break once you've eaten. We need to be in top form once we arrive at Narenda. Lynx and Shiloh are counting on us to woo the people into taking part in our festival."

"No one knows much about the species who live on Narenda."

"I know. I attempted to do some research since Lynx and Shiloh told me they'd visited once. The ship's data banks tell of the atmosphere and the planet's composition. It's tropical—much warmer than Viros, so I'm glad I brought my shorts and T-shirts with me—clothes to relax in—as well as suitable gear for meetings."

"Shorts are an Earth garment?"

"Yes. Very comfortable. Anyway, that's the extent of my research. Nothing else showed up, apart from the fact the people weren't friendly." Gweneth glanced at her timepiece. "Ah."

The wealth of satisfaction in the sound raised a warning signal in Ellard. His feline went on alert, senses stretching outward.

"I believe you owe me another kiss." She beamed at him. "We'll take care of that before you go and rest."

Take each cycle as it came.

Right then.

Ellard calmly ate his meal—a tasteless dehydrated meal of malpack strips and perknoods, a type of soft dough cut into long pieces. The gravy should make the meal taste better. Instead, it clogged up his mouth.

Gweneth pushed hers away. "As I said, not much to eat."

Ellard set the remains of his meal back on the hover tray, and Gweneth sent the tray back to the galley. He scanned the instruments one final time to satisfy himself they appeared to be heading in the correct direction before standing.

"I'll take care of that kiss now." The words and the idea came easier now that he'd considered and discussed the matter. Friends. Someone to stand with during court functions and to laugh with instead of appearing a ninny. Jarlath and Keira were right. There was no downside to Gweneth's proposition.

"Ah, all right." Instead of appearing pleased, Gweneth's dark brows drew together. She stood, her uncertainty clear.

She'd thought he'd keep objecting and his acquiescence confused her.

"Come here," he said, confident now that he had the upper hand. The thing was—if he aimed for honesty—and he tried not to lie to himself, he'd enjoyed kissing her.

Gweneth advanced, closing the distance between them. When they were almost touching, she lifted her head and met his gaze. An instant later, her chin lifted, and he smiled at the sight.

She reached up and skimmed his jaw with her fingertips.

His feline twisted beneath his skin, the leashed power of the beast almost breaking past his control, all because of her innocent touch.

"Is that your feline?"

He nodded since a lump had lodged in his throat, preventing him from speaking.

She ran her palm over his cheek, and heat roared through his body. Not his cat this time, but the man's body reacting to the proximity of a beautiful woman. One who wanted a kiss.

"Come here," he said gruffly, reaching for her and pulling her against his chest.

They both sighed then grinned.

Friends who enjoyed kissing each other. It couldn't be that bad, he thought as he claimed her lips. He'd wanted to keep the kiss quiet and friendly, but the elvetine flower-soft touch of her lips responding to his roared through him in a flash flood of emotions. He wrapped both arms around her slender form and deepened the contact, sliding his tongue into the warm softness and falling into a world of feminine mysteries. Heat and pleasure.

He'd meant to kiss her and go on his way, but the sec his brain thought about ceasing the contact, his arms locked in position.

In urgent need of a breath, he parted their lips and nuzzled the fragrant flesh of her neck.

"Ellard," she whispered.

He licked across the rapid-beating pulse below her ear, and wonder filled him. This storm of lust and longing affected her too, since she appeared just as lost.

He sighed again and pressed his forehead to hers. "I should probably go and get some rest. You're right about us both needing to stay alert once we land on Narenda."

"One more kiss?" The hopeful gleam in her beautiful green eyes unmanned him. No one ever looked at him this way. Not a woman.

Their lips met again before the thought registered in his mind. The last bit of his sanity told him to place distance between them since his cock was reacting in a predictable manner. He'd hate to frighten her, not that she seemed the nervy type, but he distrusted his instincts when it came to females. He forced his lower limbs to obey the order to move and made room between them.

She groaned and reclaimed the space. Firm breasts pushed into his chest, and she didn't seem to mind his shaft digging into her belly. The thought shot pleasure through him and drew his balls so tight he thought he might burst.

"Enough." He pulled away with a tortured groan and took an additional two steps back to negate temptation.

She nodded. "Thank you for the spectacular kiss."

"Two kisses," he corrected, his voice croaky and strained.

"You still owe me one tomorrow," she said. "It's not my fault you decided to steal an extra one."

He stared at her, nonplussed by her casual manner. Just as he thought he understood her, she said or did something that jolted him out of rhythm.

"Call me if you have a problem."

She sat in her seat and fastened the safety harness. "I might call

Lynx and Shiloh and tell them we've made contact and should arrive on the morrow as we predicted."

Ellard glanced down at his erection and back at Gweneth, calmly pushing buttons on the controls. The last thing he wanted was for Lynx or Shiloh to see the results of Gweneth's kiss. "See you later."

She lifted one hand. "Sure thing."

Ellard sighed and left the bridge. Women. He'd never understand them.

Chapter 4

Planet Narenda

The *Gallant* thudded onto the landing pad late in the next cycle and, without warning, listed to the side. Gweneth, who had already unbuckled her seat harness, flew off balance, and Ellard's arm snapped out to grab her. An arrow of pain transmitted from his artificial arm and down his shoulder, and then Gweneth plopped into his lap, jolting the discomfort from his mind.

"As much as I enjoy cuddling with you, I think the delegation from the chieftain's office is waiting for us."

Her eyes twinkled and her warm weight felt so right he had to bite back a groan and resist dragging her even closer. She smelled of flowers and sunshine, but he caught a hint of feline, and his cat took notice. Stronger than the cycle before, it called to him, tempted him to wallow and play with the scent.

"Ellard, are you listening to me?"

"Yes. We need to go and meet the delegation and fulfill our mission."

She patted his cheek, her touch like a caress. "Let's do this."

Ellard ran one hand through his hair, mystified as he helped her to her feet. Half the time, he didn't understand her. Shiloh had told him the proximity with Camryn and Earth ways had rubbed off on the *Indy* crew. He removed his safety harness and stood, careful with his balance since it appeared the ship had sustained damage to the landing gear.

"Do you require assistance?" The rich masculine voice came from behind them.

Gwen started and rammed into him. Ellard whirled them both to face the intruder.

"Who are you? How did you get on our ship?" Gweneth demanded, taking care of the interrogation before Ellard had a chance. He growled and slid his arm around her waist—a let-me-take-care-of-it gesture that got lost in the translation. Their communication skills required work.

Ellard eyed the new arrival. His face was very pale—white really—while his cheeks were flushed with delicate pink. His white eyes with glacier-blue pupils held amusement while his hands, raised in front of him, held no weapons. Long white hair hung in curls to his shoulders, and he wore tight black trews and a flowing white shirt. A colorfully embroidered waistcoat in red and green topped his shirt and it glittered in the light cast from the planet's nearest star. Ellard stared a fraction harder. Were those valuable stones in the design?

"I beg your pardon." The new arrival bowed from the waist. "I did not wish to intrude, but Ransom and I were concerned when we saw the state of your ship's hull."

"You are part of the Narenda delegation?" Ellard regarded him with suspicion while Gweneth relaxed against him and showed no desire to move.

"Yes, do forgive me. I am Niran Vasilakis, leader of the Incorporeals who also lives on Narenda along with the Drake Tribe."

"I'm Gweneth Swithin, and this is Ellard Tetsu." Gweneth took charge again. "As you can see we have had an interesting journey. We will be out shortly."

"Of course," Niran said smoothly. "We anticipate the formal introductions with joy." As he finished speaking, his form faded until nothing remained. The man had vanished.

"Well, that was interesting. Ghosts. Did you know about another race?"

"No. We'll have to take care when we speak in private. Anyone might be listening if they can pop in and out at will."

"True, but it's not as if we're full of trade secrets. We come in peace and hope to entice them to participate in our festival. This is turning more interesting by the sec. A handsome male. I'm going to have plenty of chances to test my flirting skills."

"No—"

"Ellard, they're waiting for us. No time for a discussion." She pulled from his protective embrace and carefully made her way from the bridge to the exit ramp.

Ellard followed, his feline grumbling at him. Neither of them had enjoyed the way Niran had looked at Gweneth or the speculation in his gaze. Maybe they had a shortage of females on this planet, and if so, they were *not* keeping Gweneth.

Gweneth belonged with him. She— He broke off the thought with a scowl and stomped down the exit ramp stairs. The woman was screwing with his mind. His gaze followed her as she strode over to Niran and the big male standing beside him. He imagined her smile and increased the length of his strides into the clammy heat of the planet.

"Hello," Gweneth said. "We're pleased to arrive on Narenda."

"We can see that," the second male said. "I am Ransom Drake, chieftain to the tribe. Would you like my repair team to look at your ship? You won't be able to leave with it in that condition."

A big male of an equal height to him, Ellard smelled the *other* part of him. The dragon shifter smelled of amber—warm, musky, and of honey, yet with a hint of burning and earth. A black tattoo of a dragon coiled around and down his right arm, and a scar went from the corner of his right eye and down his cheek. He wore arrogance around his shoulders like a cloak, which made Ellard's feline rumble to meet the challenge, especially since Gweneth seemed smitten by the handsome dragon shifter.

She sighed and made no secret of her interest. Ransom's grin widened.

"Thank you. That would be much appreciated." Ellard decided to wrest the lead and attention from Gweneth. "Ellard Tetsu." He extended his hand palm up to show he carried no visible weapons and came in peace. He placed a hand on Gweneth's shoulder. "This is Gweneth Swithin, who came up with the idea we're about to put to you."

"I believe you have already met Niran. Come. We will have refreshments and conduct our business before we give you a tour of our town. We have arranged accommodation for you."

"We didn't come prepared for an extended stay," Gweneth said. "Is there somewhere we can purchase a few necessities?"

Niran smiled at them, a blaze of approval, which prodded Ellard's battle senses to the fore. "We have everything you require."

"This way," Ransom said with a charming bow. At least Gweneth found it charming because she issued another of those sighs.

Ellard bit back his snarl and nodded, then he and Gweneth followed the two males. Although he'd never met a dragon shifter in person, his father had told tales of their ferocity during battles. They were a private race, and their invitation to visit still surprised him. With Ransom's looks, most females would take a second glance, despite his casual clothing of lightweight trews and plain blue shirt. Ellard reserved judgment on the arrogance since a leader required strength and confidence to lead. Whether he was trustworthy, they'd soon discover, but he decided to take him at face value—for the moment. As for Gweneth...

He frowned inwardly. Wasn't this what he wanted?

"I hope you don't mind a stroll. We are not far from my quarters," Ransom said. "Mostly, if we wish to travel any distance, we shift and fly."

"Not an option for us." Gweneth offered a cheeky grin. "But if you wish to exercise your wings, go right ahead. I've never seen a dragon shifter before and would love to before we leave."

"Gweneth," Ellard warned.

Ransom laughed, an infectious sound that made Ellard want to join the joke. "I value openness and honesty."

Ellard's back prickled as he followed Gweneth and the two males down a gravel track that wound between lush plantings of flowers. Beyond, trees filled the landscape, and on the horizon, a range of mountains thrust up from the landscape like jagged teeth. The sweet scent of the flowers lay heavy in the air. White. Red. Purple. Blue. The shades ran the gamut and made for attractive surroundings after the dust generated by numerous building sites on Viros.

"We directed you to land near my estate rather than in the town," Ransom said over his shoulder. "We will show you the town later, but it will be easier to conduct our business discussions here."

The track widened. Ellard wiped the sweat off his forehead and strode along beside Niran. While he listened to the man discuss the main town and its amenities, part of his mind attempted to follow Ransom's discussion with Gweneth. Both males had brightened on seeing her, and he now struggled with jealousy. He had no right, given he kept pushing her away. He knew that, but try telling this to his agitated feline.

"Ah." Niran's pale cheeks glowed with pink. He lifted his nose and drew in the air in the way a feline did to scent. "Delicious."

"Pardon?" Ellard frowned at the man's tone. It was...weird, he decided. The man appeared... He hesitated again. Sexually sated was the word that came to mind, yet he hadn't appeared that way when he and Gweneth disembarked from their ship.

"Have you never heard of my race before?" The corners of Niran's eyes crinkled, and he emanated agreeable humor and joy.

Yep, plain weird.

"No," Ellard said.

A loud *whop-whop* overhead had him flinching. He managed to hold back his gasp but felt his eyes widen at the immense scarlet dragon that dive-bombed toward them. A smaller royal-blue dragon lagged behind, its stubby wings working at double time to keep it above the treetops.

Niran chuckled, the rich sound pulling at Ellard and inducing him to share in the joke.

The scarlet dragon opened its mouth, and a blaze of flames shot free.

"Cut it out," Ransom ordered, a snap in his voice.

The royal-blue dragon opened its mouth, and a smaller, less impressive blast of flames emerged. This dragon lacked the same control, and the flames ran along the treetops. Several dry twigs caught fire, and the blue dragon squeaked.

"Gryffnn," Ransom roared. "Come back and put out this fire."

"Who is that?" Gweneth asked, awe in her voice.

Ellard didn't blame her because he was experiencing the same wonder. While he'd heard of the dragon race of shifters, he'd never seen one. Lynx and Shiloh were right. They needed a peace treaty with the dragons.

"My brother," Ransom said in a dry tone. "And his son."

Gweneth stared up at the flaming branches. "Can all dragons

breathe fire?"

"The ability grows with age. As you can see my nephew has little control and has just started fire breathing while my brother can repeat his party trick four or five times before he needs to rest."

"How much rest is required?" Ellard asked, interested in learning more. He watched the red dragon hurtle through the sky while the blue dragon fluttered above the treetops near the fire.

"It varies, but several cycle portions. The older the warrior, the more powerful he becomes," Ransom said. "In case you're thinking of declaring war on us."

Gweneth smiled and patted his arm. "We come in peace. Ask Ellard. None of our people wish for unrest. I am a new arrival to Viros, but the city is recovering from a war with the House of Cawdor."

"Is this true?" Ransom's bold gaze demanded answers.

Despite the bristling of his feline, Ellard nodded. "We want to rebuild and prosper, and we would like our neighbors to grow with us. That is what we have come to discuss."

Niran glanced at Ransom, and Ellard caught Ransom's imperceptible nod. He wondered at it until the red dragon distracted him. A stream of water doused the flaming tree. The red dragon trilled at the blue one and they flew ahead of their party and disappeared as he and the others continued along the tree-lined track.

Questions filled Ellard, his curiosity roused by all he'd learned. Gweneth chattered like a curious bird, peppering Ransom with queries about life on Narenda. His feline growled, jealousy rippling through the creature. He tried to contain the emotions, but they bled from him, and Niran noticed.

"There is no need to worry about Ransom. Your woman is safe with him."

"She is not my woman."

Niran's brows rose, and that weird smile played around his

lips. "I beg to differ. As I was saying before Gryffnn and his son interrupted me, you haven't heard of our race before. The Incorporeal race feed from sexual energy. Without that energy we have no substance and cannot bear young. You and Gweneth are giving off enough energy to give me a good buzz."

Ellard blinked, so shocked words failed him. He just stared with his mouth hanging open. Finally, he coughed and flapped away the bug that attempted to dive-bomb down his throat like one of Narenda's dragons.

Niran chuckled. "While Ransom does not have a mate, he would never poach from another male, not since you are so obviously meant for each other."

"No, Gweneth and I are not mates."

Niran sighed. "Some males are stubborn."

"I am not stubborn," Ellard gritted out.

Gweneth glanced over her shoulder. "Ellard?" Her expression held chiding and disappointment, and he felt heat collect in his cheeks.

"I apologize," he said stiffly.

Niran flapped his hand, the glow of amusement never leaving his expression. "Not necessary. I poked my nose into personal matters. Come, tell me more about Viros. We had heard about your battle with the House of Cawdor and that you have new rulers. A triad," he mused. "Unusual. Is it working well?"

Ellard welcomed the other man's easy manner and accepted the peace offering. "My younger brother is one of the new rulers. He and his two mates seem very happy. They're rebuilding the city and bringing a new vibrancy that we have long needed. Much of our infrastructure fell to ruin during the war. We are taking the opportunity to modernize and hope to attract tourists to bring wealth to our people."

"Growth and opportunity is good," Niran said. "My people, too, need to grow and expand our reach. It is a delicate balance."

The trees around them began to thin, and buildings became visible. Built of stone, they blended with their surroundings. A stone wall surrounded the main building and the six smaller ones. Although substantial, it wouldn't keep enemies out. Not that these dragons would have many enemies. He wouldn't want to tangle with an angry fire-breathing dragon.

"What is the main trade on Narenda?" Ellard asked, wanting to fill the gaps in his knowledge. Lynx and Shiloh would want to learn as much as possible about the secretive races who lived on this tropical planet.

"We specialize in jewelry and precious stones," Ransom explained. "This way. I have requested my housekeeper to prepare refreshments for our arrival. We have guests for the evening meal in order for others to meet you."

"Thank you," Ellard said. "We will enjoy meeting other members of your tribe so we might extend the invitation from our king."

Ransom opened a wooden gate and gestured for them to enter. To their right, beds of colorful flowers—in more colors than he could begin to describe—surrounded a wide green expanse. Half-naked children frolicked and chased a red ball. They shouted greetings but continued with their play.

"Your children?" Gweneth asked.

"No, I do not have a mate," Ransom said. "My employees, however, are a fruitful lot. They live in the cottages. My brother and nephew, my two sisters and I live in the main house. You'll be staying with us while your ship is undergoing repairs."

"Thank you," Gweneth said. "But I thought we were staying at a hotel in the main town."

Ellard frowned at the look Ransom tipped toward Niran. The two males knew something and they weren't telling. Frozen in place, he tested his senses and his feline went on alert. Nothing raised the hair at the back of his neck, and some of the tension leached from his limbs.

"No, I think we can get to know each other better here." Ransom's expression remained enigmatic. "We would enjoy visiting Viros."

Gweneth smiled. "And we would like to learn more about Narenda. Now, tell me. Could I have a ride on a dragon?"

A sensual glint appeared in Ransom's eyes, and Ellard's warning signals shot to an all-time high. "The sole time a non-dragon female might fly with a dragon is if he is courting her." He cast a sly glance at Ellard, his eyes shifting a fraction. "Would you like to fly with me?"

Ellard growled, and Niran gave a bark of delight.

"I knew I was right," he said.

Gweneth frowned. "Stop teasing Ellard. His bite is truly worse than his bark."

Ellard bristled some more. He didn't need Gweneth to stand up for him.

"You haven't seen my bite yet," Ransom said in a silky voice as he opened an ornate carved wooden door and ushered them inside. "Ah, let me introduce you to my sisters."

A woman appeared in the doorway of a room to their right. Tall and slender, she wore her beauty with confidence She'd swept her brown hair up in a pile on her head and wore a flowing golden tunic over black trews—the sort of woman who would never give him a second glance. Ellard allowed himself a polite nod and turned his attention to their surroundings. Tasteful wealth. He'd seen riches in the castle, yet the former queen hadn't had the knack of furnishing with an eye to comfort and elegance. Light spilled through a jeweled window, casting a rainbow of colors across the plain stone-tiled floor. The scent of spices wafted on the air—delicious cooking aromas—that made his stomach grumble with hunger.

"Jacinta, come and meet our guests," Ransom said. "Where is

Sable?"

"She is conversing with the housekeeper about the domestic arrangements. She will be here soon since Gryffnn signaled your arrival."

"This is Gweneth and Ellard."

Ellard shook the woman's hand and frowned at the frisson of sensation that swept up his arm. Gweneth elbowed him in the ribs, jerking him from the trance he'd dropped into at the dragon woman's touch. "I'm pleased to meet you," he said belatedly.

A man tromped in behind him, followed by a small boy.

"Out," Jacinta pointed. "Remove your boots. If you stomp that mud over the floors, Sable will cry. She's spent all half-cycle cleaning."

"I can smell berry snacks," the boy said.

"You'd better listen to your aunt." Ransom ruffled the boy's black hair. "Sable and Jacinta are quite capable of withholding berry snacks if we make them more work. This is my brother Gryffnn and his son, Hallam."

"But Niran can fix it for us," the boy said.

"No, he can't," Ransom said in a stern voice. "We learn to do things for ourselves. We do not rely on the largess of others."

"Niran does things for us of his free will," Gryffnn said with a chiding note. "We are lucky he chooses to gift us with his presence. You must never forget that."

"Enough." Ransom effectively closed the conversation. "We will have refreshments. Maybe some berry snacks, if we all behave." He ushered them into a large square room, one also full of light.

Ellard scanned the exits and the contents for possible weapons. Tiled floors covered by large thick rugs. All of the furniture bordered on large, built sturdy for big males. The room spoke of comfort and relaxation.

Ransom seated Gweneth and sat near her. Ellard's feline bristled at the other male's attentions to his woman, and Ellard's brain slammed to an appalled stop. They'd kissed and nothing more. No promises made. No future between them. This man held a position of responsibility. A leader. A chieftain. She could do worse.

Ellard forced his legs to move to a chair near Gweneth and Ransom. He sank into the comfort of the brown fabric and forced his feline into submission.

"I must go," Niran said without warning.

"Problem?" Ransom asked.

Niran frowned, his brow creasing in concentration. His form shimmered. Finally, he said, "No, I believe it will be all right. I will return later."

Ellard gaped at a repeat of the ship visit. He...the man appeared transparent. He blinked, convinced his mind played tricks on him. When he looked again, Niran had vanished.

"How did he do that?" Gweneth demanded. "Can he pop in and out at will?"

"Yes," Ransom said. "He will be back later to arrange your accommodation for me. Those of the Incorporeal race are able to fade and appear when the desire strikes them, as long as they have fed recently."

"Fed?" Gweneth asked.

Ellard frowned but remained silent since Gweneth was obtaining information well enough without him.

A door opened at the far end of the room, and two women entered. One carried a tray of drinks and the other wheeled a cart of plates and food.

"This is our other sister, Sable, and our housekeeper, Jewel. Jewel comes from Scothage."

"Our friend employs a man from Scothage to oversee her farm and animals," Gweneth explained. "I'm pleased to meet you all. You have a beautiful home. I can't wait to explore more of your planet. The things we've seen so far have whetted my appetite. I cannot wait to hit the shops and the rest of the sights."

Ransom sent her an indulgent smile. "You had a trying journey here. This cycle is for relaxation. We have a pool at the rear of the property. We could spend the rest of the cycle out there and keep proceedings on a casual basis."

The tray thumped to the table, and Ellard started, his attention claimed again by the tall dark-haired woman who had carried the tray. A faint flush had crept into her cheeks. On first glance, he'd considered her plain next to her sister, and he experienced a surge of shame for judging her as others judged him.

"This is my youngest sister, Sable," Ransom said.

"I'm sorry about the tray." She shared her apology around with a tight smile. "I'm still becoming used to my new arm."

His gaze focused on her limbs but found it difficult to discern which was the artificial one, given the enveloping black, long-sleeved tunic she wore.

Sable caught him staring and raised her chin in challenge. A familiar reaction and one from his personal arsenal. He grinned.

"It's not a subject to cause amusement," Sable snapped.

"Of course not." Ellard sobered rapidly. He'd hate to hurt her feelings.

Ransom stood from his sprawl, his eyes flashing to dragon and back.

Ellard took heed and rose too. "Please, don't misunderstand. I lost my arm during the war with the House of Cawdor and have recently had a Stores implanted. I'm pleased to meet someone who shares the same problems as me. That is all I meant." He nodded at Sable. "Please forgive me. I—"

"You have a Stores? Which version? The second or third?"

"Come and sit beside Ellard in order to compare notes." Gweneth rose from her seat. "I can take care of refreshments for everyone."

"Jacinta will do it." Ransom's iron will and determination

echoed in his words. He offered his arm and drew her to a two-seater. "Tell me more about Viros."

Ellard eyed Ransom and Gweneth for long seconds, his feline vibrating beneath his skin.

"I've never met anyone with the same injury." Sable blushed, and Ellard corrected his first impression regarding her looks. The unrelieved black of her apparel made her appear plain and colorless. "When other dragon shifters lose a limb they manage to grow it back."

"But you can't?"

"My mother comes from another race. She came from Blackon and arrived here to work in the town." She shot a swift glance at Ransom. "Her beauty attracted Ransom's sire, and she became his mistress."

"I'm sorry."

"It's all right. Once Ransom discovered my presence, he ordered me to come to live here. He has been—is—very good to me. He arranged and paid for my arm. Normally I manage to contain my clumsiness and visitors fail to notice my arm, but for some reason the nerves returned and made me ham-fisted."

Going on instinct, Ellard claimed her natural hand and stroked it with an aim to comfort. "I'm still learning to use mine. How long does it ache? Does that go away? They told me it would, but the stump is forever aching."

"It's the neural attachments doing their job. Once all the implants grow into place, the aching ceases. Did they not tell you that?"

"They did, but I'm impatient. My Stores still feels foreign to me."

Sable leaned closer and he smelled her perfume—something sweet yet spicy. He rather liked it. "And everyone around you stares and studies you like a specimen."

"Yes, which makes it even harder to relax and trust in the Stores."

Sable grinned. "Exactly."

"I've poured you both a glass of Mexes," Jacinta snapped as she placed two glasses filled with scarlet liquid on the solid table next to their chairs. "I did inquire as to your preference but neither of you answered."

"Thank you," Sable said.

Ellard scowled at the irritable sister. "That will be fine. Thank you." He watched the sister stomp back to the table with the refreshments. "Is she always so grumpy?"

"She argued with Ransom's decision to let me live here at the mansion."

"How long has Ransom been in charge?"

"Our father died two rotations ago. He never paid me any attention. Things are much better now that Ransom is our chieftain."

"It is the same on Viros. Before the present king took the crown, most citizens found life difficult. It made us vulnerable to attack." He picked up his glass of Mexes with his artificial hand, taking care to temper his strength. "What is in this drink?"

"It's a local fruit, which grows on tall trees. The dragons must use flight in order to harvest the fruit. It's tart yet sweet too. Very refreshing. Most people enjoy it."

Ellard relaxed even further, enjoying socializing with a woman who didn't judge him lacking, a woman who didn't want something from him. He found her far more restful than Gweneth, and perhaps a woman he could accept in his future. He would never need to guard her, and he could enjoy a stable relationship. Sable would never betray him or leave him for another because she knew the pain of being different, as he did.

Yes, he and Gweneth would not suit—despite his attraction to her—and she would have to accept this decision.

CHAPTER 5

E llard spoke to Sable naturally, participating in a way she had
to work hard to achieve. Gweneth ripped her gaze away
before she did something rude—like bash Ellard over the skull with
the nearest ornament. Probably that dragon sculpture since it had
lots of pointy bits to dent his stubbornness.

"You shouldn't worry about Sable." Ransom sounded amused
at her possessiveness.

"No? That is not the way it appears to me."

"You're an attractive woman. You know how to dress, how to
behave in a social situation. Your confidence radiates from you and
is second nature. My sister is young and lacks seasoning."

"That is not the way I see it." Gweneth darted a quick look at the
couple. They had their heads together and were laughing at some
joke. "They have much in common."

Her breath caught halfway up her throat as Sable turned a

fraction. How had she ever thought the woman plain? At present, she lacked confidence and dress sense, but Gweneth saw her inner beauty. Sable would shine once she gained the poise Ransom mentioned. Add some makeup, some suitable clothes... *Oy, oy, oy!*

"As I said, Sable is young. She needs to learn to stand up to Jacinta and not let her sister boss her around."

"Half-sister," Jacinta snapped as she handed them drinks.

Hallam wandered over and smiled shyly at Gweneth. "Uncle, where has Niran gone?"

"I don't know," Ransom said. "He will tell us if he is able. It might be a secret, so that means you do not pester him with questions when he returns."

"Oh, Uncle."

Gweneth laughed, amused despite her disquiet over Ellard and Sable. "We saw you flying with your father. How long have you been flying?"

"A long time now," Hallam said.

Ransom chuckled. "Three cycles."

Gweneth managed to maintain an impressed expression, but her lips quirked. "Three days, I mean cycles. That is a long time. You're doing a great job."

"Apart from setting my trees on fire," Ransom chided.

The dragon child's round face turned pink. "Uncle, I'm sorry. I promise I won't do it again."

Gryffnn plonked onto the empty seat opposite her and Ransom. "You'd better not, squirt. If Ransom's forest burns down, we'll both be in big trouble."

"Did I tell you about the time your father burnt the entire west wing of our house?" Ransom asked. "After that mishap our father ordered the house rebuilt in stone to prevent further mishaps."

"He did?"

Gryffnn groaned. "Don't tell him that."

Gweneth chuckled, this discussion reminding her of others that took place amongst her friends during their long space voyage from Earth to Viros. She missed the teasing and camaraderie. Things had changed now that Camryn and Ry were expecting their first child, and Jannike had mated with the king and the duke. She had also become pregnant.

Ransom straightened, his gaze on something on the far side of the room. The indulgent uncle and brother retreated to leave a leader. The chieftain.

"What is it? What's wrong?"

Finally, Gweneth saw who claimed his attention. Niran, and she could see right through him.

"My nephew Leeam and his prospective mate Sheera are missing. They haven't been seen for two cycles, but no one raised the alarm because each of their parents thought they were staying with friends."

"Do you require help to search for them?" Ransom asked.

"Not yet," Niran replied. "We are questioning their friends and plotting their last movements."

Ransom nodded. "We're here if you require help. All you need to do is ask."

"Thank you."

"You morph in and out at will," Gweneth blurted, momentarily diverted from her jealousy of Sable.

"There are limitations to our powers," Niran said with a smile.

Gweneth leaned forward in her seat. "Do tell."

"No," Ransom ordered before Niran could reply. "Too much knowledge is dangerous. Wariness is good at this point."

Niran inclined his head. "That is true, but credit me with sense. I have read them both. They are who they say and mean us no ill will." His tone held a bite, and Gweneth sensed Ransom's surprise.

He shrugged his wide shoulders, the hard lines of his expression softening as he turned back to Gweneth. "You're right, of course. We discussed this meeting. Please, you've mentioned your ideas in general terms. Give us some specifics so I can begin to make my decision."

"We wish to bring more visitors to our planet to give our people employment and bring more currency into our economy. Our idea is to hold a festival featuring food and goods from our planet and our neighbors. King Lynx bade me to tell you that we wish peace and prosperity for Viros and our neighbors. We want a collective approach to help us reach our goals and provide greater security for each of us." She pulled a letter from her vest pocket and handed it to Ransom. "This is the formal invitation to participate in our festival."

Ransom tapped his finger against his chin, never taking this gaze off her. His golden eyes mesmerized her, and although she attempted to move, she remained fixed in place and at his mercy. Relief suffused her when he broke the connection to accept the invitation she held.

"Is the invitation for us too?" Niran asked.

"No, it's too dangerous." Ransom returned to the barking, imperious leader.

"We need to find a new habitat for some of our people," Niran stated. "We've discussed this."

"And we'll discuss it further, but not here."

"We weren't aware of your existence, but yes, you are very welcome to participate in our festival." Gweneth sensed the undercurrents swirling through the room.

A masculine chuckle sounded, and she glanced over at Ellard and Sable. The bolt of jealousy physically hurt. She rubbed her chest, but the ache remained. They looked so cozy together. Right somehow. Closing her eyes briefly, she wished Olivia lived closer, but they'd left her with Kaya's brother on Slyvia because of the proximity to Earth. Ry had given Kaya's brother instructions to ship Olivia back to Earth at the first opportunity. A pity that stowaway Olivia's plan hadn't worked out quite as they'd envisioned. She would've welcomed input from her Earth friend.

"I will give you my decision soon," Ransom said. "I wish to discuss this with others first."

"Of course." Gweneth kept her gaze on Sable. What would Olivia do in the same position? She wrinkled her nose as she thought of her friend. First, she'd tell her not to be a ninny and to fight for what she wanted. A fair fight, of course. Actually, Olivia would tell her—

"That is perfect advice, my dear," Niran murmured.

"What?"

"You have never faced competition because you are beautiful. You manage to wind men around your little finger," Niran explained.

"You're reading my mind. Stop that right now." She rapidly built a wall in her mind like Mogens, the *Indy*'s seer, had taught her. A necessary skill since Ry had been able to read minds when she first joined the *Indy*. Of course, that had changed since he and Camryn mated. No one knew why, but it had been a relief to all of them. "Can all of your people read minds?"

"Pardon me. You're right, of course," Niran said. "You were broadcasting your stress, and it is in my nature to assist those in pain. We have the ability, but do try not to trespass because that is rude. You're right to chastise me."

"I don't require assistance," Gweneth snapped. "I want a fair fight. It's right that Ellard should have a choice. I don't want him to think he's unattractive to other females." She turned to an amused Ransom. "If you decide to join the festival, what sort of goods would you highlight?"

"Would you like to visit our business and trading center this cycle after all?" he asked. "We can check on your ship repairs, and you can get an idea of what type of products we make."

"Yes, please." Gweneth shot a glance at Ellard and Sable. "Perhaps Sable could come as well. That way, I will have a feminine shopping companion."

Ransom studied his younger sister before turning back to her. "Yes. That is a good idea. I will inform Ellard and Sable of our plans."

Niran reached over and patted one of her clenched hands. "Well played, my dear. The perfect response."

A tingle zapped up her arm, and she let out a tiny eep of surprise. The sensations ceased the instant Niran lifted his hand.

"I believe I will participate in this jaunt to the shops," he said. "It promises great entertainment."

"I live to serve," Gweneth retorted.

Niran chuckled. "You are offering a distraction, my dear. I am worried and you are helping me function."

Gweneth snorted.

"Ellard and Sable will be ready shortly," Ransom told them. "Gryffnn, Jacinta, do you wish to come with us?"

Jacinta glanced up from where she sat with Gryffnn. "No, thank you. I am going flying with some friends. We might go swimming at the green lake."

"I'll stay to supervise my son," Gryffnn said. "We need to practice fire starting."

"Also putting out fires," Gweneth said with a grin. "That part seems just as important."

Ransom barked out a laugh. "True. The youngsters are always setting fire to things. We have an area set aside for them to practice their fire breath, but accidents happen."

"Let me show you your quarters before you leave," Niran said.

Gweneth stood, surprised that Niran was the one showing her to her room.

Niran smiled at her. "Ellard had better come with us."

Five mins later, she and Ellard followed Niran through an ornately carved wooden door, the last one in a long passage.

"This is it," Niran said.

Both she and Ellard came to an abrupt halt just inside the large and very empty room.

Niran gave a full-out belly laugh, and without warning, a looking glass appeared before them. "I wanted you to see your expressions," he managed once he'd finished laughing.

"But there is no furniture." Ellard shared his puzzlement with Gweneth. "Where did the glass come from?"

"I conjured it," Niran explained. "We receive sexual energy from Ransom's tribe, and in return, we gift them with material possessions. There is a catch, though. The items we conjure last as long as the user requires them. Once the need ceases, the magic dissolves the gifts."

"What if an enemy got hold of you?" Ellard asked, his military mind working differently to hers.

"We starve without sexual energy," Niran said. "We continue to exist, but no one can see us, and we can't communicate easily or use our powers."

"You become ghosts?" Gweneth asked.

Niran frowned. "Ah," he said, his expression clearing. "I understand ghosts now that you have ceased to block me. Yes, a little like ghosts. Now, I want each of you to imagine the room furnished to your specifications." He stared at them expectantly, then barked out a laugh.

"This is Ellard's vision." Niran waved his hand with a flourish.

Gweneth stared at the austere furnishings and realized he'd imagined his room at the castle. She'd peeked inside one day when he and Jarlath were sparring with the other feline males. The sturdy metallic bars, however, were telling.

"You hate me that much?" she demanded. "So much you want to keep me incarcerated?" She took satisfaction from the tinge of red that crept into his cheeks. Was she wasting her cycles? Maybe she should grit her teeth through the rest of this visit, return to Viros and retire to her room with the food that closest resembled

Earth ice cream. Olivia had told her Earth women did this after disappointment in love.

"What would you suggest?" Niran asked. "Whatever you choose will remain for as long as you require the item. Once you are no longer in need, the things we conjure disappear. That works for food, drink, clothing, or any other object."

The kindness in his expression tightened her chest, and she had to swallow twice before she attempted to speak. Part of her wanted to suggest to Niran that she would like a sumptuous bed—large, of course—since Ellard took up a lot of space. Storage units and a clothing replicator. A decadent bathing area. A bath. Candles. Perfumed cleansing tabs. A maid to wash her hair and help her dress. Pretty clothes. She drew a deep breath. No! She was smarter than that. Besides, Ellard would expect her to push her agenda.

"Are you ready?" Niran prompted.

"Almost." She slid a quick glance in Ellard's direction and intercepted a scowl.

Blast the man with an explosive. She had no idea why her feline insisted on this grumpy cat. After her initial surprise and rush of hormones during their first meeting, she'd tried to keep her distance. That had worked for all of two mins. Something inside her compelled her to check on him, to speak with him, and generally annoy him until he noticed her in return.

Blatant hadn't worked, so she needed to tamp down on the urgent instincts coursing through her mind and use subtle. She'd step away—apart from the kiss. She didn't intend to forgo her kiss because a bet was a bet. A point of pride.

"I'm ready," she said.

Niran smiled in the way Jannike and Camryn smiled at her if she'd done a good job. As she watched, Ellard's room vanished, and a new one appeared in its place.

"Well?" she demanded of Ellard once he'd surveyed the suite of rooms she'd imagined.

"I'll take the room in here," Ellard said, after checking both rooms from the doorways.

"The bathing facilities are between our rooms," Gweneth said. "There are locks on the doors, so neither of us need to fear a disturbance."

Ellard dipped his head in a decisive nod. "Are our bags here yet?"

"They're not necessary." Niran offered another of his approving smiles. "I took the liberty of stocking the clothing replicators. You'll find everything you require within your rooms."

"I'll use the sanitizer first." Ellard disappeared into his room, closing the door behind him with a click.

"Well done, child," Niran said. "You've made your move, made him aware of you. Backing off to give him time to process is a good plan."

Her chin jerked upward, but she left the mental barrier in her mind down as she regarded him. "I will be claiming my daily kiss."

A delighted chuckle burst from him. "I think that is fair. After all, a bet is a bet."

"Exactly." Gweneth stepped into her suite room, the musical sound of his laughter still ringing in her ears as she closed the door.

The business center of Narenda was much smaller than that of Viros. It consisted of a main cobblestone street, a central market square with cover from the constant heat and a series of small specialist shops lining the street.

Gweneth's heart sank. First impressions didn't bode well. The shops were so small. What could they sell that would appeal to festival visitors? Her hand tightened on her compad, disappointment a sour taste on her tongue. But, mindful of her duties, she went through the motions and used her compad to record the sights.

"Ransom, do I have permission to take depictions of the shops, the market area, and the goods on sale?"

He radiated approval. "Thank you for asking. General shots are fine. Please check with each store owner, though."

"Of course. Can I take a group shot of us in the marketplace? I would like to send it with my daily report." Top marks today, scoring endorsement from everyone except the man she desired.

"I will see your report before you send it," Ransom ordered.

"Of course you can," Gweneth said. "I understand the need for security. King Lynx suggested I discuss my report with you before I sent it to him. He wants allies as his neighbors rather than enemies."

"I think a depiction over there would work well," Ransom said.

Before she could blink, he had everyone arranged in a grouping in front of a decorative pond surrounded by red-and-white plants. Gweneth set the timer for the remote and her compad floated from her hands to a position in front of them. Secs later, a distinct click and whirr sounded then the compad returned to her.

"It is perfect. Now the shops. I would like to purchase a pretty outfit to take home to Viros. Sable, where would you suggest?"

Sable froze—a sort of a cat-spots-prey kind of freeze. "I...I...people stare," she finished miserably.

A whoosh of sympathy struck Gweneth. She knew how it felt to have people stare at her, how it felt to be invisible in a crowd and to feel small and insignificant. She'd experienced rejection. She tucked her compad in the satchel she'd discovered in her room and stalked over to Sable.

"Not today." She took Sable's Stores arm. "I think we both deserve a new outfit. What do you think?"

"I d-don't have any credits," Sable whispered.

"I have plenty of credits," Ransom offered into the resulting silence.

Gweneth glanced at each of the three men. Wow! Niran, Ransom, and even Ellard were looking at her in approval. A cause for celebration.

"Should we start at the beginning of this side of the street? If we don't finish, we can visit the other traders on the morrow."

Ellard groaned. "Can't we go quicker than that?"

"This is business," Gweneth chided, although she winked at Sable. "Here, you take charge of my compad. Lynx wants notes of the goods that the traders would be willing to bring to the festival. We'll need depictions too." She handed over her compad.

Ellard stared at her. "I can't, not with my hand."

"Of course you can," she said. "Ransom will help."

Gweneth headed to the first shop and entered, scanning the contents with growing approval. Better than she'd hoped. Much better. Colors—every one of the color palette—filled shelves. Scarves and everything a woman would want to groom or wear in her hair. When she couldn't hear Sable following her, she turned and gestured for her to hurry. "Come and tell me if I'm imagining things. The colors. They're gorgeous."

Sable entered, her footsteps dragging. She reminded Gweneth of a timid mouse.

"Look." Gweneth decided to take charge. "This scarf is the exact shade as your eyes. Such a gorgeous mixture of blue and green. And this..." She plucked a jeweled comb from a shelf and held it against Sable's long black hair. "This would be perfect in your hair."

"I have no experience with combs and such."

"I do," Gweneth said. "I'll show you, and you can wear it for dinner. Ellard, we need a depiction."

An elderly woman—a dragon, judging by her thin golden eyes—bustled through a doorway. She hesitated on seeing Ransom. "Chieftain Ransom."

"We are here to do some shopping," he said. "The ladies have taken a liking to some of your goods. This is Ellard Tetsu and Gweneth Swithin from Viros." He explained their mission and obtained an agreement for Ellard to take depictions along with relevant information about her goods.

SHELLEY MUNRO

They ambled along the street, the number of packages that Niran and Ransom carried steadily growing.

"This is one of our shops." Niran took Gweneth's arm and guided her to an unimposing building. "We take great pride in setting up a business since we had to learn new skills in order to produce stock for our shop."

Gweneth stared at the lackluster window display and tried to think of an encouraging response. "It's very clean," she said finally.

Ransom chuckled. "There, Niran. I told you your people needed a better display to attract customers."

"We want intelligent customers and have built up a loyal following. You forget, my friend, we do not require money or material possessions. This enterprise is a way for our people to fit in to the world of other races."

Gweneth took a deep breath to center her mind since she thought her tact might get a workout in this instance. "What do you sell?"

"Ladies' apparel," Niran said.

"I don't require any clothes," Sable said. "I'll stay outside with Ellard."

Over her dead body. "Remember, we're splurging and both purchasing something to wear tonight," Gweneth said. On seeing Sable's frown, she added, "Word-of-mouth advertising is crucial to any business. We would be helping the owners of this business by showcasing their clothing tonight." Gweneth peered inside the very white shop and prayed she wouldn't live to regret this spur-of-the-moment strategy.

"My allowance is spent," Sable protested.

Gweneth wanted to stomp her feet and shake the other woman. She did neither and managed a strained smile instead.

Ransom winked at Gweneth. "I will purchase a gown for you, Sable. Go inside with Gweneth. Ellard and I will discuss business while Niran introduces you both." He cloaked his words in an order.

A tiny crease of stubbornness etched into Sable's forehead.

Gweneth shrugged and maintained her strained smile as she entered the shop with Niran. Camryn and Jannike would tell her that competition was good for her. Personally, she didn't like it one bit.

Inside, a single rack of garments claimed her attention. The fabric shimmered and made her long to caress the jewel-bright colors.

Two women shimmered into focus. Both possessed long, straight white hair, their faces were pale with prominent rosy cheeks while their white eyes held pinpricks of glacier-blue. Their dresses reminded Gweneth of the ones she'd seen in Earth history books during her quest for knowledge. Vintage period with full skirts, fitted bodices and nipped-in waists. Pretty.

Niran beamed. "May I present my wife, Aurora, and my oldest daughter, Patrice? This is Gweneth who is visiting from the planet, Viros. And, of course, you know Sable."

Gweneth offered a polite smile of greeting. "I am very pleased to meet you. Did you make your gowns?"

"We plucked them from your mind," Patrice said.

"Patrice!" Niran said.

"They're beautiful," Gweneth said, starting to rebuild the mental brick wall. "They're Earth designs." She needed to keep that wall intact all the time. She'd grown sloppy with her mental defenses since Ry lost the ability to read her mind.

A silent Sable stood beside her, and Gweneth decided to work on her plan.

"Sable and I wish to purchase something new to wear this evening. Is that possible? Do you have suitable garments?"

Patrice rounded the counter and glided toward them. "I think I have the perfect gowns for you both. Come with me, and we'll get started. Mama will organize refreshments for the men."

She led them into a separate room with small cubicles for privacy and a large reflective wall. Not a mirror but something similar. Patrice slid another door open to reveal an entire wall of completed gowns.

"Normally, we use wish fulfillment to dress ourselves or satisfy our needs," she explained. "We're capable of doing that as long as we have enough sensual energy to feed us. Making apparel for others has been a challenge since we needed to find a way for the individual garments to retain their physical presence even if their owner no longer requires them. My mother developed a way of spinning the thread from the fibrous worm and combining it with a secret Incorporeal technology. The fibrous worm thread makes the garments permanently visible. Don't ask me the particulars because they're top secret, but that is the basic explanation."

"What you're trying to say is that we won't find ourselves naked during an important function," Sable said in a dry tone. "I am relieved."

Gweneth nodded. "I'm with Sable. Strangers shouldn't get to see my assets." Not unless they're Ellard, she added silently.

Patrice grinned, and Gweneth realized she'd forgotten to screen again. Must remember.

"Now, which colors would you like to try?" Patrice asked.

Sable glanced at the profusion of colors, and that tiny crease appeared again on her forehead.

Red, Gweneth thought. "I would like to try one of your gowns in that gorgeous blue-green color. I think it will make my eyes pop."

"Pardon?" Sable gaped at Gweneth. "Nothing should pop! I suffer enough trouble with a Stores arm."

"Sorry. Earth-speak," Gweneth said. "I meant that the color would match and highlight my eyes. It will attract attention."

Sable shuddered. "I don't want to do that."

"I'll choose several styles and bring them in for you," Patrice said.

"I can't wear these gowns," Sable said. "People will look at me."

"Do you want to find a mate and maybe have your own dwelling? Have children?" Gweneth asked.

"I can't have any of that."

"Why not?"

"I'm flawed. I'm a half dragon. I can't fly, and I have an artificial arm. None of the males take a second look at me."

"Rubbish," Gweneth said. "The male dragons on Narenda must be blind. I have an idea. If Ransom agrees to participate in the festival on Viros, you should attend. Come and stay with me at the castle. King Lynx won't mind. You can meet my friends and the males our age. At the very least, you'll have a holiday and make friends."

"I hadn't thought of leaving Narenda."

Gweneth strove for patience and tact when she ached to rescind her impulsive offer. She did not need the competition of a beautiful woman. Sable possessed the raw materials to eclipse her—if she took more care with her appearance and started raising her gaze instead of studying the ground so much. "Think about it now. Ah, here's Patrice."

Patrice handed three gowns of various shades of blue-green over to Gweneth. "Will you be all right on your own? I thought I'd help Sable. I can call Mama if you want help."

"I'll be fine." Gweneth eyed one gown with doubt. "Are you sure these are the right size? They look roomy."

"Don't worry. Put on that one. It's my favorite." Patrice nodded. "You'll see."

"Call me when Sable is ready. I want to see her in the gowns."

Gweneth whipped her comfortable pale blue tunic off and discarded the rest of her clothing. She picked a gown at random and slid it over her head. The second the fabric touched her skin, it shrank to drape perfectly. The short sleeves felt restricting, and she tugged at them. Immediately, the fabric gave. The second she ceased yanking on the fabric, the growth of the fabric halted. Gweneth stared at her reflection in the reflecting wall. It needed to be shorter. She tugged it up, and the fabric disappeared until it hovered about six inches above her knee.

"Wow!" she said, spinning to observe the gown from the rear. It dipped to show the curve of her spine, the fabric starting again at the small of her back. "What is this fabric?"

Patrice opened the door of a cubicle and poked out her head. "We call it shrinkton."

"Will it reshape and go longer or looser again?"

"Yes, although the garment maintains the basic style in which you purchase it, you can resize and drape to your heart's content. Come out, Sable. Show Gweneth your dress."

"I...I..." Sable hesitated. "It's different from what I normally wear."

"That is the idea," Patrice disappeared and came back out, shunting an unwilling Sable in front of her.

The red gown did things for Sable. It brought color to her face and clung to stunning curves. One arm remained bare while a sleeve covered her Stores arm.

"No, you're right," Gweneth said. "Take that dress off right now. I can't face having such tough opposition."

Sable sidled back into the cubicle and then halted, obviously replaying Gweneth's words.

Patrice laughed. "Look in the reflecting wall, Sable. I dare you."

Sable lifted her shoulders and marched into the middle of the room. "Is that...is that me?"

"I told you so," Gweneth said while inside, she railed at fate. Sable looked stunning, and once she updated her hair and makeup, Gweneth would face stiff competition. Ellard would love Sable...maybe more than he liked her. She swallowed and turned to Patrice. "Do you sell lingerie? We might as well get the works."

Ransom's residence, later that eve

Sable touched her face with her real fingers, an expression of wonder on her face. "Is that me?"

Despite her sour mood, the sense of impending doom that stalked her mind, Gweneth managed a sincere smile. "You look beautiful. The dragon males won't know what hit them when you enter the room."

Sable gasped. "Please, I can't walk in alone." She turned on the small stool in front of the reflecting wall and grasped Gweneth's hands. The Stores hand felt degrees cooler than her real hand. "Promise you'll walk in with me."

"I promise." Gweneth disengaged and whipped off the coverall she'd used to protect her gown. "I believe we should go, or we'll miss dinner."

A tap sounded on the door, and Gweneth opened it to find a smiling Patrice. "Ransom sent me to tell you the visitors have started to arrive." She beamed at Sable. "I love the way Gweneth has done your hair. You look beautiful."

Sable wiped her hand down her ruby-red dress. "Thank you. I've never felt so nervous in all my life."

"Gweneth and I will be with you or nearby. You have known this group of people for a long time." Patrice's gesture—a sharp downward motion of her hand—spoke of unconcern, but Sable still dragged her feet as they approached the source of the chatter.

They poised at the entrance to a large reception room, Gweneth and Patrice flanking a trembling Sable.

Immediately, Gweneth sought out Ellard and her heart soared when their gazes connected. Distinct approval glowed in his green eyes, and he dipped his chin in acknowledgment. Triumph flooded her until she noticed his gaze had wandered to Sable. His eyes widened and a slow grin slipped across his lips. He started walking toward them before pain struck Gweneth in the middle of the chest.

He was her mate, the one male who brought her cat to life and he wanted Sable.

She must've made a sound—a croak of protest—because Patrice frowned at her.

"Gweneth, I'd like to introduce you to my brothers. Sable, will you be all right with Ellard?"

"What?"

Gweneth noticed Sable couldn't take her eyes off Ellard either, who appeared striking in his all black attire tonight. There was an air about him—a confidence that hadn't been present in the time she'd known him. Her stomach churned with nausea, and even she heard the low, pained groan that squeezed past her frozen lips.

"I want to introduce Gweneth to my brothers. Would you like to come with us?" Patrice repeated.

"No, Ellard is over there. He will talk to me."

Patrice nodded and gripped Gweneth's arm, forcibly directing her in the direction. Her fingers sent a cool blast along Gweneth's arm. "Snap out of it, Gweneth."

"It hurts," she said, not trying to pretend with her new friend.

"Yet you're mature enough to realize that acting mean to Sable isn't the way to win Ellard. Come and meet my brothers. They will love you and fall over themselves to give you compliments to boost your morale. Ransom might even decide to have dancing later. He does sometimes, and he likes you. You intrigue him, and he is pleased you have taken an interest in his sister."

"My feline doesn't react to him."

"How do you know?" Patrice asked, guiding rather than tugging her across the room. She stopped and introduced Gweneth to several elders during their trip to the far side of the reception room. "Have you given other males a chance?"

Gweneth blinked. "I...no. My cat reacted so strongly that I haven't considered anyone else."

"Maybe you should. At the very least, you will make more

friends. I would love to have you visit Narenda again."

Gweneth studied her new friend. "You could visit me on Viros. It's not a long journey—unless you manage to stray into a debris field."

Patrice's smile faded. "I seldom leave Narenda. It's dangerous for me to leave others of our race, which is why we live in groups, amongst people we trust. I'm sorry, but I can't tell you much more."

"Of course. I'll ask your father if my curiosity gets too much for me. You're right, Patrice. I can't make Ellard love me. All I can do is show him the possibilities of a relationship between us."

"Exactly." Patrice linked their arms again. "I see my oldest brother over there. Jacinta is hanging off him. He's demanding that I rescue him."

"What is your telepathic range?" Gweneth asked.

"It's not that far, and we need to be healthy and well-fed in order to communicate. Another reason it is difficult for any of us to leave our clan groups. There have been instances of long-distance telepathy, but it is rare. Normally, we can do it if we're in the same building. Across the city is difficult."

"I'd better reinforce my mental walls then," Gweneth said.

"I try not to intrude, but I find you fascinating," Patrice admitted.

Gweneth wrinkled her nose. "In a non-stalkerish way, of course."

"What is a stalker? Oh," Patrice added as Gweneth provided a mental picture for her. "No, I'm not one of those. Ioannes, this is Gweneth."

A handsome male with messy white hair—the style her friend, Olivia, referred to as bedroom sexy—smiled at her. He wore more casual clothes than his father—plain black trews that molded to his muscular body and a shirt of a mixture of blue and green.

He held out his hand. "I match your dress."

"Your shirt changed color during our shimmer from home to here," Patrice said in a tart sisterly voice.

"Go away, little sister, so I can acquaint myself with this lovely visitor." He squeezed Gweneth's hand, one of his white eyes closing in a sly wink.

"I promised Father I would introduce Gweneth to Wendron and Urvan," Patrice said.

"I'll do it." Ioannes' grin died a fraction as he glanced across the reception room. "I have promised Father I will make the introductions."

"Will you be all right with Ioannes? Father wants me to make nice with two of Ioannes' friends." She pulled a quick face. "Neither of them is very interesting."

The rest of the night passed in a blur of faces, interrogations by elder dragon shifter females who had beckoned her with imperious fingers for an audience, and a slightly better part—meeting the single males. Patrice's brothers were all handsome and attentive. Gryffnn and some of the other dragon males danced attendance on her too, but not one of them dragged a reaction from her cat. Her feline expressed her boredom with an inner yawn and drifted back into slumber.

Gradually, the guests started to depart. Gweneth had repeated her spiel about the Viros festival so often she scarcely needed to think to answer questions. She scanned the remaining guests for Ellard and found him with Sable, their heads close together in discussion. A pang of distress pierced her chest again. She wanted to confront Ellard and tell him he belonged with her. She took half a step before forcing herself to halt. Making a scene wouldn't aid her cause.

"You look fatigued," Patrice said.

"I am," Gweneth said. "I didn't get much rest during the trip here to Narenda. Would it be rude if I retired for the evening?"

"Not at all," Ioannes said. "Father is summoning us. I believe we intend to leave now."

Gweneth smiled. "We enjoyed meeting you all."

"Good eve," Ioannes said as he faded from sight.

Patrice gave her a quick hug before she blinked out too.

Gweneth checked her vicinity and noted that all the Incorporeals had departed. She strolled over to Ransom. "Would you mind if I retired for the evening? It has been a long cycle."

Taking her by surprise, he leaned over and brushed his lips over hers before stepping back. His amber eyes glowed with humor. "I will see you on the morn. Maybe we could even arrange a flight for you."

CHAPTER 6

RANSOM'S CLAN HOUSE, THE NEXT MORN

Ellard sprawled in a feline-size gel-chair, the black synfabric and padding fitting to his back with perfect comfort. He studied the view of the profusion of bright flowers in the garden and endless forest from his chamber window and sipped from a white cup of hot tay—the fragrant green liquid refreshing in the dawn heat. A knock sounded on his chamber door, and Ellard's cup hovered in midair before he set it on a float table. When the knock repeated, he stood and grabbed a pair of trews.

"I'm coming," he shouted.

With his trews in place, he strode to answer the summons.

Gweneth stood on the other side, fully dressed in black trews and a pale gray tunic. "I know it's early, but I came to tell you I'm going to town to speak with several market holders. Ransom said he'd go with me."

"I'll come too." Ellard turned away from his door, and Gweneth entered and shut it behind her.

"There was something else," she said.

He turned at the strange note in her voice, and his feline stretched beneath his skin, wide awake and eager to sidle closer and bask in her scent. This morn, she'd chosen to leave the cat tattoo on her cheek uncovered, and seeing it gave him pleasure, not that he stopped to analyze the sentiment.

Instead, he remained rooted to the spot. He didn't trust his instincts or his feline with the opposite sex. They'd played him false in the past—the last time directly responsible for the loss of his arm. Now that he had a Stores, the young feline women still whispered and stared. He had no need of a mate. He had friends, lots of friends. He could have a happy life without a mate.

"Ellard."

He blinked and found Gweneth so close to him that he retreated before pride bade him to take a stand.

Something shifted in her face, her impassive expression slipping. Pain? No. He blinked again to stir his sluggish brain.

"I can go on my own to the market. I'll be perfectly safe with Ransom. Why don't you stay here and relax? Send a report to Lynx and Shiloh."

Ellard considered the matter. Splitting their tasks made sense. "Sable offered to show me around the area. We are going to do our strength training together."

Gweneth's face went blank. A pause. "That's good. I like Sable."

Ellard nodded and walked to the door to escort her from his room. When she didn't follow, he turned in puzzlement.

"Wait." Gweneth approached him, almost stomping as she crossed the distance between them.

His feline pricked its ears, alert and happy at her presence. Stupid creature.

Ellard willed his body not to react, willed his feline to behave.

"Yes?"

"You owe me a kiss." And she boldly walked up to him, wound her arms around his neck, and pressed her lips to his.

Ellard froze, yet every one of his senses leaped to hyperalert. And his feline—he gave a happy sigh and purred. Traitorous creature.

Gweneth pulled back to scowl. "I thought we'd discussed this and decided on a proper kiss. Not this half-arse attempt of yours."

Ellard felt his mouth gaping and snapped it shut. "Half-arse?"

"Earth term," she snapped. "Give me my kiss, and I'll leave."

This woman... He shook his head, unsure of how to deal with her. She didn't behave in the same manner as other feline women. He considered Keira, Camryn, and his new sister by mating, Jannike. Not true. Gweneth emulated those three. Determined and independent and maddening.

A challenge.

"I'm waiting." She had the cheek to start tapping her foot.

Slap. Slap. Slap.

Bang. Bang. Bang.

"Fine," Ellard snapped and grasped her by the shoulders. Although an impulse simmered within to give her a brief peck and send her packing, he knew better. He drew her against his chest.

Her green eyes still glinted with irritation, so he closed his, not wanting to see her accusation or any other flashes of emotion. And especially her feline. The female might be unable to shift, but he saw her feline during and after their skirmishes.

Soft lips greeted his. Warm lips. Eager lips.

They shaped and molded to his, opening to encourage him to deepen their kiss into more intimate territory. He hesitated even as his feline part urged him onward.

The prick of her fingernails pushed him, and with a groan, he stroked his tongue across hers. Rough and a touch abrasive. Feline in nature. His feline purred through his mind, happy and at ease.

Ellard stroked his hand down her back and fell into the kiss, the piquant taste of her—rich with berries and a hint of minty freshness—the feel of her strong body within his embrace, the fit of her curves against his hardness. Her feline-tinged scent.

The contact with Gweneth flooded his body with emotions he hadn't experienced for many, many cycles. Happiness. Contentment.

He pulled back without haste and opened his eyes to glance down at her. He thought he saw pleasure in her pretty green eyes, definitely satisfaction.

"Thank you," she said, reaching up to caress his cheek.

His eyes slid closed again without volition. Her touch. Something about her caress lowered his inhibitions, made him vulnerable.

"You are very good at kissing once you put your heart in it. I can't wait until the next cycle."

She pulled away, and Ellard let his arms fall to his sides.

"I will see you after my market visit. You can call me if you have any messages to pass on from Lynx."

Before he could reply or even attempt to regather his wits, she slipped from his chamber, leaving behind confusion and turmoil.

Ellard sighed and wandered off to the sanitizer room. Maybe a cold wash in the sanitizer would aid his sluggish mind.

After claiming her kiss, Gweneth shared a morn meal with Ransom, Gryffnn, and his son. "I'm interested in visiting the market. Last cycle was so productive, and I found every shop owner enthusiastic about taking a stall at the festival."

"We haven't had a chance to show off our talents before," Gryffnn said.

"We need to expand," Ransom said. "It's no longer sensible to remain isolated. I see many positives about this festival. It will give us a chance to meet our neighbors in a neutral setting for one."

Gweneth helped herself to another portion of local berries.

Bright red and tart in flavor, they tickled her taste buds. Delicious. "I'm so glad. We are offering each planet ten stalls. It will be up to you which retailers take part or you can send a selection from each one and share the space. If it were me choosing—"

Niran popped into view, worry broadcasting clearly on his countenance. "My nephew and his friend are still missing. None of us can sense their presence. We've searched everywhere we can think of but to no avail."

Ransom pushed aside his half-eaten meal and stood. "Could they have left the planet?"

"No." Niran began to pace, rising off the floor and pacing air in his agitation. "We would have noticed if they drew enough power to fashion a craft or transport their essence from here to another planet. They wouldn't leave because it is dangerous. They understand they cannot survive without sexual energy. Sheera and Leeam applied to be part of the next split-off group. I doubt they'd risk their good status to run away. I've come to ask for help. None of us can leave here for extended periods at present. We've been searching all blacklight and must imbibe energy and refuel. Could you arrange for volunteers to help us search?"

"Of course, my friend," Ransom said. "I'll organize the guards to begin a sector search and fly over."

"If you provide us with transportation, Ellard and I will help," Gweneth offered.

"No, you intended to visit the market," Niran said.

Gweneth stood and strode to Niran, where he hovered in the air. "The festival is not as important as finding your missing people."

Niran sighed. "Sheera and Leeam are your age, a young couple who wish to bind. They are good. Responsible. This behavior is most uncharacteristic."

"Ellard and I would be happy to help."

"Thank you, Gweneth. I will provide a vehicle for your use." He glanced at Ransom. "Perhaps they could search near the mountains. Both Sheera and Leeam have visited the area with a gathering group. If Ellard and Gweneth comb that region, it would make our search thorough and keep everyone else away from danger."

Gweneth frowned at his response. "What danger?"

"The mountain range where we get the stones from to make our jewelry emits resonance," Ransom said. "It is dangerous to dragon shifters and too much can send us mad. Too much glittery."

"But how can you make jewelry if the stone is dangerous to you and your people?"

"It's the mountain ranges that are the problem. Too much rock in one area. The small stones we work with can make our younger dragons go a bit silly but eventually develop immunity. The mountain ranges, however..." He shrugged. "Not possible. Even the older dragons can't fly over the region."

"Will Ellard and I be safe? We want to live to attend the festival."

"My people suffer no ill effects. I think you will be safe," Niran said.

Ransom scowled. "We fall out of the sky if we get too close. It's not dignified for a dragon to fall on his arse."

A chuckle burst from Gweneth, and she clapped her hand over her mouth. When he didn't get huffy, she uncovered her smirk. "And the glittery?"

Ransom shrugged this time, the beginnings of a smile twitching at his sensual lips. "Dragons love jewels. We possess a natural gift to find valuable stones, and that can be...distracting," he ended with a rueful shrug. "Older dragons find the lure easier to resist, but the younger shifters do not have the same ability to resist the glittery. Niran, I'll set the younger dragons to search the grids closer to the town. Don't worry, friend. We will find your people."

"This glittery physically disables a dragon shifter?"

"Yes," Ransom said, shifting firmly back into his chieftain status.

He planned their search with military precision, and Gweneth couldn't help thinking how much the dragon man resembled Ry. Why couldn't her feline pay attention to him instead of grumpy and distrustful Ellard? And this glittery thing. It sounded like a weakness, something an enemy could exploit, given the opportunity. Every muscle in his body had tensed at her last question, and he'd changed the subject. She should mention this to Lynx and Shiloh. The thought brought a flash of disloyalty, even though she hadn't known any of the dragons for long. They'd made her feel welcome, and she liked them. She'd need to consider this for longer, and she wouldn't tell Ellard. Immediately, her brain fastened back on her main problem.

Ellard.

She sighed and, for the first time, started to doubt herself. Was she doing this for the right reasons? Her background, her family life—perhaps she was overcompensating and trying to force feelings and emotions where they should never go. Maybe she should give up and move on with her life. She had options. Something to think about during the next few cycles.

Ellard entered the dining room at that point, and her feline stood to attention, aware of his presence before her. Something else to ponder. Did she trust the feline who had remained silent until she met Ellard? Perhaps she should rely on her intellect instead.

"Good cycle, Ellard," she said with an incline of her head. "Niran's nephew and his friend are still missing, and I volunteered to help with the search."

Ellard sat beside Gryffnn. "Of course. We would be happy to help."

"Thanks," Ransom said. "I want you and Gweneth to fly over this sector here." He tapped the chart he'd retrieved from another room and set it on the table. "It's mostly jungle and mountains. I doubt you'll find the youngsters there, but we should do a thorough search to set Niran's mind at rest."

"No problem," Ellard said.

"How long will it take us?" Gweneth asked.

"Given good weather, you should be there and back by blacklight." Ransom studied them both, worry creasing his brow. "You might experience turbulence due to the debris shower. Since you strayed into it, we have tracked the progress of the field. It has moved and is now closer to that side of the planet. I'm not sure how difficult that will make your search."

"Ellard? What do you think?"

"I hate the idea of two Incorporeal people out there alone," Ellard said. "We'll fly as close as we can to our search area. If necessary, we'll land and search on foot."

Ransom gave a curt nod, but Gweneth sensed his approval. Satisfaction and pride bloomed in her chest until she wondered if her frame could hold it inside without an explosion. While Ellard appeared grumpy and remained uncommunicative at times, his heart kept her coming back. She knew a little of the events that had occurred during the war with the House of Cawdor. Males with damaged pride roared like wounded beests. This, according to Amme, and after observing the species, she had to agree. Yes, she'd keep persevering. And Sable...well, if she lost to the half-dragon woman, so be it. At least she wouldn't go down without a fight.

Niran blinked into prominence, dragging her thoughts from her romantic life. "The ship is ready for you. It's full of safety equipment and food supplies." The male wrung his hands and couldn't seem to sit still. "I pray we find them this cycle. My sister..." He trailed off, his voice hoarse and strained with worry.

Gweneth grasped his arm as he flitted past, tugging him to a stop. "Niran, we will find your people."

"What are their names?" Ellard asked. "If we do find them, will they trust us?"

"Sheera and Leeam. You can tell them their parents and uncle intend to ban them from outings for the near future," Niran said.

She squeezed his forearm, ignoring the cool tingles that sped across her skin. "We will find them. One of the search parties will locate them, and they'll be home with their families before you know it."

"Soon," Ransom added. "We will find them before they fade from lack of essence."

"Thank you." Niran's voice broke, and he cleared his throat. "I'll go and report back. We're conducting our own repeat searches in the town and the surrounds."

Gweneth hesitated. "Would they consider stowing away on a vessel leaving the planet?"

"No," Niran said. "Definitely not. Unless they were with a mated couple, that would mean eventual death."

"No," Ransom agreed. "We seldom have visitors. Until recent times, we haven't welcomed them to Narenda. We haven't had any deliveries since your arrival because of the debris storm moving closer. It made flying conditions dangerous. I've sent your search coordinates to the ship."

"We'll contact you and let you know how our search goes," Ellard said. "You ready, Gweneth?"

Gweneth gave Niran a quick hug. "Don't worry. We'll find them."

"The ship is parked on the training ground," Niran said.

She and Ellard left the house together and walked down the gravel path leading to the open training ground.

Gweneth inhaled the fresh life force and caught a hint of something burnt in her quick breath. "Do you smell that?"

"Yes. I haven't smelled anything like that—" He broke off to stare at the ship that waited for them.

Gweneth let out a piercing whistle. Small. Sleek. Streamlined for speed. "Nanu would love it. I can't wait to tell him about this ship. Wait, let me take a depiction. Go and stand by the wing."

Ellard grumbled but stood as she directed. "It's fitted out with weapons."

"Do you think they're expecting trouble?"

Ellard frowned. "None of them give off that vibe. Let's get going. I don't like the look of the weather."

Gweneth tested her senses, and it felt as if someone stroked her skin in the wrong direction. Chill bumps pebbled on her arms and legs. She scanned the horizon and understood what Ellard meant. The point where the land met the sky carried a sluggish gray color. Streaks of mustard yellow and some red dissected the gray, and as she scanned the region, she caught a flash of light.

"The debris storm is coming closer, but there is something else going on with the weather. I wonder how often they get the storms."

"No idea. I'd hate to fly through another one. The first was bad enough."

"Agreed," Gweneth said. "The last one was scary."

The ship reminded Gweneth of a high-tech Earth sports car but without the rubber wheels. Marcus, Amme's mate, had kept one in his shed. Garage, she corrected herself. As they neared, two steel-gray panels rose. Gweneth slid inside while Ellard trotted around to the other side and clambered into the ship. This transport was made for short jaunts and not deep space travel.

Once seated, his knees were up around his chest. "How am I meant to fly and search folded up like one of Keira's herb twists?"

No sooner had he muttered the words than the ship's shape lengthened to accommodate his longer legs.

"Cool." Gweneth scanned the instrument panel. Everything bore a label in the Universal language. She tapped a button for computer voice control.

"This ship is equipped with voice control. Please state your names so that you can operate the ship during the journey." The voice sounded pleasant yet non-gender.

"Gweneth Swithin," Gweneth said.

"Ellard Tetsu," Ellard stated.

"Thank you, Gweneth. Thank you, Ellard. Would you like to follow the set search coordinates for this cycle's flight?"

"Very cool," Gweneth said. "I want one."

Ellard grinned at her, and some of her earlier apathy lifted. "Yes, we will follow the given coordinates." Their ship purred to life.

"I brought my camera—my depiction machine—with me. This is exciting, even with the circumstances."

Ellard shared another smile with her, and her pulse rate did a type of bump and grind, leaving her momentarily breathless. He scanned the instruments. "The ship is equipped with heat-seeking vision. Phrull, I forgot to ask about their appearance. Computer, do you have depictions of Sheera and Leeam?"

"Bringing up depictions," the computer stated.

Two pale faces appeared on a screen. Both had a rosy glow in their cheeks despite their pale skin. Their hair, however, didn't resemble the normal pale white of most adults. Nor did their clothes. Gweneth figured they wanted to express their individuality. Sheera wore her hair long and in curly blue spirals that matched her clothing, a soft pale blue tunic and darker blue trews. Leeam had colored his hair black and it fell down his back in a straight shiny curtain. His clothes were black and contrasted with his pale skin.

"Attractive kids," Gweneth said.

Ellard frowned at the screen. "They don't seem old enough to think about mating."

"Different species have different habits and expectations."

"True. Computer, state the basics of the mating habits of the Incorporeal race," Ellard instructed.

"Ellard! That is personal."

"Information is power," Ellard stated. "It might save our lives. Computer?"

"The Incorporeal people are an old race. Their powers have made them valuable to those who seek to benefit from a symbiotic relationship. Greed has led other races to snatch Incorporeals from their clans, and this has caused widespread loss of life."

"Explain," Ellard said.

"Each clan must live near a species that produces energy during their mating process. Without that energy, the Incorporeal fades from sight and loses the ability to function. It is possible for them to exist in this state for many rotations, but they are unable to become visible. Each clan has a leader, and when the clan is in a state of hunger, the other Incorporeals give their energy to the leader so that he may function. It is his responsibility to search out food."

"Computer, what happens if there are too many Incorporeal beings?" Gweneth asked.

"There is not enough food. The clans search out a new compatible food source and split for both groups to prosper."

"Niran mentioned this," Ellard said.

"If the Incorporeal race can conjure anything out of air, no wonder other races seek to harness that power," Gweneth said. "They couldn't force them to make everything they asked for, not if they can blink out of sight at will."

"They could if someone threatened their families or other races they care about," Ellard said. "And no doubt, there are other ways of controlling them. Most of us have a weakness of some sort."

Gweneth flinched at a flash that shot through the sky on the horizon. The storm did seem closer. "That is true."

"Not all races would produce the correct type of energy for them to feed on. Some races lay eggs or have artificial breeding. Others don't require a mate and can breed without another."

Gweneth turned from the window to stare at Ellard. "They can?"

"Yes."

"But what fun is that? Sex is about pleasure."

He scowled and stared out the window at the nearing storm. "You shouldn't be discussing this with me."

"Why not? I mean, I know about sex. I can give myself pleasure—"

"Enough," Ellard snapped, his glare off-putting as he turned to scowl at her. "I don't want to know about that...that stuff."

Interesting. Gweneth turned away to stare out at the scenery. The buildings gave way to trees. She could see an occasional clearing, the glint of water and splashes of yellow, red and blue flowers. She bit back a grin as she thought of sex and Ellard. The sec she mentioned anything relating to sex, he turned into a grumpy cat. Keeping him off-balance might be the key. Keep him confused, and maybe she'd find a way forward.

Ellard concentrated on the scenery and the instruments. The instruments picked up several heat patches, but since they flew over farms and dwellings, he didn't worry about stopping to check on identities.

"Have they searched the outlying villages?"

"Niran said they've been checked already. The search parties are investigating the outer zones and taking another look at places they've already searched." Gweneth glanced at him, and his feline sprang to attention, every one of his senses engaged by this sprite of a female, no matter how hard he tried to ignore her presence. "I presume they've talked to their friends and questioned their siblings."

"Niran said they had."

Ellard scanned the lake below, a clear and brilliant blue. "According to the instruments, the flight will take another forty mins."

"Do we pass over those mountains? The storm seems to have settled there." She peered at the instruments. "Do you think the weird colors are to do with the debris or something else?"

"No idea. I'm thinking it might be best to attempt to go around the storm rather than through it. Niran implied the ship would handle anything, but we'd still get tossed around."

"I vote for your idea," Gweneth said firmly. "We don't want to lose contact with Ransom. With luck, another search team will find the missing Incorporeal people, and we'll get a recall." She paused. "Ellard, can I ask you something?"

His stomach turned with sudden foreboding. He shot her a glance, expecting to find her impish humor. Instead, he saw seriousness and the birth of a frown. "Yes?"

"None of the feline women seem to have ambition. All they talk about is mating with an eligible feline, and they complain about the dust from the rebuilding dirtying the hems of their dresses. I've tried to make friends with them, but they seem shallow and stupid. None of them has ever traveled off-planet. They can't defend themselves. They haven't known true hardship. Oh, they talk about the war, but they remained hidden in their homes with their families. Some of them attended the ball where the showdown occurred, but they didn't have an active part in protecting the House of the Cat. Not like you and your friends. They have no interest in learning new things. When we were on the *Indy* together, we were a family and did stuff together. Ry made sure to keep us as safe as possible, and that we understood how to defend ourselves."

"You're still a family." He spoke nothing less than the truth because the *Indy* crew was a tight unit. And thanks to his brother and Jarlath, he'd become part of this group of strong felines.

"Things have changed now that Ry and Camryn have decided to use Viros as a base. While he hasn't discovered any relations here on Viros, he and Camryn want to bring up their child amongst other felines. They want their child to know their heritage. I understand that. I do, but it means I have to build my life here because they're my family."

"That's not true, Gweneth. In the short time you and your friends have been on Viros, we've followed several of your suggestions and recommendations. You must understand that after years of following tradition, this change, the need to keep up with our neighboring planets, has shocked many of our citizens. Some of them prefer the old ways where they lorded it over those of a lower position. There are still pockets of resistance who fight Lynx and Shiloh because they dislike change."

Ellard scanned the instruments and, after seeing nothing out of place, continued with his thoughts. "This festival idea of yours, Gweneth. It's brilliant. If you hadn't crashed the council meeting, none of us would have come up with an idea of this scope. Not that I approved of the way you did it," he added hastily in case she decided to repeat the action.

"That's what I mean," she said. "The older council members looked at me as if I had rocks in my head. They were shocked to the core that I dared to enter male territory. I don't feel as if I fit any longer. I don't fit anywhere."

The forlorn note in her voice tore at him. His feline gave an uncharacteristic whine, and the human part of him wanted to offer comfort. "I understand. I do," he said at her snort. "Things have been different for me too. Jarlath met Keira and fell in love. I knew Jarlath would mate. He had to since he stood first in line to the king until he stood aside for Lynx. I thought my job and my life would continue in the same way as my father's. Then, I lost my arm, and Jarlath mated with Keira. Everything changed, and the life I enjoyed shifted. Don't get me wrong. I like Keira, or at least I do now. I thought her a troublemaker at first."

"I think you're strong, Ellard. It can't have been easy losing a limb. I admire the way you haven't let it stop you from doing anything. You still train. You're still a bodyguard and train the younger soldiers."

A laugh escaped him, unbidden yet truthful and from the gut. "When I realized Jarlath had let them cut off my arm, I wanted to die. I found it difficult to accept. My anger fueled me for a time." And at himself for letting the enemy have entry to the castle.

"But you're okay now?"

"Jarlath is my best friend. We grew up together. Once I calmed down and asked myself what I would have done under the same circumstances, I knew Jarlath didn't have an alternative. I would have made the same decision if I had needed to make it for him. Jarlath gave me a chance to live, and that's what I need to do." Ellard heard his own words, and they struck him. He wasn't truly living, not if he decided to run from Gweneth. His feline liked her, wanted her. Maybe he should take this chance and embrace the possibilities, consider promises and final decisions later. But like Gweneth, he could enjoy life more, try new things, and savor new opportunities.

For some time, he'd been aware of a restlessness.

"Have you thought about what you do want?"

"My friend, Olivia, wanted me to stay with her on Slyvia. Ry and Camryn said they'd let me if Kaya's brother agreed, but I'm a feline. Ry's need to find his roots resonated with me. I decided to stay with what I knew rather than leap into adventure like Olivia. She's much braver than me."

"Where did you meet Olivia?"

"Amme—she used to be my nanny and my companion when I grew older. She married Olivia's brother and stayed on Earth. That's where I met Olivia. I want a chance to grow into myself." She shrugged and gave a self-conscious laugh. "That probably doesn't make sense to you."

But once again, her words paralleled thoughts he'd never had the courage to voice. "It does make sense. This assignment to visit the dragon shifters of Narenda is a start. You're meeting beings of different species. They like you. You're good with them.

You suggested the festival, and you're taking a huge part in the organization. I'd say you've already started growing into yourself and becoming your own woman. Just be yourself," he ended in a rush. Aware he drifted into territory too intimate, if he wished to stay away from Gweneth, he turned his attention to the instruments. Everything normal.

"Nanu will wet himself when he sees depictions of this ship. Maybe I should take inside depictions too." Gweneth picked up her device and aimed it at him. Her device clicked and she pointed it elsewhere, repeating the action.

"What do you mean? Wet himself?"

Gweneth placed her device on her lap, her green eyes twinkling with mischief. One quick glance had his feline reacting with a purr. He liked her in this mood, even if it did raise his suspicions.

"It means he will be envious. More Earth speak, I'm afraid." She sighed. "We had such a good holiday on Earth. I miss Amme, but she is happy with Marcus."

"Tell me about your holiday. Why do you like Earth so much?"

"Every day, I mean cycle, we did something new. We went shopping, to the beach. We helped Marcus on his farm and swam in his pool. We went dancing and to the movies. Camryn taught us how to cook different Earth foods. We cooked our food outside. They call that a barbecue. I met Olivia, and she took me shopping and showed me about makeup."

Amusement bubbled up in him. So much enthusiasm and zest for life. The feline who claimed her would be a lucky man. His feline gave a silent snarl, which Ellard ignored. Maybe he should ask Jarlath and Keira for names of eligible felines for her to meet.

"We could have a special day." Gweneth's excitement burst through his reluctant thoughts. "A day of celebration to spend with our friends and families. I wonder if Lynx would agree to a holiday so everyone can celebrate. And maybe during blacklight, we could have a dance or music in the square outside the castle gates."

"That's not a bad idea."

"You think?"

"Yes. You should suggest it to Lynx and Shiloh. Did Jannike enjoy your holiday?"

"We all did. Ry said we can visit Earth again, but that won't be until their child is born and is older."

The ship dropped without warning—a series of bumps causing his stomach to plunge.

"Whoa," Gweneth said. "That's one good thing about deep space flight. No turbulence."

Ellard scanned the controls. "Computer, report on the storm."

"The storm remains on this side of the planet in the upper atmosphere."

"That's what the instruments are telling me. It looks safe enough to fly over the search area. Computer, is the turbulence caused by the debris storm or the resonance the dragons mentioned?"

"The predominant cause is the resonance. However, conditions seem more unstable than usual due to the debris field, which has drifted closer to Narenda," the computer stated.

"There is something odd about that debris field," Ellard said. "It seemed to have an energy field of its own rather than just debris drifting through space."

"Do you think it's safe?" Gweneth asked.

"I'll try to go lower. Maybe we can get below the turbulence."

"Ten mins before we enter our search area. I'll watch the heat seeker and let you concentrate on flying. What is that?" Gweneth asked, gesturing at the screen that registered their position and the landscape.

Ellard studied the shimmering blob on the screen. He scanned their surroundings through the viewport and saw nothing but the slate-gray sky and putrid mustard-colored streaks that dissected their path. "Computer, identify anomaly on screen."

"Checking...checking... Anomaly unknown," the computer announced.

"I can't see it outside, only on the screen," Gweneth said. "It's getting bigger."

Their ship bumped through another spurt of turbulence. Ellard took the ship off autopilot, wanting the illusion of control. His hands gripped the controls, the knuckles of his good hand turning pale with each rapid buck of their vessel.

The last plunging dive swept them into a blanket of mustard-colored clouds. Ellard cursed, holding their ship steady through a series of gut-swooping bumps.

"Computer, what course should we set?" he demanded.

"Checking...checking..."

Ellard gritted his teeth, muscles and his Stores arm straining to hold the ship level. At least, he thought they were flying straight. Difficult to tell with this barlarkos-soup atmosphere. "Computer?"

"Checking...checking..."

"The screen has gone blank." Gweneth thumped her hand on the screen. "Nothing. Computer?"

"Checking...checking...checking..."

"I don't think it's working. All the instruments are blinking out," Gweneth said.

Ellard peered through the viewport. "I think we're exiting the cloud. The cloud is— Phrull, what is that?"

Instinct had Ellard shoving the controls to the right, but they worked as slow as his cambeest in a stubborn mood.

"It has the appearance of a space gate, but it isn't mapped on the charts," Gweneth said.

Ellard fought to turn the sluggish ship, but the shimmering blob pulled them closer. Their ship accelerated, and it wasn't because of anything he'd done.

Gweneth reached over and laid her hand on his Stores. His

imagination and the embedded sensors told him her fingers were clammy, yet she didn't panic, didn't scream, didn't demand he save them.

The mustard color dispersed, the sparkle becoming red, brighter, and larger.

A threat.

Ellard struggled to turn their ship. His feline snarled, a harsh cry of fury.

Without warning, their velocity increased, and they slammed into the shimmering object.

Gweneth's safety harness gave with the force of the collision. She crashed into the viewport despite his grab for her. The ship shuddered and groaned, and the computer burst into speech.

"Checking...checking...checking..."

They whooshed into darkness, going faster, faster, *faster*.

The pressure within the cabin grew until each breath strained his chest.

"Gweneth!"

No reply, and he couldn't see her.

"Gweneth!"

The weight on his chest grew, his mind going dark. Couldn't think. Couldn't breathe. Couldn't function.

CHAPTER 7

The steamy heat woke Ellard. Sweat poured down his face and beaded on his torso until his tunic stuck to him like an extra skin. He attempted to move and couldn't. Panic roared through his feline, leaping to the fore and tensing every muscle in his body. A groan slipped free, and he swallowed. Thirsty. Stuck. Sore head. Chest. Dark.

His mind returned slower than his body function.

His eyes flickered, and he realized something covered his face. His arm lifted, sluggish yet working. He'd landed in a bush, a tree of some sort. Something soft and abrasive brushed against his cheek. Immediately, fire consumed his face, and something sucked at his skin. The suction eased then began again. He thrashed, attempting to move, his eyes now fully open, reality sinking in its hooks.

The phrullin thing—the plant—intended to eat him.

Move. Move. *Move.*

He struggled, forcing his good arm free. His feline snarled, the testy panic echoing through his mind. His other arm refused to work despite the instructions his brain sent through the neural transmitters.

Shift. Shift. *Shift!*

The transformation began almost before he made the decision, but tendrils of plant held his arm firm. He felt a pull on his arm stump. A wrench, then debilitating pain. Too late, he recalled his Stores.

Needed to detach it properly.

The tug and pull continued from the plant as he corralled his panic enough to halt his shift.

Nothing happened.

Too far gone.

Agony writhed through his stump where the special connections slotted. He heard as well as felt the separation, the wrenching of his Stores from his body. Fur rippled across his skin. His tunic ripped—another hindrance to movement—but he wriggled and thrashed and crawled from the mouth of the tubular plant.

Tendrils grabbed for his limbs and tail. Ellard roared—his anger echoing through the sun-blasted clearing. But finally, he scrambled free.

He retreated and whirled to study the plant. It stood as tall as him with a cream-and-yellow tubular body. Half a dozen green leaves, covered with fuzz, protruded from the base. Something—maybe his Stores—bulged out the side. As he watched, the bulge reduced and disappeared. The plant released a sound, almost like a belch, and rotated in Ellard's direction. Then, the plant moved, dragging itself along the ground. The tangle of roots extended in front of it and propelled the tubular body in a forward motion.

Ellard found himself gaping at the weird sight.

Phrullin' hell. Seemed as if his Stores was gone unless he managed to cut it from the plant somehow.

No weapons. He scanned his vicinity, his mind still not functioning at full speed. Must've hit his head. He retreated farther to get away from the plant, which seemed to be stalking him and—

Gweneth.

His feline growled, fear a red-hot spear ripping through him. He lifted his head to scent for her. Grunted. A putrid scent lay in the air—one of rotting flesh and damp soil. He tried again, searching for the fresh green scent—the familiar bouquet of Gweneth.

Nothing.

He spun and tested the air in each direction. He backed up, sat on his haunches and tried again. He had to find her.

Strong, wiry tendrils slid around his tail and spread around his belly before he could blink. He leaped from his sitting position, every inch of him aching. The tendrils broke, and a pained cry came from the plant. He blinked in horror. Phrullin' great. Not only did they want to eat him but they had feelings too.

Nothing but those bloody plants. And...targool! The phrullin' things were moving, massing around him.

Which one had swallowed his Stores?

They all looked the same—tubular bodies—white and mustard yellow in color with furry red tongues. The tongues flickered in a rude gesture, the tiny filaments covering them flickering in ceaseless quivers. The green tendrils that had held him prisoner ran along the ground in front of the mass of plants, grasping, searching, reaching for food.

Phrull.

He searched for a weapon again and saw nothing useful. No, better to remain in feline form. He was stronger and felt marginally better, thanks to a feline's speedy healing and recovery.

The nearest plant moaned with such longing and desperation

that Ellard's hackles rose. He growled, low and menacing, but the tube plants kept coming.

Screw his arm. He'd run and search for Gweneth.

While his mind had dissected his choices and come up with a decision, the plants had surrounded him, cutting off his escape.

Gweneth. He had to find Gweneth.

Ellard leaped at the tube plant before him, mowing it down as he scrambled over the top of the white-and-mustard body. The plant shrieked—an ear-piercing scream—that cut through him like a sharp dagger, twisting his thoughts. He hesitated, scratching his scalp and then knocking it to clear his confusion.

Green tendrils snaked toward him, twisting under his tender stomach. They burned through the lighter fur on his underbelly. The sting worsened, and he roared. He wrenched his body, rotating and leaping at the tube plant behind him. Smaller in stature, it didn't seem to expect him. It shrieked at his sudden attack. *Must find Gweneth before these plants hurt her.*

He scrambled over the plant, snarling when the green tendrils attempted to fix him in place. Using the power in his hindquarters, he sprang away. For a sec, he thought the tendrils might hold him, but they snapped without warning.

The plants cried out, their unholy shrieks grating on his mind. He staggered at the sharp pain in his brain, his momentum keeping him flying forward. He landed awkwardly, his balance off due to his missing front leg. A pained grunt escaped, the air bleeding from his chest.

Ellard rolled and scrambled to his feet. He lurched away from the plants. *Gweneth. Got to find Gweneth.*

The whispers and screeches coming from the lumbering vegetation made every hair along his backbone stand to attention. Phrullin' creepy.

Determination propelled him onward, even as he cursed his slow ineptness. Lynx and Shiloh made him shift and practice, but they were always there to help him remove his arm. Jarlath encouraged it too, and the confidence they showed in his abilities helped jerk him past self-pity. Gweneth needed him, and he wouldn't fail his bright sprite.

His?

Huh. He continued his awkward run-hop-lurch action until he couldn't hear the plants' shrieks and whispers. Once assured of his safety, he paused to scent the air.

Forest. Plants—he'd never forget their putrid scent. Water.

No Gweneth.

Panic began to swirl through him. Had the plants found her already, eaten her?

He listened intently.

Nothing.

Think. What to do? He needed to go back to where he'd woken and move outward. They'd been together. Gweneth should be close.

Ellard slinked along a path, which wound between the trees. Tall, pale pink and uniform trunks stood in rows that reminded him of the castle soldiers on parade. The plants hadn't followed him into the trees, which told him they needed the heat of the glade, the direct light. Perhaps if he circled the open ground.

The hiss of the plants followed him, and they turned to watch his progress.

Ellard growled. Phrull, those plants were creepy. They were watching him from the clearing, and those closest had already sent out seeking tendrils. *Keep moving. Don't stop.* He lurched around the edge of the plants.

Blood. He smelled fresh blood.

He hastened his pace, going so fast that the lack of one leg didn't seem so bothersome. Phrull, it was Gweneth. Her still form lay on the far side of a small pond. No sign of the ship.

Although urgency urged him to enter the water, he slowed.

No knowing what lived in that. Better to go around. Curse those phrullin' dragons. Why hadn't they mentioned the carnivorous plants?

Ellard skirted the pond and approached Gweneth with trepidation. Phrull, she couldn't be dead. She couldn't.

Blood tricked down her cheek. He nudged her, and when she didn't move, he licked her face, clearing the worst of the blood coming from a gash in her skull. Gweneth. *Gweneth.*

Ellard stood back and shifted.

A series of shrieks snared his attention. The tube plants had arrived, circling the pond in a mass, moving in a ponderous fashion, their roots dragging their bodies across the open ground. Already, their green tendrils crept toward the water.

He'd have to move her, go deeper into the trees. Assess her once they reached a safer location.

He bent to scoop her up, grunting at the pressure on his one arm. He almost dropped her before a burst of energy had her sliding against his chest. Phrull, he couldn't carry her. He'd have to dump her over his shoulder and hope he prevented further injuries. Her limbs appeared normal, but her lack of consciousness bothered him. And the blood...

Panicked urgency gave him extra strength, and somehow, he lifted her until she dangled her over his shoulder. On shaky legs, he straightened and almost face-planted. Gods, this was why he shouldn't be with Gweneth. His limitations made him a liability.

A sibilant hiss made him jump. How had the bloody plant crept so close? Gweneth slid off his shoulder and he cursed at his inability to save her. A quick glance showed the plants had built a bridge of green tendrils across the pond, and the tubes at the front of the pack were starting to cross.

"Phrull." He struggled to lift Gweneth again. "Gweneth?"

"Burns," she croaked.

"Ah, phrull." A green tendril had slid stealthily around her wrist and burned her skin. Ellard freed her with a jerk and slid his arm around her waist. "You'll have to help me."

Gweneth gave another pained moan, and it spurred him to action. He directed her limp body from the path of the seeking tendrils. She moaned but staggered beside him. He followed a narrow path into the trees, trying to help her as much as he could. Once he could no longer see any plants, he halted.

"Gweneth, tell me where it hurts." He stared down at her, concerned at the renewed path of blood running down her cheek.

"Head. Ankle. Chest," she croaked after a pause.

"I'm going to check you for injuries. Just want to make sure we're safe."

"What were those things?"

"Plants. They tried to eat me."

A shudder ran through her. "What happened? I remember the storm, and I think I struck my head in the ship. That's all I remember."

"We crashed. I couldn't see any wreckage."

"So we're stuck here?"

"For the time being," Ellard said. "We have no way of contacting the dragons."

"I know."

Ellard frowned at the place where his hand used to be. A burst of cold attached to his stinging stump and he felt as if he possessed an arm again. He blinked because there was nothing there. No arm. No fingers. But it felt...

"Dragons," a voice whispered.

Ellard started and whirled around, his heart thudding against his ribs. "Who's there?" A reply wasn't forthcoming, so he made a wild guess. "Sheera. Leeam?"

Silence reigned, and he couldn't decide if he was hearing things or not.

"Your uncle is worried about you," Ellard said. "Your parents are desperate to find you. Everyone is searching for you."

The voice didn't reply, and he shrugged, turning his attention back to Gweneth. Her usually vibrant features were pale, the wound leaking blood again, and her eyes had slid shut. He stroked his thumb across one grubby but silky cheek. At least she was alive. Her breasts rose and fell with each even breath. Phrull, she looked so small, so defenseless. The weight of responsibility for her safety crushed his confidence.

"I don't know what to do," he whispered.

A tiny smile played around her lips until she attempted to sit upright. A groan slipped free, prodding at his insecurities.

"Don't move."

"Not going anywhere," she whispered.

He stared at her, and unable to resist, he brushed a kiss on her pouty lips. She sighed, a murmur of something resembling satisfaction. Some of the weight on his chest lifted. He repeated the caress because he'd enjoyed her sigh. Then he squirmed a little because, in truth, the contact lessened his panic. He tasted her sweetness, a hint of blood.

"What would you do if Jarlath injured himself?"

"I wouldn't kiss him," Ellard barked out.

"Good to know. I'm sure Keira would be reassured."

Ellard snorted, but her question had pierced his panic. If it were Jarlath, he'd assess his injuries then he'd do his best to treat him. He'd stop the bleeding. "I'm going to touch you, check for injuries."

Gweneth opened eyes that had closed and licked her bottom lip with one slow lash of her tongue. "Sounds like fun."

Ellard snorted again, this time the sound closer to a laugh. The woman killed him with her persistence, her charm, her love of life. "Tell me if I hurt you." He sucked in a breath and pictured Jarlath. If he pretended this was his best friend, then maybe he'd manage the task. He started with her legs.

Jarlath. Jarlath. *Jarlath*.

Nope, not working, not with her warm flesh heating his hand. Slim, yet strong thighs, shapely calves. His gaze stopped on the hole in her trews. The skin beneath appeared blistered. "Is it still burning where the plant burnt you?"

"Yes, a bit." She jumped.

"What?" He hadn't been touching her.

"Something cold touched the burn. It gave me a fright."

Ellard scanned their surroundings. Nothing. But even so, he thought they'd managed to stumble upon Niran's missing people. He failed to understand their continued silence. "Is it helping?"

"Yes."

"Thank you," Ellard said with another glance around them to check for danger. When he saw nothing except tree trunks, he turned back to Gweneth and sucked in a fortifying breath before he touched her again. Arms next. Before he could second-guess himself, he checked her arms one at a time. She winced. "Sore?"

"A little. Bangs and bumps, I think."

Ellard gave a curt nod and ran his hand over her torso. His fingers skimmed her breasts, and heat blasted through him like combustible rocket fuel. He swallowed and jerked his hands away. A quick glance showed distinct humor, and her white teeth tugged at her bottom lip as if to halt a smile or a laugh at his expense.

"Stop it," he said sternly. "This is hard enough for me as it is."

"Why?"

"I hate seeing you hurt."

"And?"

Curse the woman. How did she read his mind? "And touching you unsettles me."

"In a good way or a bad way?"

"Undecided."

"Oh."

"Nothing wrong with your thought processes. You're teasing

me."

"And your point is?"

"What is the word Camryn uses? Ah, yes. Smart arse. You are being a smart arse at my expense."

She flashed a grin, and it warmed him through. His feline issued a purr of pleasure, and blood poured into his cock, taking him from confused to ready for action in half an eye blink.

"I think you're right. You're going to have a few bruises. Let me try and clean up your wound. I need something to bandage it, stop it from bleeding again."

"Use the bottom of my tunic. It's cleaner than yours." She wrinkled her cute nose. "What is that yellow stuff?" She leaned closer then reared back. "Stinks."

"I woke up and found myself halfway inside a tube plant. I *was* the dinner menu." Ellard stared at her tunic. "I've no idea how I'm going to rip a strip off your tunic. It's not easy with one hand."

"What happened to your Stores?"

"The plant swallowed it."

"Oh. I'm not sure I have the strength to rip a strip free either," Gweneth said. "Not yet. I feel as if the entire *Indy* crew have pummeled me during a training session. Oh, wait. Stars, I'm an idiot. I have a knife in my boot. The right one. There is a small knife concealed in the heel. We all had our boots modified after Jannike's abduction."

"I don't suppose you have a communicator stuffed somewhere."

"Nope. Mine was in my messenger bag."

"Your what?"

"It's a type of bag. I can't believe I've lost it. You didn't see any of the ship debris?"

"Nothing," Ellard said. "I have no idea how long I was out." He studied the heel of her boot. "How do I open it?"

"The stud at the back. Push on it and hold it down until you hear a click."

SHELLEY MUNRO

Ellard followed her instructions, and secs later, he managed to cut an uneven strip of fabric off the bottom of her tunic. "You are a very unusual woman."

"Is that a good thing?"

"Yes," he said firmly. Gweneth and her female friends were different from Virosian women. "Can you turn onto your left side for me? Wait, I'll help you." He rolled her over, holding her in place until she breathed through the pain. "Okay?"

"Yes. I'll have to get over it. It's getting late. We'll need to find shelter for the blacklight. We have no idea what might be wandering around."

"I'll check your injuries first." He smoothed the tangle of locks off her cheeks to reveal a small cut. His breath hissed out.

"What?"

"It's just a small cut. I thought it might be worse."

"Head injuries always bleed a lot. Jannike bled all over the bridge because she didn't have her safety harness on and slammed into the wall."

"Ouch," Ellard said. "That's why you should—"

"Always wear a safety harness," Gweneth finished for him. "That's what Ry says."

"How did you meet Ry and the others?"

She hesitated, uncharacteristic for her, since she usually sprayed her words everywhere without much apparent forethought.

"You don't have to tell me." He eased her up a fraction and attempted to wind the makeshift bandage around her head.

"I can hold the end." Her small fingers covered his, and the muscles of his arm tensed.

He inhaled sharply, fighting the surge of lust that grabbed him by the nuts. Such an innocent touch, but now that she'd kissed him, allowed him to kiss her, his mind kept diverting to thoughts of closer contact. Sex. "I... All right." He withdrew his fingers, his feline snarling through his mind in protest. "Let me put the

120

bandage in the right place." He did and gently pressed her fingers in position. "Hold that there, and I'll wind the bandage into place."

Between the pair of them, they positioned the bandage, and with her help, he fashioned a knot to hold it in position. With the bandage secured, Ellard turned his mind to the next step.

The endless expanse of forest offered little in the way of shelter, but there was no way they could venture into a glade, not with those tube plants. They required a steady stream of whitelight, or else they would've followed them. Unless something else in these forests kept the plants confined to the clearing. The heavy weight of responsibility had him scanning the trees, casting out his feline senses to detect trouble.

This easy and quick jaunt to Narenda had turned into an adventure. A flash of humor struck him at a recollection of him telling Jarlath he enjoyed routine. Jarlath's change of behavior had rattled him, yet he had to admit—despite the danger and the radical life changes—he did enjoy adventure.

"How is the head? Do you think you can walk, or do you want me to carry you?"

"It would be better if I could move. I need to try. I'm slowing our progress. Besides, we don't know what creatures wander the forest during the blacklight. We need to find a place to hole up for safety."

"Kiss her."

The soft voice offered temptation, and Ellard froze. His gaze cut to Gweneth. No, she hadn't heard. He frowned in indecision. Somehow, his feline must be sending him messages. Either that or they had invisible company.

Still, a kiss wasn't a bad idea. Gweneth deserved one, given her pragmatism and sensible reaction to their situation. Before he could talk himself out of the idea, he bent over her and kissed her pink, tempting lips.

She never hesitated, kissing him back, enticing him to linger and savor. When his brain began to work, he lifted his chin. For a long sec, they stared at each other.

She swallowed, and her tongue darted out to soothe her full bottom lip. "Um, what was that for?"

"A thank you," he said gruffly. "You're injured, yet you're not panicking. Instead, you produce a knife from your boot. Thank you for not behaving like one of the castle ninnies."

"Ninnies?" A smile curved her lips, drawing his avid attention. "Ellard?"

"Kiss her again. Please."

The small voice sounded close to his ear. Not his imagination.

He closed the distance between him and Gweneth. "I think we have company," he breathed against her lips. "I'm going to kiss you again. Watch behind me to see if you can see anyone."

He didn't give Gweneth time to reply, settling in to kiss her. He'd previously restrained himself and kept the kisses as innocent as she'd allowed him. This time, he sank into the pleasure and gave her one of his very best, using every bit of technique he'd learned since he became sexually mature.

Gweneth responded so sweetly, her soft groan like a caress down his back and over his arse. A shudder worked through him as she opened to him. Unable to resist, he explored the silken depths of her mouth. Her tongue danced with his, and she issued another sexy moan.

When he pulled back, they were both breathing hard.

His gaze darted to her mouth. Her lips appeared redder than normal and swollen. A sense of satisfaction suffused him. "Did you see anyone?"

A flush collected in her cheeks. "Sorry. My eyes closed. I couldn't help myself. Can you help me up? I can't see anyone."

"Sheera? Leeam?" Ellard swung in a slow circle but saw nothing but trees. "Maybe it's my imagination. Give me your hand, and I'll pull you up."

"No. I need to crawl to my feet. Just hold on to my arm and help me balance." As she spoke, she rolled and used her arms to push to a crouch.

Ellard watched her face, saw the strain in her features, and a sense of pride engulfed him at her lack of complaint. He helped guide her until she stood fully upright. "Are you okay?"

"I'm sore, but we need to move. I can't see anyone," she added.

"You go first. Cast out with your feline senses, test the air to scent for danger."

Gweneth wrinkled her nose. "I can't do any of that."

"Trust your gut. We need to proceed with caution."

Gweneth set a slow pace, and he watched her for a time. When she didn't flag, he paid more attention to their surroundings. The sense of someone observing them persisted, yet he couldn't hear a sound. He would have thought the Incorporeal couple would have made their presence clear since he'd mentioned Niran. Must be a reason because his instincts weren't playing him false.

Someone had attached themselves to them. Someone was observing their every move. Someone followed them through the forest.

Gweneth limped along the natural path that wound through the trees. Smooth and well-worn. Something...someone had made the path.

Up ahead, bright whitelight shone on the trail.

"It's quiet. There should be birds and insects." Gweneth came to an abrupt halt. "This clearing is full of those weird tube plants. Oh my stars! Did you see that?"

"What?"

"A small bird was perching on a bushy olive-green tree on the edge of the clearing. That tube thing sent up a green tendril and snatched the bird right out of the tree."

"I hope the one that ate my arm gets indigestion," Ellard muttered. "Those things aren't cheap. I cleaned out my savings to make the purchase." And even worse, the Stores was a one-time installation. He forced his mind off the unpalatable fact.

"Part of the clearing has rocks. None of the plants are anywhere near them. I think they have to stick to the soft ground."

"And near water. This clearing has a pond too. We'll have to go around." Ellard checked for a suitable route. Thick tree growth surrounded the glade. Off the beaten path, bright green plants grew in thick abundance. Each stalk carried a series of sharp spikes. "We'll circle the clearing. Let me go first so I can break through the undergrowth."

"Wait." Gweneth grabbed his arm. "I can hear something."

Ellard sent his senses soaring, his feline stirring as if he anticipated danger.

"No danger," the voice whispered.

But Ellard didn't move and remained still, casting out his senses to understand what might make the cracking noise. He caught Gweneth's gaze, and she mouthed at him, then turned a quiet circle to take in their surroundings. So, she'd heard the voice too this time.

The crashing sounds continued, coming closer. Ellard signaled Gweneth, and they both edged off the path and hid behind a tree.

A bird appeared, but not like any bird he'd seen before. A weird grating moan came from the clearing, and the plants pulled back from the edges until they stood in a solid mass of white and mustard. Their writhing green tendrils retracted until they were short stubs attached to each plant. A second and a third bird trailed the first, equally huge in size. Their hefty legs and talon feet crushed the twigs and sticks on the path. Their bodies were birdlike but on a large scale, and they possessed long necks with small heads and beady yellow eyes. Their brown feathers appeared almost furlike.

"They made the path," Gweneth whispered, her breath warm against his ear. "Let's hope they're vegetarian. I've seen something similar on the planet Ornum. The birds I'm thinking of are rare, but they're plant-eaters."

"I wish the dragons had told us about the dangers here," Ellard murmured, not taking his gaze off the approaching birds.

"Maybe they don't know," Gweneth said. "If they can't fly over without getting pulled at by the glittery fever, why would they travel here?"

"But Niran and his people come here. He should've mentioned something."

Gweneth shrugged then winced. "Maybe he was too worried."

"No danger," the voice whispered.

"I hope you're right." As Ellard spoke, the nearest of the huge birds stared straight at him. Ellard froze, and the bird gave him another searching look before it ambled past. At the edge of the clearing, it waited. The moans from the plants increased in intensity. The other two birds lined up beside the first, and without warning, they charged.

The plants shrieked, but the birds ignored the cacophony. They seized one flower tube, and with combined effort, they dragged it from the group. The tube screamed and struggled, helpless in the grip of the birds. They dragged it from the clearing and into the trees. As soon as they reached the dim light, the tube's struggles ceased.

"That answers two questions," Ellard said. "The plants need the whitelight, and the big birds prefer vegetables. Let's go. If we hurry, we can skirt the clearing while the tubes are in a tizzy."

Gweneth nodded and stepped onto the path. She muttered under her breath, pausing to stretch her right leg before hustling toward the clearing.

The birds had devoured the tube and strutted back toward the massed plant tubes. The high-pitch screeches resumed, but Ellard didn't pause to look, instead striding after Gweneth.

The track reached the base of a hill, and the gradient increased.

The trees were thinner here and the rocks glittered different colors in the whitelight.

"Might find a cave," Gweneth said.

"Maybe." The top of the hill appeared flat. "If we climb up here, we might see where we are. The dragons will send out searchers if we fail to return." At least, he hoped that would be the case. Ransom had struck him as an honorable male.

"Danger," the ghostly voice whispered, so faint Ellard wondered if his imagination played him false. But that little voice hadn't steered them wrong so far.

"Let's stay in the trees during this blacklight," Ellard said. "Stay under the cover of the trees and observe before we make any decisions."

Gweneth gave a tired nod. "I'm not sure I could make the journey at present. Every single muscle is singing a protest in time with my brain."

"Why didn't you say?"

"Wasn't safe to linger."

Ellard bit back his protest at her logic. She'd done what she needed to do to get to safety, and now he needed to do the rest.

The familiar drone of a ship had him peering through the trees. The pilot wouldn't see them through the mass of vegetation.

"Quick, run back to the clearing. Try to hail them."

CHAPTER 8

E llard took half a step and bumped into a cold but invisible
wall. The icy wall engulfed him at his next step, and a
shudder sped across his skin. His feline grunted, and each of his
senses—humanoid and feline—spiked to full awareness.

"Ellard, hurry."

"No." He had to push out the word, the cold so bad he couldn't
think.

"Kiss." The weak demand sounded next to his ear.

He took a step back toward Gweneth, and the cold disappeared.
He studied their surroundings and couldn't feel or sense anyone
dangerous.

"Why aren't you trying to get help?"

Ellard turned to face her. "Our invisible friends attempted to
stop me. Can you hear them talking?"

Ellard closed the distance between them and slid his arm around

Gweneth. Before she could voice the questions shining in his eyes, he kissed her. He dived straight into the experience, tasting her lips and the silken depths beyond. After her initial start, she slipped her arms around his neck and clung, pressing her breasts against his chest. A pleasurable shudder worked down his body to sink into his cock. Phrull. He closed his eyes and focused on the buzz of enjoyment, her scent, her taste.

The squawk of a bird had him raising his gaze to scan their surroundings. He remained close and allowed the truth to simmer between them.

Gweneth quirked a brow at him, her luscious lips tilting up at the corners. "What was that?"

"You don't know? I must not be doing it right."

Her smile broadened to a smirk. "You know you're doing it right, Ellard. I want to know why."

"An experiment."

Some of her good humor faded, and he wanted to kick himself. He wanted more than kisses, yet maybe this was better. He shouldn't encourage her when she could do so much better than him. His one experiment with the opposite sex since he'd lost his arm hadn't proved a success. His partner had refused to continue unless he turned off the light, even though he'd paid her for the privilege. Gweneth could have her choice of lovers.

"I thought we were past that." Her sharp tone spoke of irritation. Anger.

Face the problem. "You're beautiful, Gweneth. I wasn't much to look at before I lost my arm. I'm a handicap."

"What you are is an idiot. Why the experiment if you think we have no future? Our kisses are a rousing success. Don't try to tell me you feel nothing because I won't believe you."

"I haven't been with another female for ages."

"Good. I don't like to think of other females touching you."

Ellard blinked.

"The experiment," she prompted.

He blinked again, his mind not working at its normal pace. She almost sounded jealous of his other lovers.

"Ellard!"

"The voice keeps telling me to kiss you. We must give off sexual energy with each kiss."

"Sheera and Leeam are hungry? That's what you're saying?" Gweneth curled her fingers to a fist, fighting the urge to jump up and down and cheer. Yes. Yes. *Yes!*

"I think so. I think that's why they're having difficulty communicating with us. I'm hearing snatches of words, sometimes very faint."

"I felt something extra—a shove when you lifted me."

"My theory is that helping us that way drained the last of their power."

"We must keep them alive. They're kids starting out."

Ellard's brow furrowed. "They're old enough to mate. They're not youngsters any longer, not according to their Incorporeal race."

"They stopped you running to find a clearing."

"Yes, and they didn't want us climbing to the top of the flat hill."

They'd wanted her and Ellard to kiss. She could use this to nudge their relationship along in the correct direction. Stars, she could kiss Leeam and Sheera even though she hadn't met them yet.

"The ship is heading back this way," Ellard said.

Gweneth drew in a breath and clapped her hand over her mouth.

The ship came closer and appeared to hover above them.

Ellard eased up beside her. "They know we're here. Must have heat-seeking equipment."

"Friend or foe?"

"The voices say danger."

The ship continued to hover.

"Off the path," Ellard whispered. "The birds are heading back this way. Maybe they'll think we're birds too."

Gweneth slipped into the trees with Ellard close on her heels. A thought occurred. "Stand close to me. They might think we're bigger."

"Good idea."

Gweneth smothered her grin against his chest. What did Olivia used to say about kismet? Something about if it came calling to cast away doubt and embrace that bitch until you sucked it dry.

"They're leaving."

"Could be any number of reasons. What should we do?"

"On the assumption they've found us, I think we should stick to our plan. Find shelter and reassess in the whitelight. Hopefully, the dragons will realize something is amiss and find a way to get us out."

"Makes sense. Can we use those leafy plants over there to fashion a shelter and something to rest on? They're not the hungry type?" Gweneth straightened from her lean against Ellard and winced at the combined pain of several bruises. Not for the first time, she wished she could shift to feline to help speed her recovery.

Ellard trotted over to investigate the plants. When he started tearing the large green-and-pink leaves free from the main plant, she joined him.

Once they had a pile, she grabbed an armful and followed Ellard. He plunged off the track again and into the trees until he neared a large rock formation.

"This will work. The rocks at our back and the trees are thick here. We can't see the path, but we're still close enough to get to it." He dumped the leaves he carried. "Stay here. I'll get the last of them."

Despite the unrelenting aches and jabs of pain, Gweneth started to fashion a bed. If she stopped and sat down, she didn't think she'd manage to start moving again.

Ellard returned with the last of the leaves. "I saw some sticks we can use to make a framework. The air feels wrong. It's going to rain."

"Delightful," Gweneth muttered as he strode away. "Cold, wet, and sore. A triple treat."

Ellard returned, and together, they constructed a rough frame. They draped the larger leaves over the top, layering them to make a roof.

Gweneth sank to the ground with a groan.

"Take off your tunic, and let me check your bruises. In this heat, infection will set in quickly."

Gweneth opened her mouth to argue, then pressed her lips together. Getting naked with Ellard might spur him onward and give him a nudge in the right direction. She raised her arms and hissed. "You'll have to help me."

It took him longer with one arm, but their combined efforts finally worked.

"Phrull, that's a big bruise on your ribs." He traced the region with one gentle finger, and her breath caught at the scatter of sensations that darted from the point of contact.

"At least nothing appears broken. We were both lucky."

A howl sounded in the distance, and they both lifted their heads, automatically scenting in the direction of the disturbance.

"Better grab a pile of stones and a stout stick. We possess one knife between us," Gweneth said.

"The creature—whatever it is—isn't close. Not yet. You stay there. I'll collect a stash of sticks and stones. I want to check your wound while it's still light enough to see."

"My head isn't too bad, not as painful as my ribs."

"Yes."

Ellard left, and Gweneth attempted to relax. While she hadn't planned her cycle to end this way, at least she was with Ellard.

By the time he returned, blacklight had settled in, bringing the area to creepy life. Shadows loomed, spread by the faint starlight that pierced the trees. The sounds were different, although the creature hadn't howled again.

"Do you want to put on your tunic?"

"It's still muggy. I think I'll sleep better without it." While Ellard had been away, she'd rolled it up into a neat pillow.

"It's started to rain."

"I hadn't noticed."

Ellard sat down beside her. "Thank you for not panicking."

"Panic won't help us." She rolled closer until she felt the heat coming off his body. "We'll get out of this mess alive. Ransom will come for us."

"It might take them a while."

"The Incorporeals will come."

"Maybe not. There must be an explanation, a reason why Sheera and Leeam are trapped here."

"You think it's them and not something else?"

Ellard sighed. "If it's another being, we might be in trouble. I prefer to stay with my theories until I have proof to the contrary."

Gweneth smiled into the blacklight. Her too, because she could use this to advance her courtship. She rolled closer, and Ellard's good arm came around her. Without hurrying, she aimed in the general direction of his mouth. Her lips grazed his shoulder and moved on to the base of his neck, where it met his shoulder.

A small rush of air escaped him, and she grinned. This time, she pressed a harder kiss in that spot and added a bit of suction.

Ellard froze. He moaned and jerked from her touch.

"Is something wrong?" Gweneth knew of her crime. A cheeky move, but necessary if she wanted to keep Ellard off-balance.

"Don't kiss me there."

"Why not?" Despite the reduced light, her feline half allowed her to see him. His green eyes held a storm of confusion and sensual heat. All emotion that offered encouragement. Somehow, she needed to maneuver him into taking the next step. She wanted him. Her feline wanted him, yet she sensed he needed to make this decision on his own. In this, she shouldn't push.

"Gweneth, playing dumb doesn't suit you."

His terse words stung, and she glanced away from his stern visage. He was right, damn it. Manipulation wouldn't win his love. She needed to fight fair and square, to seduce and show him her heart. They had to get to understand one another, their strengths and weaknesses. No tricks.

"I'm sorry. I...I got carried away. Ellard, I wish you would see yourself in the way I see you." The words, while impulsive, grabbed his attention. His frown dispersed.

"How do you see me?"

"I see a good and loyal man, a feline with a true heart. I see someone who would do anything for his family or friends. I see a feline male I could love and trust."

The silence throbbed between them, and she wondered if she'd gone too far.

"Women never take a second glance at me," he said finally.

He watched her with his cat-green gaze, his attention solely on her. Her heart began to thud instead of simply beat. *Thud, thud, thud.* Impossibly fast.

"Who do they look at? What do you think they see?" she whispered.

"Before Jarlath found Keira, they looked at him, and the women from the upper level families decided if they paid attention to me, they might have a chance of Jarlath returning their interest. The felines we met and the ones we socialized with used me to get to Shiloh and Lynx. The House of Cawdor used me to put a plan in place to cut the House of the Cat off at the knee. The fact a beautiful woman paid attention shocked me, and I never looked deeper or asked the questions that might have stopped their plan."

"You can't let the past color your actions."

"Why not? We learn by experience. It's how we grow."

"That's true, but we shouldn't feel sorry for ourselves either. People are blind not to see the real you. When you smile, your eyes glow. You have beautiful eyes, Ellard. Seeing you that way makes my heart beat faster, my insides turn to mush, and I start thinking about—"

"Don't finish that thought."

"You're not frightened of a little frank talk about sex?"

His sharp intake of air and the subsequent gritting of his teeth made her pulse race even faster. "You're too young for me, and you're so beautiful. Looking at you makes my teeth hurt."

Gweneth stared in astonishment. Was that a confession of his sexual attraction to her?

"What happens if you change your mind?" His low, impassioned words held fear and betrayal and truth, yet a thread of hope underpinned the emotions.

Gweneth sensed she might have a chance if she handled his objections carefully. A faint one, but she had to find the right words, which meant sharing part of her hidden self. "You think I'll change my mind? That my feline is steering me wrong?"

"I think you're young. You've spent time with Ry and Camryn, exploring different worlds during your voyage to Viros. You haven't met many males your age. You should have fun rather than stress about your future."

"I'm not too young to know my own mind."

"There are hundreds of eligible males on Viros. The dragon shifters we met are interested too. I saw their stealthy glances, their appreciation of your beauty and brain."

Pleasure suffused her at his words. He spoke of her intelligence. No male had ever complimented her in that way before.

"The lack of an arm is a handicap. My Stores made me whole, but losing it again has made me a liability. Don't you want children? I've thought about bringing up a child and how I'd do things differently than my parents. But with one arm, it's not easy to hold a child. How do I teach my son? How do I pass on the knowledge I've accumulated with my physical restrictions?"

"Stop feeling sorry for yourself. It's not attractive. So what if you don't have your brother's or friend's looks? So what if you've lost an arm? No matter what you think, you can't let the horrible things from your past define you."

"What would you have me do?"

"Forge a path for the future. Do it your way. Don't let others try to tell you what you can and can't do. You've listed your shortcomings before, and I grow tired of your excuses. You are an intelligent male, one of position. You will fail if that is what you want. You can grow into a bitter old feline who snarls at everyone or you can embrace the life of your dreams. A child would be lucky to have you as their father."

Ellard flopped over on his back to stare at the fern roof of their shelter. "You make it sound easy, doable. It's not that simple. You haven't faced the same handicaps. You're beautiful, and your looks make things much easier for you."

"Crap," she spat out. With one quick move, she straddled his hips and glared down at his startled face. "I will tell you this once, then we won't discuss it again." She ignored the surge of his cock beneath her bottom, the tensing of his big chest, and the watchfulness in his beautiful green eyes. "My father is the governor of the planet Ornum. Ornum is an inhospitable hole—the armpit of the Citron universe. It's where neighboring planets send their prisoners, those who have committed terrible crimes. My mother was feline, yet she never shifted and didn't bear a cat tattoo on her cheek. I believe my parents were happy and had a good marriage, but my mother contracted an illness and died when I reached ten rotations."

"I'm sorry," Ellard said. "That must have been difficult."

"I still miss her every cycle."

"You've made your point," he said. "You had a difficult childhood. You can get off me now."

"I haven't finished," she snapped.

Ellard fell silent, and she took that as a sign to continue.

"My father hired a nanny for me. Amme. He grew distant, and I believe that occurred because he missed my mother so much. The depiction I have of her—we look a lot alike. As I matured, the cat tattoo became visible on my cheek. My father didn't approve. The mark horrified him because it meant my mother had kept secrets from him. He ordered me to wear a mask while in his presence or whenever I ventured from his mansion. He insisted I cover my face." Their gazes connected and held. "I know how it feels to be judged for my looks. My father couldn't bear to see my face, and whenever I went out in public, people whispered and gossiped about why I wore a mask. How is that any different? People still stare at my tattoo, which is why I cover it with makeup sometimes or use a potion Mogens developed during our Earth visit." Her lips twisted. "Just so I can feel normal."

"Your father ordered you to wear a mask?" Horror reverberated off each stiff word, and she could see his feline close to the surface.

At her clipped nod, his breath hissed free. He raised his hand to brush his fingers over the small black tattoo on her cheek.

"How did you come to join Ry and the *Indy* crew? I've always wondered."

The question—one she knew would come—hurt all the same. She braced as pain and shame struck at the heart of her. She scrambled for equilibrium, but not before the backs of her eyes smarted, and her hands clawed into her thighs. A foreign snarl echoed through her mind, shocking her as she recognized her feline's distress. Surprisingly, she became more aware of her with each passing cycle.

"Gweneth?"

She nodded in response, her thoughts tossed back into the past and the moment when her world had rocked off its axis.

She and Amme had returned from a shopping excursion in the better part of the town. They had entered the house and given their packages to the junior servant.

"Miss Gweneth," the butler had intoned.

"Good morn, Gastonique."

"The master wishes to see you in his study."

"Thank you. I'll go and change. I stepped off the path just as a wagon drove past." She gestured at the muddy hem of her gown. "I won't take long."

"Your father wishes to see you." Not a shred of expression crept into Gastonique's stern and craggy features. "He has summoned me twice already."

Gweneth nodded and stiffened her spine. Amme gave her arm a reassuring squeeze as she turned toward her father's study. Before she tapped on the carved wooden door, she took a sec to check that her fabric mask remained in position and none of her face would be visible to her father. She sucked in a quick breath and tapped twice before pausing to listen for her father's permission to enter.

"Come."

She pushed open the door, stepped through, and after closing it again, she approached his large desk. He spoke on a communicator and spat directions at one of his aids like a robotic machine. *Bang. Bang. Bang.*

Two upright chairs sat in front of his gleaming black stone desk, but she knew not to take a seat. This meeting would be short. She stood to attention, hands clasped behind her back, gaze downcast. He would notice her muddy hem. He noticed everything.

After another series of orders to his aid, he disconnected.

"Where have you been? I requested your presence this morn."

Gweneth stared through the eye slits of her mask. Her father lacked presence, a short, squat man with an uncertain temper to make up for the shortcoming. He ruled the prison planet of Ornum with a steel glove, and his underlings jumped to his every order. She often wondered why her mother married him—that was until the cat tattoo formed on her cheek. Her mother had kept secrets and taken them with her to the grave. Sometimes, she wondered if her father intended to punish her or her mother.

"Answer me."

"Amme and I did some errands. I required new masks." A spurt of satisfaction filled her at the subtle barb. Her father could hardly castigate her since she merely followed his orders.

"I have decided to hold a hell-horse race. A special one to raise funds for the city."

In other words, to fill his deep pockets. She didn't think he required a response, so she remained silent.

"The race will be called the Dowry Derby, and the winner will receive a cash prize plus your hand in marriage."

"What?"

His mouth twisted, and his brown eyes bore an expression she hadn't seen before, one she couldn't decipher. Triumph. Pain. Embarrassment. His features bore all of those fleeting emotions. He blinked and his expression shifted into one of determination. "You will be part of the prize package for the winner of the Dowry Derby."

Horror swept her, her skin prickling and a sweat broke out on her arms and legs. Her father hated her so much he wanted to give her away to whichever man won a hell-horse race. A stranger.

"Gweneth. Gweneth!" Ellard's voice pierced her memories, ripping her from a moment that had been one of the worst of her life.

She swallowed, the movement painful because of the lump that had lodged in her throat.

Ellard moved, lifting her off his chest and wrapping his arms around her trembling body. "Phrull, I'm so sorry," he whispered.

"Can you tell me what happened next?"

"My father dismissed me. I can't remember walking up to my chamber. I think the shock...it paralyzed me." She shivered, frozen to her core.

"Understandable." Ellard drew her closer and pressed a kiss to her temple. The gentle caress melted away the chill in her body.

"I wanted to refuse because I knew the type of man who would enter the race. There aren't many females on Ornum. It's the perfect place to incarcerate prisoners because it is isolated. My father knew the race and the prize would bring a lot of interest."

"How did you come to meet the crew of the *Indy*?"

"Ry entered a bet with his brother. He was an outlaw at the time, falsely accused of murder, with a reward for his capture."

"Ry?"

"The rest of the crew were wanted too, for acts of piracy. Ry's determination to win the bet drove him. His brother promised to help him clear his name if Ry beat him. Ry wasn't guilty. His brother used magic to execute the crime and implicated Ry."

Ellard stroked her back, diverting her thoughts. "Go on."

Gweneth swallowed again, her angst fading because, although she hadn't thought so then, the race had changed her life for the better.

"As I said, Ry resolved to win, so he and his crew hatched a plan. They decided to kidnap a horse trainer from Earth, but they made a mistake and ended up snatching Camryn instead of her twin brother."

Ellard barked out a laugh. "That must have caused consternation."

"From what I hear, it did, but Camryn talked them into keeping her instead of returning for her brother. She helped them catch a hell-horse and train the creature."

"What is a hell-horse? I don't believe I've heard of one before."

"It's native to Ornum. Not the nicest creature. They are furry with sloping backs. They're usually black or brown and very aggressive. They eat meat and like to scavenge. It's challenging to capture one and an even bigger challenge to race them successfully since handling them is dangerous."

"Camryn trained one of these?"

"She did. She not only trained Gabby, but she changed the hell-horse racing history by riding Gabby to victory. That might not sound impressive, but generally, in a hell-horse race, they attack each other, and the last one standing is the winner. Gabby had a foal, and they used her maternal instincts and rewards to get her over the winning line first."

"What happened next?" Interest shimmered in him, and despite the circumstances, she enjoyed his focus on her.

"Camryn managed to get Gabby to the finals. By then, they had all become attached to her and her foal. None of them wanted her injured, and Camryn decided she would ride Gabby during the race. You should have heard the fuss. The biggest upset in hell-horse racing history, but the rules never specified how the race should run. I believe the attendance numbers were the highest ever recorded."

"Did you see the race?"

"No, women don't generally attend. Not that I wanted to watch. Hell-horses are gruesome creatures. The races are a blood sport. Camryn won, and at the celebration ball, my father presented me to Ry. Ry had fallen for Camryn by this time and didn't want me. He'd wanted to beat his brother, which he did, and the winner's purse came as a bonus. He'd never wanted a wife."

"So, how did you end up with the *Indy* crew?"

"My father took a liking to Camryn and had her kidnapped and placed in his harem. He also neglected to pay Ry his winnings because Ry didn't want me."

"Ry and the crew rescued Camryn, then came to confront my father. He refused to hand over the currency unless they took me. Ry agreed—finally—and Amme said she wouldn't let me go without her, so we both went with the *Indy* crew. Once we were on the ship and on our way to Ibrox, Ry ordered me to remove my mask and never wear it again. My tattoo shocked him. It stunned the crew, but it worked out for the best. I found new friends. A family."

"Phrull, Gweneth." Ellard sought her mouth, and passion exploded between them at the first touch.

She poured all her feelings into the exchange. Her need for him, her desire and passion. His hand roamed her back and came to rest on her butt. The press of his hand ignited a storm in her, the thrust of his cock against her belly a welcome sensation. Ellard parted their lips, and she thought he'd retreat since he usually did.

"I didn't realize," he whispered.

"Why would you? I never talk about my past. I enjoy my present and dream of the future. I've learned it from Ry and Camryn, although they both say the past shapes us. We learn lessons and take that knowledge into the future."

"You are wise beyond your years." He kissed along her jaw and moved lower to nibble on the vulnerable skin of her neck. "I've tried not to want you, Gweneth. I've tried so fiercely but I'm so hard I hurt. This is your last chance. Please tell me if you're playing with my feelings or want to use me to get closer to Jarlath and Lynx. I can't take my heart getting ripped out again."

Gweneth sucked in a harsh breath. "If you're doing this because you feel sorry for me, I will—"

"I don't feel sorry for you." He kissed the upper swell of one breast, his breath warm and seductive.

A spike of pleasure lashed her nerve endings and sank to her pussy. Everything in her focused on the warm spot where his lips lingered. "Speak," she said hoarsely. Stars, didn't he understand? She was as vulnerable as he was in this relationship stuff. Apart from Ry and Camryn and Jannike and her men, she knew nothing of males. However, she thought her observations of her friends had helped.

"I admire you even more since you told me of your past. Could we...could we take one cycle at a time? At least until we get back to Viros?"

A howl echoed through the forest, and she puffed out a laugh. "You mean we mightn't live to return to Viros."

"Yes." The stark truth.

"If we do not survive, I want to know you intimately. I want to feel what the sexual act is like with a compatible male." Her gaze didn't waver, although heat traveled up her neck and settled in her cheeks.

"I want to experience loving with you, Gweneth." He gave her the same steady regard but didn't blush.

"Yes, please."

"Show me how to remove this clothing," he said, his tongue tracing along the lace of her bra cup. "I haven't seen one of these before."

"It's an Earth garment. A brassiere. Bra for short. The Virosian women have the little support tops that do the same job, but I favor the lace on my bras. They're prettier."

"They are," he agreed, and the warmth in his green eyes sent her insides swooping. "Show me how it works."

"They fasten at the back with small hooks. I'll get it this time. I'll show you in the morn once it is easier to see."

The howl echoed again, and a shiver ran down her spine. Her hand trembled at the hook-and-eye closure of her bra, and she had to make two attempts before the garment loosened around her breasts. "What do you think that is?"

"Something high on the food chain. At least it doesn't appear to be coming any closer."

Gweneth stripped her bra down her arms and tucked it near her tunic.

Ellard sucked in an audible breath. "Phrull, Gweneth."

She lifted her gaze and attempted to pierce the blacklight to see his expression. His glowing green eyes were all she could see. "Should I keep going? Take off the rest of my clothes?"

"Please."

"Will I get to see you?"

"You'll see my arm." His hesitation was clear, and she understood the vulnerability.

"I won't laugh or poke fun at you or make you feel you're lacking in some way. It takes guts to start again, to take that first step. I know because I've been there. I still feel the sting of my father's rejection. It's not something that fades easily."

The howl came again, farther away this time, and some of Gweneth's trepidation faded. Maybe they'd get to the next stage without an interruption. Another thought occurred. "Is your arm, your stump all right? You didn't remove it carefully like you do when you shift."

"It's strange," he said. "I woke up inside that plant and ripped myself free. The stump hurt initially, but a ghostly surface appeared when I needed to help you and worked with my thoughts. The cold from it seemed to help heal the injury on my stump. I mean, it's tender but bearable."

"Our mystery friends," Gweneth said. "If it is Sheera and Leeam, do you think us having sex will help them?"

"We're not doing this for them. If you're trying to help them and using me, we're stopping right now."

"No. Ellard." She fumbled for his shoulder in the blacklight and squeezed with considerable force. "I have been open about my interest in you since we met. Consider this, Ellard. Think hard. Would I do that to you?"

A tight pressure formed in her chest and spread up her throat. He couldn't think she'd treat him that way. Not after she'd shared her past with him. She didn't discuss her time on Ornum with anyone.

The tension in his shoulder released, and she loosened her grip.

"No, I'm sorry. My past...the things that have happened play on my mind. I worry about making more mistakes, ones that might hurt my friends and family."

"At least you're talking. That's a start. If I ever do anything to make you uncomfortable, you have to discuss it with me."

"Maybe."

She opened her mouth to castigate him, then changed her mind. Luck had helped her find a family and a support group. She'd had longer to regroup than Ellard. He was still finding his way, and she needed to make allowances. She pushed off him and stood to shimmy out of her trews and the matching lace panties.

"Gwen," he whispered.

"What?" She quite liked how he shortened her name, the husky note of awe in his voice.

"You're beautiful."

"Thanks." She hesitated, not wanting to make him uncomfortable. She puffed out a breath because although this might not be easy for him if she let him hide now, their future would never come from a place of honesty. "Please take off your clothes too. If you're worried about my reaction, don't. I have a strong stomach. Mogens says I would make a good medic if I chose that path. I won't scream or faint or do anything girlish. If I do, I'll let you off the bet for the morrow. No kiss demands."

His groan held a hint of humor, and she knew it would be all right. Secs later, he stood and disrobed.

"I can't see much detail. Your eyesight is better than mine."

"Maybe that's a good thing."

"Ellard, say that again, and I will box your ears."

CHAPTER 9

E llard adored that pissy tone of hers. She made him laugh even when he didn't want to react. "Come here."

She approached him without hesitation and pressed against his chest, the warmth of her breasts forcing a groan past his lips. His left arm came around her, their lips met, and the sensual contact hurled Ellard straight into pleasure. Phrull, he'd never thought he'd have a woman like Gwen. Once—yeah, once—he'd dreamed, he'd acted and received the equivalent of a kick in the balls.

But Gwen...

He wanted to believe in her. He wanted her, plain and simple. So much. And his feline had craved Gwen for far longer. Stubborn beest.

Her arms curled around his neck, and the last of his restraint snapped. A very feline snarl squeezed past his lips, echoing in their rough forest shelter. The pitter-patter of tiny paws scraped over the ground nearby, then scuttled away at his cry.

Mine. Mine. *Mine.*

His fingers slid down her smooth back to cup her arse. Soft warmth. Plump and curvy yet strong with more muscle tone than most women. Ry's doing as he taught her skills to survive. Her confidence came from her interaction with her female friends, and while her forthright speech rattled him, he liked that aspect of her personality. Her father...phrull, he couldn't imagine why a parent would reject a beautiful and talented daughter like Gwen. Governor Swithin's loss and his gain.

The friction of her sensual mouth drove his thoughts away from what should and shouldn't be, and he wallowed in the taste and the scent of her, the way she threw herself into their exchange. He parted their lips, dragged in a breath, and smelled arousal. Hers. His. The herbal bouquet from the crushed leaves underfoot, and the earthiness of the soil filled his next draft of lifeforce, and he smiled, the curve of his lips feeling natural and right.

"I like this. Touching you, Ellard." She rubbed against his torso, squeezing his erection between their bodies.

One last chance. "Are you sure? Birth control?"

"Taken care of, thanks to Mogens. Remember that threat to box your ears?"

"Yes."

"Threat holds for this too. I know some stuff, so don't think I won't carry out my threat."

"Let's get comfortable. I would lift you off your feet, but I'm handicapped at present. How are you? Your ankle?"

"A few bruises. I'm sound of mind and body. Last time I intend to reassure you." She pulled away and sank onto their makeshift bed of pink-and-green leaves, and he gave thanks for his feline genes. She mightn't be able to see him as clearly, but he wouldn't miss a thing. Creamy curves. Smooth skin. Black hair in a messy braid. Full lips. Pale green eyes. *Beautiful.*

He stared for an instant longer, imprinting the sight in his memory before he joined her and slid close. He nuzzled her neck, drawing in her piquant scent of flowers and green herbs. The far-off cry of some sort of animal, quickly silenced, made him start. Gweneth jumped a fraction too, and he stroked his hand down her back in silent comfort while he cast out his feline senses for danger, then relaxed. They were safe. "You're going to need to help me here since my range of positions is limited with one arm."

"Ooh, what are my choices? Let me choose." Her eagerness made him chuckle.

"We can have you astride me or I can take you from behind with you on all fours."

"Both."

He spluttered out another laugh. She made this fun instead of the awkwardness he'd experienced in the past. "All right. Which first?"

"You from behind," she said without hesitation. "I can't see much in the blacklight anyway. This way, I'll get to feel surrounded by your muscles and heat."

"Touching and exploring first," he countered, his grin broad and toothy. At least it felt that way since his cheeks ached from the open display of his happiness.

"I can work with that. I get to explore first."

"Gwen."

"Ellard?"

"I'm going first." Before she could protest, he kissed her mouth—a dominant liplock. He crushed his mouth against hers and took control, using every bit of his expertise. Her hands wandered his back, his arse, and his feline purred at the sensual stroking. His lips trailed down her neck, his teeth scraping across delicate skin, his rough tongue soothing the prod of nerves. He moved lower to the mounds of her breasts. Instead of going slow, he upped the pace and latched his mouth on one nipple, drawing hard while he fingered the other.

"Ellard," she whispered, holding him close. "That feels so good. I want...I want...more."

He scanned her face, not fully trusting her words. Women had fooled him before and instinct drove him to check, to second guess things everyone told him. He found her eyes squeezed shut, her cheeks flushed, a soft smile etched into place.

When he plucked her nipple, tugging to a point shy of pain, she moaned, the sexiest sound he'd ever heard.

"Kaya spoke the truth," Gwen whispered. "This is so much better with a male. When do we get to do more?"

For a fleeting sec, suspicions rose to the fore. His feline snarled, the fury so great that Gwen jerked.

"What is it? What's wrong?"

"My past," he said, striving for honesty since she'd given him the same.

"You're scared."

"I'm not scared," he snapped.

"I've seen Ry and Camryn together. Jannike with her men. I know what scared looks like."

"I am *not* scared."

"*Bawk. Bawk. Bawk.*"

His mouth dropped open since he'd heard that weird expression—an Earth one, apparently—before when Jannike was taunting his brother. "Would you like me to spank you?"

"Yes, please. Kaya says it's very stimulating."

Ellard gaped at her, so sexy and alluring with that naughty little smile. Phrull, what did Gwen and her female friends discuss when they got together? "No more talking."

Something thumped to the ground, not far from their shelter. They both paused, tensing and relaxing when they heard no other sound.

Gweneth sucked in a quick breath. "But how will you learn if I enjoy what you're doing?"

"I'll know."

"But—"

"Talking later," he said, forcing a note of finality into his order. Maybe her chattiness came from nerves. He watched her closely and saw nothing but eagerness and excitement. Arousal.

She sucked in a breath, her mouth opened. Gwen intended to speak. He cut off her words, trapping them with his lips while he used his one arm and hand with good effect. He ran his fingers over her breast, down over her waist, to land on her hip. She shuddered against him, another of those sexy little moans battering his kiss.

Fun. She made this fun and new again.

His worries dispersed like a cloud fog meeting the determined rays of a solar star. He'd given her a chance to walk away, yet she hadn't taken his offer. The truth—he wanted her. His feline craved her, and he wouldn't give her another chance to slip away.

He moved down her body, only pausing to kiss and lick where she least expected his attentions. Her ribs he gave a quick lick, light enough to make her giggle and wriggle. He dragged his tongue around her navel. 'Round and 'round until he drew a reaction from her—this time a low moan and a restless stirring that told him she truly was enjoying this experience.

He urged her to part her thighs. He wedged his body in the gap between, biting back his groan of anticipation with difficulty. Her scent. He wanted to roll in it and mark her with his. He wanted to combine their scents as a warning to any other male who dared to glance in her direction. And taste... A shudder went through him as he leaned closer.

A thin line of dark hair guarded her pussy, and his hand trembled as he parted her folds. The rich and enticing bouquet of her filled his next breath. His pulse rate jumped to fast and choppy while his feline chose the moment to purr, satisfied with their path. He leaned closer, suddenly nervous, the air seeming thick on his tongue. No pressure, but this was her first time with a male.

"You'll tell me if I hurt you?"

"Why would you hurt me? I know what to expect. I'm more aroused than I've ever been when I played with my vibrator or my other toys. Besides, sometimes a little pain is a good thing. Pain and pleasure are closely related. Kaya told me, and she should know since she's had some experience."

"Silence."

She giggled but didn't speak again.

He licked the line of her cleft, stopping just short of her nub. Her exotic flavor burst across his taste buds. Beautiful. He could lose himself in her. Be himself. He lapped and teased and added his fingers, stroking around her entrance and dipping his digits in her juices. She *was* ready for him, and some of his trepidation faded.

He kissed her warm, swollen flesh, circled her clit with his tongue and teased the bundle of nerves until it throbbed against his mouth.

Her hands came down to smooth over his hair. Each flicker of his tongue resulted in a sharp tug until his scalp smarted. She moaned, the sound gripping his balls, and he worried he might embarrass himself.

"No more. Please, Ellard. I want to feel you inside me. I want you draped over my back and pounding into me."

He groaned, from both her words and the vision she painted. "Soon. Give me a sec." He was a big male, and he'd rather rip out his beating heart than hurt her or dim the bright flame she showed to the world.

He dipped his finger inside her, pushing it into her scalding juices. Her flesh rippled around his finger, eliciting a shudder from him. Amazing. Despite their circumstances, this would rate as the best cycle of his life. He slipped two fingers into her, and she took him with one of her sexy moans. Phrull, he'd dream of that sound this blacklight.

"Ellard."

"Shush," he said without heat and moved back. "On your hands and knees for me."

She scrambled into position so fast that he laughed.

"You've aroused me, made me horny. Now fix it, Ellard."

His laugh filled their shelter and held layers of happiness he hadn't allowed himself since... He shoved aside the past, clinging to Gwen, clinging to the possibilities, clinging to a better future.

"Ellard."

No mistaking the impatience shimmering in her. He smirked until his feline gave a grumpy bark of displeasure. *Steady, boy. We don't want to hurt her, not if we want to repeat the experience.*

Unable to help himself, he ran his hand over her rounded buttocks. He urged her to spread her stance and gave thanks to every deity he could think of that his feline sight allowed him the pleasure of seeing this perfectly in the blacklight. Her juices, her swollen folds grabbed his attention, and his hand developed that annoying tremor he seemed to suffer from while in her company.

Another thump sounded as something heavy crashed to the ground. A seedpod or fruit of some kind, he decided after testing his senses. Secs later, he heard the flutter of wings. A nightbird or creature feeding up in the tree canopy.

"Ellard, this cycle would be good."

"Did any of your female friends tell you about gags?"

"They were mentioned in passing." Smugness dripped from her reply, and he bit back his instinct to laugh. One thing he could do...

He smoothed his hand over one buttock, the skin silky-smooth and warm. Unmistakably feminine. Without warning, he lifted his hand and smacked her cheek. Three quick taps in a row, to pinken her skin and give her something else to think about.

She jolted but didn't cry out, so he repeated the smacks from a different angle. While she processed the heat and the pain of the spanking, he traced the lips of her pussy with one callused finger and grazed her clit.

"Ellard." Her body trembled, the tone of his name gentler and containing none of her earlier bossiness.

"I'm going to take you now. We won't get too vigorous because you'll be sore enough in the morn without me adding to your misery."

"I'd forgotten," she murmured in surprise. "You're good."

His feline let a purr slip free while the man reveled in her praise. He smiled as he lined up his cock and pushed past her entrance. "Stars, Gwen." Heat and softness caressed the tip of his shaft, pleasure a fiery streak to his balls. He pushed a fraction deeper before forcing himself to pull out. "Talk to me, Gwen."

"Now you want to talk."

"I'd hate to hurt you."

"Kaya says my body will adjust. At least, I hope it will. You feel huge."

A grin jumped across his lips. "Finger your clit, Gwen. I would, but I don't have two hands."

He pushed into her again, drilling deeper into her channel. His eyes squeezed shut to savor the decadent friction. "Better?"

"Yes."

She sounded more relaxed and the tension had eased from her body. He withdrew and rocked back into her, setting up an easy rhythm. Her sheath rippled around his cock, and one of her sexy moans filled the air, acting as a prod on his rapidly dwindling willpower. "Gwen, phrull. How close are you?"

"Simultaneous orgasms are rare. Kaya said so."

"Kaya's not here. I am."

"Yes, you are," she purred, and the clear satisfaction stroked his male ego. She wanted him. She truly wanted him, despite his handicaps, physical and mental. "I'm close. Very close. Don't worry about me."

Taking her at her word, he released his restraint and powered into her with hard, deep strokes. She moaned, and he faltered until he realized the throaty cry contained pleasure, dragged from deep in her chest.

She shuddered, a whole-body shudder, the small mew of pleasure making him smile. Her feminine flesh contracted around his cock, and the enjoyment roared through him, fast as a leopard chasing prey. He pulled back and gave one final, hard thrust that pushed him into release. His shaft pulsed in what seemed like never-ending contractions. With his body draped over hers, his breath coming in harsh drags, he paused and rubbed his cheek over her sweaty back.

Phrull, if he were to die tomorrow, he'd have a big smile on his face. Something about Gwen pushed happiness to the fore and made every problem seem smaller.

"That was...was...amazing. When can we do it again?"

He licked the tender skin where her neck and shoulder met, her scent and flavor washing through him. She smelled different from earlier, now containing a hint of him too. He liked the change. His feline liked it a lot.

"Ellard?"

A smile burst free, feeling more natural than it had for a long time. "Give my body a chance to recover, woman."

"Oh. I thought males could go almost straightaway. Kaya says there are pills and potions to help in that—"

"I don't require pills or potions." He bit his lip to contain his humor, gave her neck one final lick, and pulled from her snug body.

He reclined on their makeshift bed, the leafy surface hard and scratchy against his skin. He ignored the discomfort and drew her against his chest. She snuggled into him, her tongue darting out to lap across his chest.

"I can wait. A cuddle is nice too."

"Nice?"

SHELLEY MUNRO

"It means I enjoyed—"

"I know what it means." Phrull, this woman challenged him on all levels. His big body scared most females. His plain countenance—often arranged in a scowl, he had to admit—had them backing off in alarm. And his lack of one arm repelled the rest. He finally began to understand that none of this mattered to Gwen. It truly didn't, and it...

A miracle, he decided. His eyes stung without warning, and he kissed the crown of her head. "Since I'm so much older and defective maybe—"

"You are not defective!" The fierceness in her brought warmth and pleasure. His champion.

"Poor word choice," he said. "I meant that since I'm not quite ready for another go yet, maybe you would like to explore me."

"I'd like that. It would be better than nice." She pulled away to stare at him, even though he knew she couldn't see him well. "It's a pity it isn't whitelight."

One of those ghostly howls echoed through the air, still some distance away. Given that he and Gwen had intended to fly over, he hadn't checked the possible dangers, the predators, and plant life. He'd never make the same mistake again.

"At least they're staying away," Gwen said.

"Yes. How are you at climbing trees?"

"I don't know. I've never tried. Can we practice on the morrow?"

Ellard grinned, amusement releasing the pressure of anxiety about their rescue and the possibility of the howling predators drifting in their direction. "If we have a chance."

"I like to learn new skills."

"I've noticed."

Gwen separated their bodies and pushed him onto his back. She straddled his hips, but instead of doing the obvious, she did the opposite.

She traced his face, her fingers learning the hardness of his jaw, the smooth cheeks thanks to a recent application of stop-beard. A sigh whispered free from him, and he closed his eyes. Fingertips danced across his mouth too fast for him to respond and suck one inside. Another time.

Her tongue flickered down the column of his neck and darted across the spot where felines placed their mark on their mates. The flash of sensation, the flash of sheer need, the flash of desire blindsided him. Temptation had never gripped him in this insistent manner. Gwen must've sensed his mood because she froze.

"Did I do something wrong?"

"No."

"Then why have you gone as rigid as a board?"

Each breath was a warm puff against his mating spot, and he and his feline remained as immobile as Gwen.

"You know about the way felines mate?"

"Jannike told me. I liked it when you licked me in the same spot." She sounded defensive now, and he hurried to make her understand.

"I do, too, but if we are to have a future, I want it to be a safe one. A happy one." He paused, and Gwen spoke before he could voice his thoughts.

"You would prefer to enjoy our new closeness without any expectations."

Crap, he'd injured her feelings. "If something happens to either of us, the other would suffer if we were mates. It would be bad enough now, but when felines are mates, they become one. Their minds link as well as their bodies."

"I understand."

He sighed.

"No, Ellard. I'm not just saying that. I do understand and agree with what you're saying."

"True mates aren't common on Viros, not like they used to be. Jarlath and Keira are unusual. Your friends are too, and Lynx and Shiloh…" The strangeness of his brother's relationship still amazed him. Shiloh's happiness shone like a star though, so he refused to refute their triad relationship as his parents did. "I want to make sure that what we're doing is real and true and not survivor's relief."

"Agreed," she said and pressed one quick kiss to the mating site at the base of his neck before moving down his body. "Ah," she said on colliding with his cock. "You're right about the pills and potions."

"I told you so." No mistaking the smugness there.

"It moved." She sounded thrilled, and he bit back a chuckle. "The idea of me petting your cock excited you."

His lips quivered with the strain. "I will enjoy your touch."

"Kaya says—"

"I don't want to hear about the blue-hair pixie when we're together this way. If you wish to know something, ask me."

"Please."

"What?"

"Please ask me."

Ellard rolled his eyes but his mouth refused to follow through, smirking instead like an actor from a bad space trope comedy. "Did you wish to continue exploring or would you like to ride me?"

"Don't rush me. I want to do both." And she set about her explorations, her fingernails scraping over his chest, darting tendrils of enjoyment across his skin. Innocent touches. Brazen touches. She progressed down his body, rubbing her butt against his erection.

"How long is your hair?"

"It reaches halfway down my back. It was longer but the length became a problem when I wanted to train with the others. Camryn cut it for me."

"I'd love to see it loose." He trembled at the thought of the silky locks sliding over his bare skin.

"When we have a chance, I want to share the sanitizer with you." She glanced up, and Ellard caught a flash of dimples. "Jannike says—"

"No! Please, not my brother's sex life."

She giggled, her teasing a warm balm to his soul. After repositioning herself, she curled her fingers around his cock. She explored him thoroughly: his shaft, the sensitive head, and his rapidly hardening balls. In secs, lust simmered through him, her touch flammable and pushing at his restraint. With great effort, he remained prone, but he trembled under her attentions. Even when she moved on to massage the muscles of his thighs, his feline wriggled and pushed and urged him to take control. Wouldn't happen.

"The thing that I'm discovering about touching is that it resembles one of those weapons with double-edges." She glanced up. "I want you inside me."

"I'm yours." The words, while corny, rang with truth. This innocent slip of a woman had lured him in, and he'd followed like Jarlath's prized cambeest trailed Keira.

"So this riding thing. Quick instructions, please."

Amusement came quick, digging into his cheeks. If he wasn't careful, this happy expression might become a permanent thing. He couldn't function as a soldier with a smiley face. "Guide my cock to your pussy and push down. Take me inside you. Rise and fall. Experiment with the angle until you find one that gives you pleasure."

"What about you?"

"I get to watch you, your breasts, and your face. I'll enjoy every sec."

A tad awkward, she clambered into place. Slowly, slowly, she took him inside her wet heat. "Ooh," she whispered. "I like that."

Another of those uncharacteristic grins flirted with his mouth. Such concentration on her face. She rose and slid down, finding her rhythm. Pleasure roared through him, both physical and visual. His eyelids grew weights, but he fought the urge to close them. Instead, he watched the bounce of her breasts, the tightness of her pink nipples.

His balls became heavier, tighter, even though she'd barely started. With each word, each action she ensnared him deeper, battering down every one of his objections. As he watched, she slid her finger over her clit, the move grazing his shaft and one taut ball. Such a joy to watch. She bore no pretense, just open joy and curiosity, a love of life. Given her story of her father, that dumbfounded him. She'd blossomed in spite of her odious parent.

Another nudge of her finger over his shaft shifted his attention, and the swivel of her hips almost did him in. "Do that again. Please," he added before she could remind him of his manners.

"Not yet. I'm enjoying the slow build."

"I've created a monster."

Her giggle held pure enjoyment, and he decided waiting wouldn't kill him. Instead, he watched her smile, the curve of her breasts and the lazy up-and-down movement as she rode him. Phrull, she was a vision.

He relaxed as much as he could and let the sensations frisk his body as they willed. The layers built one on top of another, thick pleasure in a mind-blowing stack. His cock became sensitive, so sensitive he thought he would detonate.

"I want to hold on to this feeling," Gwen blurted. "The way I feel now."

He wanted that too.

"But I can't," she wailed and came hard.

Ellard squeezed his eyes shut and exploded, the spasms continuing for long moments, each ripple of her flesh, igniting a twitch from his cock.

She drew in a sharp breath and fell forward until she lay on his chest, not even flinching at the renewed flutter of wings in the treetops above. "Amazing."

"Yes." A picture of his future, one with Gwen, flashed through his mind. Phrull, he couldn't think of anything he'd like more.

"Do we have other positions we can try?"

"I'm sure we can come up with a few." Ellard smiled. "I need a rest though."

Gwen yawned. "Me too." She drew back and parted their clammy bodies. "That was amaz— Who the hell are you?"

Ellard bolted upright to stare in the direction Gwen indicated. Two pale waifs stared back, their long, straight hair and faces as white as their garments.

"How long have you been there?" Gwen demanded. "Did you watch us?"

Chapter 10

"We...we didn't mean to peep. *Not peepers.* Cold," the male said.

"Hungry," the woman added. "So hungry."

"Who are you?" Gwen asked again, this time consciously lowering her voice since they were both shivering and looked as if a strong wind would blow them over if they didn't topple under their own steam first. She reached for her trews and her bra and scrambled into her clothes while keeping an eye on the couple.

"Sheera," the young woman whispered, the glacier-blue of her pupils a mere pinprick.

"Leeam," the man replied, tucking his arm around the woman's trembling shoulders.

"You don't resemble your depictions." Ellard, as a feline, didn't mind others seeing him in his naked form.

"We require food to look that way," Sheera said. "Thank you for gifting us with your sexual energy. We thought we might die. So sorry we peeped. We don't normally do that. Against the rules."

"Our faces remain the same, but we change our hair, clothes, and accessories as the mood suits." Leeam gave a shrug, but it held little oomph. "It's fun."

A flash of heat flooded Gweneth's cheeks, and she had to restrain herself from rubbing at her embarrassment. This couple, and they didn't seem very old, had spied on her and Ellard. While she was glad they'd provided food, getting past the voyeur part was more difficult. "I can't believe you spied on us."

"We followed you from the plants," Leeam said. "You are our best hope of escape."

"Why couldn't you return home?" Ellard asked. "Your uncle is worried. Everyone is searching for you."

Sheera bit her lip while Leeam hung his head. "We didn't mean to cause trouble. We wanted to collect some special stones so we could give them to the dragons to make into a ring for us. We've been here before with our families. We come during the hot weather and have a picnic. It's not difficult to flash from home to here and return."

"Why couldn't you do that this time?" Ellard asked.

"There is some kind of force field, and we can't move past it," Leeam said. "We've tried, and it saps our strength."

"Our ship disintegrated after we hit something. I never saw what happened because I blacked out," Ellard said. "What else can you tell us about the area?"

"The dragons fear it because the rocks or something under them gives off an attraction that can kill them."

"You spoke to us earlier, whispering of danger. What have you seen?" Ellard barked the order, stepping into bodyguard mode.

"The plants. They sensed our presence and almost ate Sheera."

"What about the thing that howls? Have you seen that?"

"No, it sticks to the other side of the Red River," Liam said.

"We've heard it before if we stay late collecting the stones, but we've never seen it."

"Good info. Wait." Ellard frowned at them. "What about the plants? Have you seen them before?"

"No. The clearing where we first saw you is where we relax and share our energy. The plants are new."

"What about the birds?" Gweneth asked. They hadn't seemed dangerous, but they were big. One kick from them and the recipient might not live.

"They were here before. They eat plants and fruits."

"That's a relief." Ellard tapped his chin with his forefinger, a gesture Gweneth was coming to recognize as his thinking monitor. "Why did you warn us not to climb up to the flat hilltop?"

"The force field trapping us here seems to originate from there. We feel the power bleeding from it." Leeam shuddered. "We have to fight the urge to climb the hill."

Another howl echoed through the forest, and Gweneth glanced at Ellard. The creature seemed much closer than earlier.

Ellard reached for her hand and squeezed in reassurance. "How did you manage to help me with Gweneth?" he asked Leeam. "Picking her up, I mean."

"Sheera had the idea. You needed help."

"But you almost wiped yourselves out helping us."

Sheera gave a shy smile. "You have already repaid us by gifting us with energy. We're still not as strong as usual, but at least we won't die if we stay with you."

"I'm not sure how I feel about voyeurs, but I'm glad we were able to help," Gweneth said.

"You are beautiful together," Leeam said, his tone sincere. "I hope we can find benefactors of your caliber once it comes time to leave our families."

"What was the special stone for?" Ellard asked.

"Sheera and I love each other. We wanted to prepare a gift for a benefactor, someone who will shower us with sexual energy and help us start our own tribe."

The more she learned about the Incorporeal people, the more fascinating they became. Living ghosts. She wanted to ask more questions but decided to save them for the next cycle. "Ellard and I should rest now. Can you sleep too?"

"We will blink out to conserve energy," Leeam said, showing more animation than earlier. "We can still communicate via voice in this form."

The two popped out of sight.

"Thanks for reminding me you can see everything I do," Gweneth said.

A tinkle of laughter pulled an unwilling grin to her lips.

"We are very discreet," Sheera whispered. "We do not gossip or even discuss our benefactors with each other."

"Good to know," Gweneth said.

"A snack before we go to rest would be nice," Leeam said, and Ellard heard the humor in his suggestion.

"A kiss is all you get," Gweneth said, trying to sound stern. She glanced up and caught the glow of Ellard's eyes. "What?"

"It's not often I see you nonplussed."

"They watched us."

"But they were discreet and didn't appear until we had finished."

"I was still naked."

"Spectacular," Ellard corrected. "Come back down here and let me kiss you."

"At least we found them," Gweneth grumbled. "That's something. They're so young."

"We are not," Leeam said, indignation crisp and combative in his reply.

"New rule," Ellard said. "You need to be visible to take part in our conversations. The sole exception to this rule is while we're traveling through the trees and trying to find a way out on the

SHELLEY MUNRO

morrow. You may speak or advise us in that case. Is that clear?"

"Yes."

"If Gweneth and I are in our chamber, and this shelter counts as a chamber, you will keep your opinions to yourself," Ellard continued. "Is that understood?"

"So, if you are outside your chamber and we are visible, we may speak with you?" Sheera queried, and she sounded worried and close to tears.

"All we're asking for is a little privacy or at least the illusion of privacy," Gweneth said. "Do you understand?"

"Yes, we do," Leeam said. "Please forgive our bad manners."

"Yes," Sheera added in her softer voice. "This experience has placed us off-balance. We are happy to abide by any rules you put in place." She paused. "But you will continue to feed us?"

The bloom of silence trembled with urgency and fear.

"Of course we will," Gweneth said. "Good rest to you."

"Thank you," Sheera whispered. "Thank you."

Gweneth cuddled against Ellard and pressed a kiss to his throat. Now that she'd had a chance to consider the matter, having the Incorporeal couple dependent on them gave her and Ellard a good excuse to make love again and often, which worked to her advantage. There was always the chance Ellard might decide to stop with the lovely touchy-feely stuff, but now he'd think twice about putting a halt to their lovemaking.

She lifted her head and aimed at Ellard's lips. He responded, a feline growl issuing from him before her mouth sealed off its escape. She sank into the kiss, enjoying the heck out of the physical contact. After all, they couldn't let Sheera and Leeam die.

Gweneth groaned as she attempted to stand the next cycle. Every muscle screeched like a hell-horse in a tantrum. Finally, upright, she cautiously rubbed her hipbone. "I hurt."

"Some of the aches will ease with movement."

164

"I hope so." No matter how much her muscles protested, they had to move, had to find a way off the planet's surface and away from the rocks that caused the dragon glittery sickness and death. She tried a few steps and bit her lip. What she wouldn't give for a hot bath to ease her throbbing muscles.

Sheera's head bobbed in front of her, and Gweneth started, a naughty curse escaping before she could self-censor. "Fuck a duck."

Sheera giggled.

"What is it? What's wrong?" Ellard popped from their shelter with one leg in his trews and one leg out.

Gweneth pointed at Sheera's floating head, the youngster's humor no longer in evidence after witnessing Gweneth's displeasure. "She gave me a fright. I didn't mean to squeak, but that is plain creepy."

"Leeam said we should try to conserve energy."

"But we shouldn't frighten them either," Leeam's disembodied voice replied.

"Damn straight," Gweneth said and wagged her finger in her best Amme impression. "Don't worry," she said because Sheera looked as if she might cry. "We will become used to each other."

"Which parts of the area have you explored?" Ellard asked, now fully clothed. "There is no point covering the same ground."

"We morphed straight into the clearing then, once we freed ourselves from the plants, we decided to climb to the top of the flat hill since it's the best vantage point." Leeam paused, and his hair and face blinked into view. "The dragons do the best aerial maneuvers when they're playing. Not that they play near the mountains in this area, but I thought we might find someone to help."

"And you came up against the force field," Ellard pushed the conversation in the direction he wanted it to travel.

"Yes," Sheera said. "Except once we started climbing, the urge to get even closer was almost overwhelming. It felt...wrong, and I pulled Leeam back to the base of the hill and into the forest. This used up a lot of our energy."

"Maybe one of us can climb up to get a good look," Gweneth said. "I didn't feel the urges Sheera described. Did you?"

"No."

"Then that's the logical next step."

"No, we need to find water and food first," Ellard said.

"Oh, that's easy," Leeam said.

Without warning, a blue canteen popped into sight and hovered in front of her, its shoulder strap dangling.

"Now that we have a little energy, we can conjure food for you."

"What about a ship? If we can get past the force field?" Ellard asked.

"Sorry," Leeam said. "We're not strong enough for something of that magnitude. Our parents or uncle could do it, but we're not strong enough right now."

"It's all right." Gweneth grasped the canteen, reassured by the solid feel of it and slung it over one shoulder. "Food and water is a big help, but how does this work? The ship disappeared after we crashed. Will the food sustain us?"

"Yes, because we offer it freely, and you need it to survive. That's the basic answer. Maybe Uncle Niran could explain it better, but anything physical we make for you exists until you no longer need it." Leeam closed his eyes, and an instant later, a dark green tunic popped into existence in front of Ellard. "If you accept this tunic, it will remain visible until you change it for another or remove this garment and leave it somewhere."

"Chocolate," Gweneth blurted. "Can you conjure chocolate?"

"I don't understand—ah," Sheera said, smiling at Leeam. "I'll do it." She closed her eyes, and seconds later, a bar of chocolate appeared in front of Gweneth. She snatched it up, glanced at the packaging, and grinned. "One of my favorite New Zealand chocolates. Kaya will start to drool the sec she hears. She's eaten the last of her chocolate stock, and none of the sweets we've managed to make have passed her discerning palate."

Ellard yanked the tunic over his head. "Let's head out. No talking. Everyone alert."

"Aye, aye, Ellard." Gweneth did a snappy salute then ripped open the wrapping on the chocolate. She handed over several squares to Ellard and shoved two into her mouth. A moan of pleasure escaped as she chewed. Dark chocolate with hints of spicy chili to counteract the sweetness. Delicious.

Ellard glanced at the chocolate with a little more interest and bit some off. He chewed.

"Nice?"

"Different. I've heard you discuss chocolate before, but I couldn't understand the attraction."

"Ye of little praise," Gweneth mocked.

"Shush." He shut off her words with his mouth, his unhurried kiss taking her by surprise. His tongue sought entrance, and the rich taste of chocolate fired her senses. Raw need shot to the fore, and she almost dropped the chocolate in her urgency to get closer. Almost. She wound her free hand around Ellard's neck and rocked against him, the burst of sensation at the physical contact roaring through her in a heated rush. This was so much better now. His kiss. His touch. His willingness.

He nuzzled her neck, his teeth nipping at her earlobe. The dart of pain made her breath catch, then an instant later, the throb sank downward to gather in her pussy. "Ellard."

He released her and stepped back, his green eyes alight with mischief. "My debt is paid for this cycle. Let's move out."

His confident swagger made her grin while his rear view brought a happy sigh. The man's body consisted of sexy muscles, and she enjoyed gawking. His kisses were also great for pain relief. She strode after him, scanning their forest surroundings as they followed a narrow trail between the trees.

As the star climbed higher in the sky, the heat intensified. Perspiration beaded on her forehead and dampened her clothes. Swarms of tiny flying insects, disturbed by their passing, flew in clouds around their heads. Flapping her hand didn't seem to get rid of them, and the insects kept dive-bombing her face. Talking wasn't wise.

Overhead, she heard the odd bird or animal, but the dense treetops meant she never saw what made the sounds. Friendly or dangerous? She had no idea.

Up ahead, Ellard slowed. He flapped his hand over his face. "Can you hear that drone?"

"Yeah."

"Force field," Leeam said, his voice coming from over to her right. He and Sheera remained invisible to conserve their energy, although their faces had shone brighter after their kiss. Such an interesting race, and unlike any she'd met before.

"So the force field is above and in front of us," Ellard said. "This doesn't look good. I'm willing to bet if we walk in the other direction, we'll also come to the force field."

"If we're in a trap, then how did we get through?" Gweneth asked.

"No idea. My best guess...it's something to do with the ship. For some reason, it could pass through the field, but that doesn't help us get out."

"A ship," Leeam said. "Can you hear it?"

They cocked their heads to listen, the uneven whine of the engines indicating the pilot had the ship hovering above them.

"They've found us."

"Heat-seeking instruments," Ellard said tersely, his large frame locked in position.

"I can flash up to the top branches," Leeam said. "Stay here, Sheera."

"Be careful," Ellard said. "Until we learn whether it's friend or foe."

"I'll be fine," Leeam said. "I won't be visible."

"But I presume you still give off a heat signature?" Ellard scowled, his serious bodyguard expression. "Don't get cocky. This situation feels wrong."

Ellard continued frowning, his attention on the treetops, and Gweneth picked up his unease. They waited and waited. Leeam didn't return, and without warning, the ship moved off. When they could no longer hear it, she exchanged a glance with Ellard.

"Leeam," he called. "You can come down now. Leeam?"

Sheera's face popped into sight in front of them. Tears welled in her eyes. "They've taken Leeam. I can't find him. I can't sense him any longer."

CHAPTER 11

"What do you mean you can't sense him?" Ellard turned in a circle, his gaze on the tangle of branches and leaves above their heads. He sucked in a breath, identifying the smells—the greenery of the plants, the earthy scent of the ground underfoot, and the faint floral perfume from Gweneth. No sign of Leeam, not a hint in their surroundings.

"It's like he has vanished. I should be able to sense him in the way I could when we were all together," Sheera said, her voice becoming increasingly higher and frazzled. "I don't understand. I never heard anything apart from the ship. Leeam blinked off my inner radar. We have to find him. He could die if he can't feed. We're already weaker than normal. If it wasn't for you and Gweneth, we would have died because we seem to be trapped in here."

"Steady," Ellard said. "We need information. We'll walk in the direction the ship went."

"If it was a friendly, they would have got Leeam to communicate with us," Gweneth said.

Yeah, his thinking exactly. No matter which way he looked at it, Leeam's disappearance didn't bode well for any of them. "We'll reconnoiter and gather information, then come up with a plan. Sheera, we need you to keep calm and help us. Can you do that?"

During the brief pause, Ellard steeled himself for tears. Tears were tears, even if they were the invisible sort.

"Sheera, you need to be strong," Gweneth said. "We need to work together to learn what has happened to Leeam. I want you to go up to the treetop like Leeam did and tell us if you can see anything."

"I...what if I disappear?"

"We will come and find you," Ellard said in a firm voice. "But I think his disappearance has something to do with the ship."

"All right," she said, but her voice lacked confidence. "I'll do it now."

"Stay alert and keep talking to us the entire time."

"I'm going now," she told Ellard. "I'll morph up to the sturdy branch up there and stand on it. Should I become visible?"

"No," Gweneth said. "Save your energy. Just keep talking to us."

Gweneth glanced at Ellard when Sheera popped from view. "You think the ship knew his location and captured him somehow?"

"Yes," Ellard said in a low voice, his gaze on the bushy pink-and-green leaves of the surrounding trees. A faint breeze had sprung up, the scent holding a pungent bouquet, which didn't agree with his feline. He sneezed.

Gweneth scowled at the mass of trees and plants. "I don't like this."

"Me neither." Ellard studied their surroundings. Narenda's star pierced the canopy, creating flickering shadows. Dead leaves crunched beneath his boots, and to his right, a bright yellow climber wound around a dead tree, a jarring contrast to the feathery pink-and-gray trunk. But no matter how hard he concentrated, he couldn't hear birds, insects, or other animal life. Instead, a preternatural silence hung over the forest.

"I wish we had weapons."

"At least we have your knife. That's a start."

Sheera's head shimmered into sight, and Gweneth managed not to make a sound, although Ellard saw the way she clamped her mouth shut. Glittery tears ran down the woman's cheeks, her panic evident. "I couldn't see Leeam or the ship."

"What about the force field?"

Sheera wrinkled her nose. "It's like a bubble over the area. I could see the curve of it over the flat hill. The sky is a weird color outside. A muddy yellow with streaks of red."

"You can see through the force field?"

"Yes, but it gives me the creeps. It's like something rubbing my skin in the wrong direction, and the field saps my willpower. I want to reach out and place my hand on it." Sheera blinked, her long eyelashes sweeping her upper cheeks. "Leeam said that wasn't natural and we should keep away."

"The field of debris has moved even closer. That would be why no one has come to search for us. That thing doesn't behave like any storm I've witnessed before. We should get moving and explore the rest of the area." Ellard commenced pacing.

"But what about Leeam?" Sheera asked.

Gweneth went to Sheera and put her arm around where she thought the girl's shoulders would be. Her arm cut through air, and Sheera giggled, the sound a welcome mood lightener.

Ellard stopped, and Gweneth ripped her gaze off his muscular backside. Not quick enough, judging by his stern look before he addressed the Incorporeal woman. "Sheera, do you have any weapons?"

"No, but I can make them as long as I have enough energy." She sent them a shy smile. "You produce tasty energy during lovemaking."

"Good to know," Ellard said in a dry tone that made Gweneth grin. "They know we're here. They'll return for us. The force field must be a trap to catch something."

"Us or Sheera and Leeam?"

"Do outsiders know you come here?" Ellard asked.

"We have always lived with the dragon shifters. Until Ransom took over as chieftain, outsiders never visited our planet," Sheera said. "We are a secretive race and don't appear to strangers."

"But you were very open with us," Gweneth said. "We haven't been here long, but already, we know a lot about your people."

Sheera blinked out. "I need to conserve my energy."

"That is fine," Ellard said. "Remain close so we can protect you."

"That is why you were given our secrets," Sheera said.

Gweneth shared a quick look with Ellard. "Pardon?"

"We can read minds. It is how we are able to fashion what each recipient requires. Niran judged you both pure and good people and worthy of our secret. Your first instinct was to protect me. You helped join the search to find Leeam and me when we went missing. You fed us, and now you're trying to keep us safe. That is why we gifted you with our secrets. Some seek to exploit us."

It was the most Sheera had said since they met her, and her words rang with passion.

Gweneth thought about the dragons. "Ransom doesn't have a mate."

A tinkly laugh rang out. "No, but he is a lusty male. His energy is piquant and sustaining. All the dragons are lusty lovers."

"I sort of want to ask how we measure up," Ellard muttered.

"We've told you already," Sheera replied. "You produce tasty energy. Leeam and I feasted well, and we needed it."

"Good to know," Gweneth murmured, shooting a smirk at

Ellard. He looked kind of cute with the hint of color high on his cheekbones.

"One more question before we move," Ellard said. "How long will Leeam's energy supplies last?"

"We feasted well last eve but we used up some of our energy providing you with food and clothes. Unless Leeam is able to find another food supply, maybe two cycles?"

"Let's move," Ellard said and strode along the defined path leading through the trees.

"Sheera, how close do you need to be to feed?" Gweneth asked.

"We need to be near the location. If a couple is in a room, we must be outside. We are not *peepers*. Not usually," she added in a sheepish tone. "Leeam and I will never disclose details either, Gweneth," Sheera said in a stiff voice. "It is a basic tenet of our culture. We rely on others to provide our food, and we never, ever wish to make them uncomfortable."

Ellard heard the hurt emanating from the girl's voice and exchanged a glance with Gweneth.

"I'm sorry. Ellard and I...this is new to us. We'll learn together, all of us. Now let's find Leeam."

"I'm sorry too," Sheera whispered. "Friends?"

"Yes." Ellard spoke for both of them. "We'd better cut the conversation. We're coming up to a clearing and it's full of those plant things. I can hear their drones."

For half a cycle portion, they navigated the trail, brushing past sharp leaves and rough vines. Sweat trickled down his backbone, his tunic clinging to his chest and back. The squawk of a bird and heavy footsteps had them stepping off the track once to allow a flock of the big birds to amble past.

The tinkle of running water became audible, and the trees thinned. Ellard slowed and scented the air in the same way she'd seen Ry and Camryn and, recently, Jannike.

Gweneth stopped at his side and jumped backward without

warning.

"What is it?" Ellard demanded, alarm tightening his shoulder muscles.

"Baby plants." She pointed at the ground then frowned at her right boot. "At this rate, I won't have any boot left. With each encounter, that hole becomes bigger."

"We'll have to cross the river," Ellard said.

"What about the animal that howled all night?"

"Sheera, did you see it? Do you know what it is?" Ellard asked.

"No to both questions," she whispered.

Gweneth stared at the river. "I guess we need to find a place to cross. It looks deep. And cold."

"Can you swim?"

"I'm half feline. Of course, I can swim."

"I can build you a—" Sheera broke off. "The ship is returning."

"New plan," Ellard said. "Sheera, I want you to become visible and stand between us. Wrap your arms around our waists, so they'll have to take all of us."

"Face the danger without hiding," Gweneth murmured. "I like the way you think."

"But—" Sheera began.

"At least this way, we will know what we face." Gweneth reached for the girl's hand as she shimmered into sight. "Hopefully, they'll put us with Leeam, so he won't be in danger of starving."

"And we'll discover if they're friend or foe," Ellard added.

Sheera trembled like a tree leaf in the middle of a violent storm. "I'm scared."

Ellard tucked her against his right side, leaving his arm free. Gweneth nudged closer and looked up at the hovering ship, visible through the bubble of the force field.

"Tracking beam," Ellard said.

A ray of illumination shot through the bubble and focused on them. Gweneth's skin tingled, and Sheera whimpered.

"It's okay," Ellard said. "This is a good plan. We'll know what we're facing, and once we're out of the bubble, the dragons will have a better chance of finding us."

He broadcast confidence, and Gweneth worked on presenting the same air of self-assurance. As the beam enclosed and lifted them, he prayed this idea worked.

Tension gripped Ellard's chest, a tight band of steel restricting his breathing as they whooshed upward toward a ship hovering above the dome of the force field. Sleek and long in shape, the hull bore a patchwork of paint, which told its age and pedigree. An older ship of military origins sold for scrap. Someone had patched her up and done a reasonable job, given the purring of her engines.

As they neared the open cargo hold, the urge to roar his frustration almost overwhelmed him. Instead, he worked hard to channel his training and keep alert for escape possibilities. Of course, one part of his plan might get them killed. Gut instinct told him they'd wanted the young couple for their special abilities and knew of their existence. If their captors decided he and Gweneth were surplus to requirements, nothing would stop them.

He might have led the woman he admired into a trap.

A trap that might end with them both dead.

No wonder he was having trouble breathing.

"Recognize the ship?" Gweneth murmured against his ear.

His respect for her rose another notch. Most women would've embraced full panic mode by now. Sheera continued to tremble and shudder between them, but not Gweneth.

He studied the black-and-gray ship again with no recognition. "Not yet."

"They might kill us."

Ah, that sharp brain of hers had already played the angles.

"At least we'll be outside the dome."

"There is that."

A frisson speared him, the sense of someone brushing his fur the wrong way as the beam drew them through the force field without difficulty. A mustard-colored cloud obscured the ship for an instant, the oily and sour stench making his breathing raspy. A cough racked Sheera, her slight body twitching uncontrollably between them. The cloud skittered away, and the hovering ship grew closer, bigger, and something about it pulled at his memory. Something familiar.

"If a debris storm didn't do us in, I have no doubt we can get through this too," Gweneth said.

"That's my girl."

Neither of them commented on the tremor in her fighting words.

She smiled and the warmth almost penetrated the anxiousness shadowing her green eyes. "Am I your girl?"

"Sheera, make yourself invisible. I want you to do something important for us. The instant we're inside the ship and on solid footing, move away and try to find Leeam. Can you do that?"

The girl sniffed and swiped the back of her hand over her nose.

"Leeam is counting on us," Gweneth said in a low voice.

The girl pushed back her shoulders at the reminder, gave a curt nod, and faded from sight. "Yes, I can do that."

The beam guided them into the open hold, a cavernous space previously used to hold military supplies. At present, the area stood empty. Ellard scowled. A quick jaunt then. They wouldn't have much time to effect an escape. The cargo doors slid shut behind them, the protesting creaks continuing for some time before the ship became sealed again. Without warning, the beam loosened its grip on them, and Ellard tensed, ready to fight. Nothing to use as a weapon in this dingy hold. The walls and floor bore evidence of rotations of service, the walls a military gray covered with dents and scratches and graffiti.

A door creaked open, as grumpy as the main hold door, and four bearded men strode through. Ellard took one look at their swinging leather kilts and the assortment of weapons—swords and blasters—and groaned. Bloody Scothage reivers. At one time, reivers had preyed on the few trade ships visiting Viros. Lynx and Shiloh had seen them off, and he hadn't heard of them traveling near Viros since.

"Where is she?" The man's bushy black beard didn't hide the knife scar on his cheek. His grease-streaked plaid shirt in checks of red and green also bore a chieftain's badge. His black boots slapped the dusty floor as he strode toward them, his leather kilt swinging.

"I suppose this isn't the best time to ask him what he's wearing under his skirt," Gweneth murmured.

Ellard barked out a laugh, the sound attracting attention.

"Where is the girl?"

"I'm here," Gweneth said, lifting her hand in a friendly wave.

Ellard slid his hand behind his back and pinched Gweneth's butt. She jumped, shot him an apologetic look, and buttoned her lips.

"I know him," one of the other bearded men declared, his green-and-black-plaid shirt straining over his barrel chest. "That be Ellard, aye." He approached and nodded. "Aye, he be the king's bodyguard. The Virosian king. I heard he lost his arm."

The chieftain halted in front of them, his fingers rubbing the hilt of a massive broadsword even as his gaze lingered on Gweneth. "Use the weapon. I want that woman contained and incarcerated with the other Incorporeal."

"Aye, laird," one said and pulled a silver box from the waistband of his kilt. He strode to the door they'd entered through and fiddled with something on the box. He slowly circled, aiming the thing around the hold. When nothing happened, he frowned and exited the cargo area.

"So you be the king's bodyguard. Have a score to settle with the Virosian people." He continued to stroke the hilt of his weapon then grinned to display teeth unexpectedly white given his grubby appearance. "I be wondering how much they pay to get you back. Aye, hurtin' their pockets be satisfyin'"

His gaze roamed Ellard before settling on Gweneth. Ellard bristled. His feline bristled, and he sensed an answering distaste from Gweneth. The man studied her as if she were a tasty morsel of food for consumption.

"Who be you, pretty bird?"

A scream sounded—feminine and rife with panic.

"Ah, we have the woman." His voice radiated satisfaction of a job well done. "Take them to the lockup. All of them. I be feelin' hungry. We break our fast while we decide our next move."

Some of the tension faded from Ellard's muscles. They had a chance of escape, and maybe now that they were outside the force field, the dragons would manage to track them.

The chieftain wandered from the hold toward the screams. As one, he and Gweneth bounded for the door but came face-to-face with two of the Scothage reivers. With weapons in hand, they smirked at Ellard, their features full of bring-it-on smugness.

Ellard pulled up, and Gweneth slid to a halt, holding her hands in front of her.

"Frisk 'em for weapons, aye," the smaller of the two said, his wiry frame and braggart attitude bringing to mind one of Keira's pouter-chicks—the birds she kept for eggs and meat.

Ellard held his hands out in the same manner as Gweneth as the beefy man neared. Ellard drew in a breath and wrinkled his nose. The Scothage needed to work on his personal hygiene. None of the Virosian felines would ever let themselves drop into that state of stinky, no matter how poor their circumstances.

The male frisked him with brisk and knowledgeable efficiency. He took his time, his search more thorough with Gweneth. When he grabbed her breast, Ellard snarled but Gweneth acted quicker and smacked the reiver over the head.

"I have no weapons, you numbskull moron, and certainly none

there. Stop trying to cop a feel."

Ellard tensed, ready to spring if the stinky Scothage decided to belt Gweneth back.

Instead, Stinky chuckled, unabashed by her chastening. "She be right. No weapons. Soft, sweet-scented breasts." He grabbed his crotch and did an offensive hip rock. "I be voting to keep her."

"Darrack won't agree if we be getting good currency in exchange for her safety," Pouter-chick said. "Though she be a tasty wench."

"I am not—"

Ellard elbowed her in the ribs, and she glowered, rubbing the spot. "Ow, that hurt."

"Don't you be beatin' on her," Pouter-chick warned. "We get top currency for her if she whole. Make someone a good rootin' wench."

"Ah...did you..." Gweneth trailed off, eyes wide and at a loss for once.

Despite the circumstances, Ellard bit back a grin. Gweneth's splutters were very cute.

"To the cells with ye," Stinky ordered. His long, single plait fell over his shoulder with the force of his gesture. "Ye be walkin' in front. No skullduggery, aye, or there be consequences."

"Consequences," Pouter-chick taunted, his black beard bristling in silent laughter, the series of small braids holding his hair back jiggling. "That be fightin' words."

"Idjit," came the reply.

Ellard witnessed the twinkle of the man's eyes. These men were a solid team and knew each other well, but then, so did he and Gweneth. Somehow, they'd get out of this mess since the reivers obviously didn't intend to kill them. Opportunists, they wanted currency. He'd heard the Scothage race practiced thrift, which would work to their advantage in this case. Arranging a ransom or selling them to the highest bidder would take time.

Ellard took in their surroundings and memorized their route

through the ship. Scuffed gray and more gray.

Gweneth walked at his side, equally attentive, and pride suffused him. She might be young, but she acquitted herself well thanks to Ry and his crew.

A feminine scream rippled along the gray corridor.

At his side, Gweneth tensed.

"Who are you torturing?" Ellard asked, with a glance over his shoulder.

"The woman who came aboard with you," Stinky said.

"What woman?" Gweneth asked, her footsteps slowing.

The two Scothage men exchanged a glance.

"We never be torturin' valuable assets," Stinky said.

Pouter-chick smirked. "Ooh with the big words."

"Shutup, idjit."

"Take the right fork," Stinky ordered.

Ellard and Gweneth turned as instructed.

"Through the double doors."

They pushed through and saw two Scothage men struggling with Sheera. Ellard wondered why she didn't blink out to evade capture then he noticed the wide silver band around her neck. It gave off a subtle blue glow.

"Who is she?" Gweneth asked. "What are you doing to her? She's young."

"She be our passport to riches," Stinky said.

Pouter-chick entered a code on a panel, too quickly for Ellard to register the keystrokes. A grate door slid open. "In there," he ordered.

Ellard hesitated until a sword prodded his side. He stepped into the windowless room—more gray—and turned to face them.

Gweneth stepped in beside him, and relief suffused him. He'd worried they might separate them.

Stinky grinned at him, displaying a gap in his white top teeth. "You be lucky yer the king's bodyguard and worth a ransom." He gestured with his chin. "One arm not much use. You shift to feline? You still have missing arm?"

Ellard glowered at him, even though the Scothage spoke the truth.

Stinky shrugged. "No matter. You be valuable. All that matters."

The door slid shut just as Sheera screamed again.

"Stars, what are they doing to her?"

"I don't know," Ellard murmured. "She didn't seem to register our presence. Did you see Leeam?"

"No. Kiss me, Ellard. Let's give her a tiny boost of energy. It might help to calm her, and if Leeam is here and languishing, it might help him too."

"You just want to grab some extra kisses." But as he said the words, Ellard gathered her closer with his arm.

"Score all 'round." Gweneth's cheeky grin urged him to share the joke.

Their lips collided, and for one heady sec, reality pushed away, replaced by sheer pleasure and satisfaction, softness, and the scent of Gweneth's arousal.

Outside their cell, Sheera broke off mid-scream, the silence welcoming and pleasing. Ellard continued to kiss Gweneth, his feline purring at the close contact. His mind drifted back to the previous eve and their loving. Somehow, Gweneth centered him and pushed his anxiety about his lack of an arm away.

He smiled down at her.

She raised a hand to stroke his cheek. "Nice."

"I thought so, and Sheera has stopped screaming." Ellard walked to the grate door and peered out. Sheera stood between the two Scothage males, the band around her neck glowing. She looked straight at him this time, and he winked in acknowledgment. Good. Gweneth's idea had worked. Sheera had stepped past her panic, and the slight energy boost had helped her center her thoughts.

"You be going in here with the other," Stinky said in a gruff voice.

Gweneth joined him at the door. The door to another cell farther down slid open. Ellard caught a glimpse of a pale being sitting in the corner of the cell and breathed a sigh of relief. Leeam. A band circled his neck, the glow of blue almost ghostly in the dim light. Kid didn't appear too healthy.

Sheera darted into the cell and slid to her knees. Skinny, pale arms slipped around her shoulders as the couple embraced. The cell door slid shut, and the door didn't return to its original opaque. The grates were easier for feeding and checking on prisoners. Nifty feature.

"What now?" Gweneth breathed next to his ear.

"Wait. Observe. Hope that the dragons can rescue us, and failing that, Lynx and Shiloh will know we're missing because we've skipped our check-in a couple of times. They'll come looking."

The Scothage men disappeared, their chatter fading. One returned and pushed tubes through the grate of their cell.

"Water. Soup," he said with a gesture at the tubes. He pushed the same tubes through the grate to the Incorporeal couple and departed.

"They have no idea how the Incorporeal feed," Gweneth whispered.

"Leeam doesn't look too good. Sheera?" he called in a low voice.

She pushed to her feet, her actions slow and almost tortured. When she reached the grate door, he saw the tracks of tears staining her cheeks, the blue glow from the throat band pulsing like a heartbeat.

"What is the collar for? Does it inhibit your powers?" Ellard asked.

"Yes, we can't blink out."

"Can you materialize items still?" Gweneth asked, coming to stand by his side.

"Yes, but staying visible is sapping our energy. Leeam is weak because he needs food."

"The Scothage don't know how you feed. How do they not know this if they know enough to make a collar to force your compliance?" Ellard asked.

"They're not particularly bright," Gweneth murmured.

"They're smart," Ellard contradicted. "They have to be to make their living as pirates. Did they say what they intend to do with you?"

Leeam struggled to his feet and lurched to the door. Sheera squawked in distress and ran to offer her support.

"Help to door," Leeam said.

She shouldered most of his weight and got him to the door. His pale fingers gripped the bars to keep upright.

"Think someone sold us out but didn't tell them everything," he whispered hoarsely. "They've been watching, waiting for half a rotation. Something about the debris storm gave them an unexpected advantage, or they caused it. Couldn't work out."

"Do you think one of the dragons would give the information to reivers? No, why would they do that? Betraying your people wouldn't make sense," Gweneth said.

Ellard studied the youngsters. "It would make sense if they'd left the planet and wanted to abduct Incorporeals to start their own empire."

"Or if the reivers are acting as intermediaries," Gweneth added.

The sound of the ship's engines changed, the throb becoming stronger.

"We're moving," Gweneth said. "That's good."

"Why is that good?" Ellard demanded. "I'm thinking that those collars will stop Niran and his people from tracking Sheera and Leeam, and if whoever gave the reivers the idea of kidnapping them knows about the feeding, then they'll have to get to them quickly. They won't want to take us. We'll stay with the reivers."

"I have a tracker," Gweneth said. "All of the *Indy* crew have trackers inserted. That's how we managed to find Jannike. Once we leave this area with the interference, Ry should be able to track me."

"Does the tracker survive shifting?"

"Yes. Mogens, our seer, is good. He has an extensive knowledge of herbs and medicines."

Leeam slumped against the door and would've fallen if Sheera didn't grab him.

Ellard caught Gweneth's gaze, her slight nod. As one, they retreated to the rear of their cell. His pulse jumped into a higher gear at the idea of touching her again, feeling the slide of skin against his.

"Can we do this and still keep most of our clothes?" she whispered.

CHAPTER 12

"We can, but you'll have to keep those sexy little moans under wraps."

Her green eyes twinkled, and her lips pursed. In the past, he would have stiffened, wondered what she'd do next to disrupt his life. Now, a surge of excitement swept him on seeing the devilment take form. It made him wish he could read her thoughts, a notion that hauled his brain to a screeching halt even as his feline purred extra loud. Reading her thoughts would become possible if they mated, if she ever managed to shift to feline. His blood pressure soared, heat and awareness sizzling across his skin, his senses, his mind.

Gwen leaned closer, her breath wafting against his ear. "You think my moans are sexy?"

"Hell, yes." No point trying to dissemble when his cock felt hard enough to drill through steellite bars. No point trying to fib when he couldn't keep his hands off her delectable body. No point trying to evade the truth when his feline kept purring like an oversized motor.

Gwen grinned at him, two dimples popping into sight. "I guess we'll need to try a new position."

"We will," he agreed, his damn smile setting up residence on his mouth and not letting go. His facial muscles ached from the unusual action, and he belatedly felt sympathy for his friend, Jarlath. He hadn't liked Keira, hadn't approved of their courtship. What he hadn't realized was the difficulty of fighting the blast of different emotions and his feline self.

"I'm going to take you against the wall," he said and enjoyed the slight widening of her pretty green eyes, the deepening of her iris coloring.

"That could be fun."

"And I might drop you on your arse since I possess just one arm."

She tugged on the empty sleeve of his tunic. "You won't drop me. I've seen you train with the others."

Her utter confidence in his abilities threatened to cut him off at the knees. Although she hadn't touched his stump, she didn't treat him different either. In that moment, everything—every truth, every doubt clicked together with the finality of a final puzzle piece.

Gweneth Swithin was not a normal feline female.

She'd faced adversity and risen above it, and he could do nothing less than meet the challenge she set him. He could imagine a future with this woman—if he forgave himself for the past and accepted felines made mistakes. He'd learned from his errors but also allowed himself to become bitter and closed himself off from his friends. Gweneth offered him a second chance if he allowed himself to believe.

Warmth pressed at his chest, embraced his heart, his feline.

He believed.

He cupped her cheek and kissed the tip of her nose. "We'll have to do this quick to avoid detection."

"My first quickie," she said with delight.

A chuckle burst free, unbidden, and he dipped his head to steal a kiss. Her lips welcomed him, and her arms snaked around his neck as she pressed closer. The sensations—almost too fast to catalog—roared through him. Pleasure frisked his nerve endings, the warmth around his heart grew an extra layer as their tongues danced together, their lips mated and he lost himself in her generous response.

When their lips parted, they smiled at each other.

"Can you take your trews off without removing your boots?"

Gwen nodded. "Mogens designed our clothing. It's stretchy but retains shape." Without demure, she yanked down her trews and worked them over her sturdy black boots.

"Underwear too. Your tunic will cover you if anyone comes."

Gweneth followed his instructions and placed her lacy underwear on her folded trews.

So calm, he mused. Nothing rattled her much. Her attitude had a lot to do with Ry and his crew. All of the *Indy* crew bore the same competence—a fact that made him grateful.

His hand slid beneath the hem of her tunic to caress her buttocks. Smooth, fragrant skin.

"Part your legs."

The instant she did, he cupped her pussy and smiled at the liquid heat of her.

"You want me."

"Always," she said. "Now that I've had sex with you, I can't wait to have your cock deep inside me again. You make me feel whole. So much better than my vibrator."

Phrull, she destroyed him with her honesty. No games. No tricks. No pretense. "I want you too. I can't wait to thrust into your hot pussy."

"Then what are you waiting for," she whispered. "Take me. Fill me. Make us both feel good."

She didn't mention the Incorporeal couple, but they sat at the back of his mind. Somehow...

He yanked down his trews and underwear until they hovered around his knees, his erect cock springing free. With a show of athletic strength, she levered herself up, opening herself to him as she curved her bare legs around his hips. Her flesh appeared pink and swollen as he guided his shaft to her entrance. They both let out a sigh as he tunneled inside. She pushed down, going faster than he would've if they'd been in more comfortable surroundings.

"Slow. We have time."

"You're not hurting me." Her smile burst free. "Not much. I'm finding I enjoy a tinge of pain. Gives the enjoyment an edge."

"I'm a big male. If the reivers are watching, they're watching. Nothing we can do about it, so we might as well make it good and move at our pace."

"Fast," she insisted, and suddenly, he sank balls deep into her heat.

They paused, then she squeezed her internal muscles around his length. Sweet stars. His eyes slid shut, and he almost detonated when she repeated the move.

"Phrull, Gwen. Slow down. I'm secs away from coming."

"Good," she said sweetly, and she slipped one finger between them to stroke her nub.

Amusement spread through him as he pulled back and stroked into her clinging flesh again. A spiral of pleasure shot from his balls and up his cock. A growl sneaked from between his gritted teeth.

"Stars, I love the way you do that."

His eyes flicked open to stare into hers. They danced with humor and passion. He watched her irises darken as he withdrew and thrust into her again.

Footsteps sounded outside their cell, and he quickened his pace. Never mind Sheera and Leeam. He thought his feline would sulk for half a rotation if he stopped now. He hadn't ceased his purrs since he'd first pushed into Gwen's sheath.

Gwen stilled on hearing the footsteps and issued a shuddery groan. Then she leaned forward and licked the side of his neck. Her tongue seemed more abrasive than normal, the warm lick raising a raft of sensations. Without warning, she nipped him. His feline roared, and Ellard came so hard he saw stars swirling through his mind. His legs trembled, but Gwen held tight, continuing to grind against him as she rubbed her clit.

She gasped, and he felt the squeeze of her internal muscles as she stilled, leaning more of her weight into him.

"Damn, that felt good," she whispered.

"Oy, what you be doing?" a voice called from the door of their cell.

"If he can't work it out, he needs a brain transplant," Gwen whispered.

Ellard shook with silent laughter but helped her to separate their bodies. She slid down his lower body, grinning at him as she gained her balance. He tugged her tunic down to cover her then bent to yank his clothes back into place.

He handed Gwen her clothes and turned to block the reiver's sight of her dressing.

"What do you want?" Ellard asked, going on the attack. Anything to distract him from Gwen.

"Chieftain say he hear from king. Willing to pay reward for your safe return. Both of you." This Scothage male possessed a tall and rangy build. His plaid shirt appeared cleaner, although the yellow-and-gray checks made Ellard long for screening glasses. Everyone would see him coming.

"When will the exchange occur?" Gwen asked, ducking from

behind him to stand by his side.

"Seven cycles from now. They need time to raise the currency."

"I see." Ellard wandered closer to the door and glanced at Leeam and Sheera. "What's wrong with them? They look ill."

"They do be lookin' sick," the reiver said. Now that he came closer, Ellard saw he wore yellow disks to stretch his lobes. They went well with his protruding ears. "Chieftain be angry if they die."

Ellard knew a few other beings who would let loose their wrath as well. "Where will the exchange take place?"

"We have to move debris field away from planet. We meet on edge of field."

Gweneth pressed against his armless side. "You're responsible for the debris field?"

"Aye. Malasses be clever. He design bubble to trap debris field."

"Who is Malasses?" Ellard asked. "Have we met him?"

"He be a Kiraxes. Clever. Help us gain power and currency in exchange for catching these two for him. Why he want, don't know. They weak and puny."

"It looks as if those bands around their necks are killing them," Gweneth said.

"Bands stay on," the reiver said firmly. "Malasses say."

"When will you hand them over?" Gweneth asked. "It should be soon, before they die."

"We deliver on Scothage. Go after exchange you. Two cycles, three at most before we hit home. Pity can't touch you." He leered at Gweneth. "You be bonny lass. And you be big. Chieftain say give more food. Keep hale and healthy." After one final pervy glance at Gwen, he pushed two tubes through the grate. He repeated the action, shoving tubes into Sheera and Leeam's cell before disappearing. His footsteps faded, and Ellard heard the slam of a door.

"They look terrible," Gweneth whispered. "At this rate, they'll die before someone can rescue us. If they knew enough to capture Leeam and Sheera, why don't they know how to feed them?"

"My guess would be this Malasses wanted to keep the price low, so he withheld information. He wouldn't want to share their powers or drive up the price for the abductions." Ellard hated seeing the couple like this. In the short time they'd known them, he'd become fond of them.

"We're okay," Leeam said and bounded to his feet. "Thank you for feeding us. I was starving."

The tension bled from Ellard when Sheera also stood, looking healthier and more robust.

"Careful," Ellard warned. "Stay down. They might have visual security."

Leeam gave a swift nod and subsided in a boneless heap to the floor.

"Have you heard of this Malasses?" Gweneth asked.

"Yes." Leeam sounded grim and much older. "Some of our people used to have a symbiotic relationship with the people of Kiraxes. They withheld food and forced them to do unspeakable things to gain material advantages. Those who could escape did so before the Kiraxes forced these collars on the remaining Incorporeal citizens. We heard they starved to death, rather than agree to follow orders."

Gweneth frowned. "It sounds as if Malasses wishes to get his hands on that power again."

"Yes," Sheera said, and fear shook her slender body.

"The collars keep you bound?" Ellard bent forward to study the lock on the cell door. Maybe he could get it open. Although the ship had some mod-alterations, this part seemed older.

"As long as we wear them, we can't escape," Leeam said. "I've tried to remove mine, and each time, it burns my palms and around my neck." His slender fingers lifted the collar, and Gweneth gasped at the vivid blue of his flesh. When he released the collar, his fingers glowed a faint blue, and he flexed them, his expression set in pain.

"How would Malasses know to set a trap in that area?" Ellard asked, trying to understand. "How could he know you and Sheera would be there?"

"Courting couples often go there to choose a precious stone for the dragons to mold into a promise ring. We go there to collect stones for the dragons and to relax. If he'd been watching, he'd know this. It's common knowledge in our town. Someone must have talked."

"An argument against letting outsiders onto the planet," Gweneth commented.

"But they can't stay isolated either," Ellard said.

"Some of us need to find new homes," Leeam said.

"And the dragons need to expand, too," Gweneth added. "If they've contacted Lynx and Shiloh, they'll know where we are." Her gaze zeroed in on the lock of their cell. "We need to be ready. I think I can pick that." She slid her knife from her boot heel and worked the lock.

"That's my girl," Ellard said, full of pride.

Secs later, the lock clicked, and she opened the door. She darted out and performed the same magic on the other cell.

"I'm going to try to get the collars off. Leeam first."

"Sheera first," Leeam ordered. "Please."

Gweneth gave a swift nod. She reached out to grasp the collar, and a faint buzz sounded. Her entire body juddered, a shower of blue sparks shooting from the metallic-looking band. Sheera moaned, her jaw clenching.

"Let go," Ellard ordered.

"C-can't."

Ellard hurried closer and peeled Gweneth's fingers free, one digit at a time. His heart beat faster than normal, and his feline clamored for release. The collar kept sparking, each blue spark that struck him shooting a shock down his forearm.

Gweneth went limp, her eyelids fluttering. Finally, finally, Ellard dragged her free and both women slumped.

"That's not going to work." Leeam stated the obvious as he crouched beside a limp Sheera. The white skin around her neck glowed a glacier blue to match her pupils.

"No. I'm going to leave the pair of you in your cell with the door unlocked. If you remain inside, the reivers might not notice. They don't seem particularly bright. Pretend to be unconscious if you hear them coming to check on you."

"What are you going to do?"

Ellard glanced down at the unconscious Gweneth. "I'll rouse Gweneth and hide. Then, we're going to capture the reivers one by one and take them out of commission. We'll find a way of removing your collars once we have control of their ship."

"I like confidence," Leeam whispered, his hands stroking Sheera's hair.

"No other way. Besides, Lynx and the others will come for us. The reivers won't make it back to their base before we're rescued."

"Thanks." Sheera's pained reply deepened Ellard's resolve. Despite his confidence, he didn't know if Lynx would arrive before the reivers met their contact. For all he knew, this Malasses might come to meet the Scothage reivers.

"I'm sorry you were injured," Ellard said as he awkwardly levered Gweneth up and placed her over his shoulder—the easiest way to transport her with his handicap.

"We had to try. Sheera and I have never experienced the collars. Our grandsire mentioned them in tales. We might not have our full powers but Ransom encouraged Niran to teach us to fight. I might manage to get some kicks in before they send a zap through the collar."

Ellard patted Leeam's shoulder. "Last resort. Play dead first. Save the surprise attack for right at the end. Shut the cell door after me."

Leeam nodded. "Some of our people are against Ransom

teaching us to fight. They're wrong. We can't rely on our ability to shimmer in and out."

"When we get out of this situation, I'll teach you some tricks," Ellard promised.

"Me too?" Sheera croaked.

"Both of you." With one final curt nod, Ellard cautiously moved in the direction the guards had disappeared.

He peeked around the corner, saw that no reivers lurked in the corridor, and hurried to the end. Here, the corridor split, and he heard several voices coming from the room halfway along. The scent of food wafted on the air. A galley or mess of some sort. Ellard took the quieter direction and loped away from the noise. He paused at each door, frustration stirring in his gut when he couldn't balance Gweneth over his shoulder and open the doors to the rooms he passed. All he could do was pause and listen, casting out his feline senses to ascertain if a reiver occupied the room on the other side of the door.

"Grata." Not much sound transmitted through the doors, despite the age of the Scothage ship. Deciding not to risk entrance, he padded to the end of this corridor and halted. Without warning, hard fingers pinched his butt. He jumped and spat out a curse, whirling so fast that Gweneth's skull connected with the wall.

"Ouch! You can put me down. I'm awake," she said in a hoarse voice.

"You couldn't have just told me," he muttered, helping her slide down his front. He held her steady and watched her rub her left temple. "You okay?"

She studied her fingers and offered a wan smile. "No blood. That's a good start."

"Can you stand on your own?"

In reply, she toddled a few steps and almost fell. "Might need a bit of help."

"That, I can do. It will be easier if you can balance. If I carry you,

I don't have enough hands to open the different rooms. I can't hear through the doors," Ellard said in a low voice.

"Have you seen any of the reivers?"

"Heard some the other way. I think it was a mess room or a galley of some sort since I could smell food."

"I could do with some food," Gweneth said, her voice hopeful. "The stuff in the tubes looked nasty."

"We'll check this way first. See if we can find any reivers on their own to increase the odds in our favor."

Gweneth nodded then winced. "Next time, I won't pinch you. Not straightaway."

"Good to know you learn from your mistakes."

A snort emerged as he slipped his arm around her waist.

A voice sounded from in front of them. "Cal, that you?"

Ellard glanced at Gweneth and found her more alert. He signaled with his hand, indicating she should go low and prayed she understood. She jerked her chin, her muscles tensing as the clomp of boots came closer.

"Cal, that you, aye?"

Ellard waited and cursed under his breath when the footsteps halted. They needed to move. Now.

As one, he and Gweneth flew around the corner, driving into reiver's chest. Both of them. The reiver toppled back with a shout of surprise, and Gweneth slapped a hand over his mouth.

"I told you to go low," Ellard muttered.

"No, you didn't."

"I signaled with my fingers."

"Oh, I thought you had a cramp and were stretching them."

"But—" Ellard snapped his mouth shut. She didn't train with his soldiers. They hadn't known each other for long, so he couldn't expect her to read his mind. "Next time I make this signal." He demonstrated with his fingers pointed at the floor. "It means go low. If I make this signal," he pointed at the ceiling, "it means go high."

"Very well." Gweneth tilted her chin, more alert than earlier.

The Scothage male moaned, and Gweneth punched him hard in the face. His moan cut off, and his head lolled to the side. Still breathing but unconscious.

Ellard sent her a look of respect.

"What will we do with him?"

"Drag him into one of these rooms," Ellard said. "Tie him up and move on."

"Let's do this." She opened the door to the closest room, scanned it, and backed out. "This one will work."

Together, they dragged him inside, Gweneth found an abandoned plaid tunic on the floor and hacked it into strips. Five mins later, they'd trussed the male like a fat pig-bird, ready to roast.

Gweneth cautiously opened the door and peered into the corridor. "It's safe. Let's go."

Ellard closed the door after them and followed Gweneth. They turned the corner and came face-to-face with two of the Scothage reivers. For an instant, they all stared at each other. The two Scothage males wore their leather kilts with plaid tunics. Their faces, the parts not disguised by bushy beards, were tan from exposure to the light of a star. Although he stood half a head taller, Ellard knew not to discount their wiry builds.

"What they be doing here?" one blurted.

"Ran out of water," Gweneth said. "We were thirsty."

"Huh?" the other said.

Ellard struck before their brains started functioning. He kicked one hard in the middle of the chest in a move he'd learned from training with Ry. The Scothage went flying, hitting the wall with a sickening thump. He slumped downward, and Ellard dragged him back to the room where they'd left the first. Galling as it was, Gweneth didn't seem to require his help, her Scothage opponent becoming more cautious with each blow she landed.

Gweneth appeared in the doorway. "Quick. We have to go. Coward turned tail and limped away."

Ellard left the groaning Scothage in a heap on the floor.

"They could at least wear underwear under their skirts," Gweneth said with a sniff. "A strong wind could blow at any time and create a show."

Ellard bit back a grin at her disapproval. "I can't believe we're discussing male dressing habits while trying to evade capture."

Shouts and running feet sounded outside the door. Ellard waited until they could no longer hear anything before cracking the door to observe the corridor. "Clear. Let's go."

"We can't evade capture forever."

Ellard grinned a feral grin. "But we can create havoc meanwhile."

They cautiously exited the room and continued in the direction away from the mess.

Gweneth halted, a furrow appearing on her forehead. "The ship is stopping. Something is happening."

"Our rescue?"

"No, if a strange ship appeared, they wouldn't stop. It's someone they were expecting."

Ellard listened, not as attuned to the ship as Gweneth since he hadn't flown as much in deep space. Grata, she was right.

"What do we do?" she whispered.

Ellard shrugged. "Keep to our plan. They know we've escaped the cell." He prowled down the corridor and peered around the next corner. "The bridge."

"Can we get closer? We might learn what is happening."

Good plan. As one, they slinked along the corridor walls, taking care to maintain silence. The familiar vibration of a moving ship recommenced. The stop had been a quick one. To let someone board or someone disembark? Ellard froze at the thought. What if they'd off-loaded Sheera and Leeam?

"You got them?" a harsh voice demanded.

"Aye, sir. They be locked in the cells."

The second voice belonged to the leader of the reivers, but it sounded as if someone else had charge of this mission. A new arrival?

"Are the collars in place?"

"Aye, sir."

"Good. That's good. Set a course to Kiraxes while I go to inspect my prize."

"There they be," a man cried from behind them.

"Phrull," Ellard muttered.

Two males appeared at the bridge entrance while behind him and Gweneth, four Scothage males stalked forward, brandishing stunners.

"How did they get loose?" the Scothage captain demanded.

"Who are they?" the big man at his side asked.

The newcomer stood taller than the captain and appeared older with a spare yet muscular frame. His face bore a network of tiny scales, and two slightly curled horns extended from his bald skull. An aurora of power simmered from him, but Ellard had never seen a male of this species before. A quick glance at Gweneth told him she hadn't either.

"They be with the Incorporeals," the captain said. "We be ransoming them."

The horned man stared at them both until Ellard wondered why, then the man smiled, and a chill raced down Ellard's spine. Whatever the horned man's thoughts, they didn't bode well for their safety.

"How fortuitous," the horned man crooned.

Fear licked Ellard now, and he felt Gweneth sidle closer, as if she experienced the same foreboding. They were outnumbered. Nowhere to run. Nowhere to hide.

"The Incorporeals will require food. You will produce it for them."

Gweneth gave a soft gasp, and every muscle in his body tightened. This new arrival knew about the sexual energy necessary for the Incorporeal survival.

"You be feeding them to the other creatures." Disappointment and a touch of horror filled the Scothage captain's voice as he saw his unexpected profit slipping away.

"Have no fear," the horned man said, amusement curling his straight mouth into a mocking joke. "You'll still have your prisoners once they feed the Incorporeals. You'll have entertainment too," he promised, his amusement creating a terrifying expression. "The Incorporeals feed on sexual energy. I thought I'd have to order all your men to touch themselves. It would've done in a pinch. This will work much better."

"Take 'em back to their cell," the Scothage captain ordered.

Two of the Scothage reivers grabbed Gweneth. She used her knee and got one in the groin before they overpowered her. Ellard bit back his amusement and didn't resist when the other two reivers pulled their weapons on him.

"A feisty woman," the horned man said, rubbing his hands—black fingernails, Ellard noted—together. "This feeding will provide great entertainment. I can hardly wait."

CHAPTER 13

G weneth stared at the man and tried to keep her expression impassive. Did he mean what she thought he meant? A quick glance at Ellard confirmed her horror. This man... He'd truly commanded them to have sex to feed Sheera and Leeam. The sex part, she didn't mind so much, but if he thought they would do it with him and the Scothage crew watching...

"No," she said.

"Yes," the man said, his voice calm. Scary calm. "You will have sex and provide food for the Incorporeals, and before you refuse again, if you don't, I will give you to the crew. They won't suffer the same sensibilities."

"We'll do it," Ellard said.

The man rubbed his hands together, flashing those black fingernails again. "I thought you might. Escort them to the cells. I expect my new possessions to be in full health when I come to inspect them. Do not disappoint me." He strode away without waiting for a reply, each step a confident swagger.

A Scothage pirate grabbed her upper arm and thrust her down the corridor. He bore a black eye and a nasty-looking bump on his temple plus a scowl. "Get off with you."

Gweneth jerked free and glowered back. "I'm going. No need to push me."

"Hush, Gweneth," Ellard murmured, striding to keep up with her. "We don't want to upset them."

"It's too late for that," Gweneth said, eying another of the Scothage reivers who appeared worse for wear. "We should have thought of that before we hit them over the head."

"Only a few of them."

Gweneth snorted.

"Enough talkin'," one of their escorts snarled. He walked with a slight limp and looked familiar. Yes, Gweneth held responsibility for his limp.

Soon they reached the cell area. One of the reivers opened the cell door and gestured for them to enter. He shoved Gweneth on the shoulder and pushed her to the back of the cell. Ellard followed secs later, and they both turned to watch the reivers lock the door. With the cell secured, both parties glared at each other.

"Lock the main door too. Make sure they can't escape again," one of the reivers ordered.

Another door slammed, the bolt slotting into the lock like a death knell.

Gweneth paced a tight circle of their cell. "What are we going to do now?"

"We'll have to give the appearance of making love, otherwise, I think they'll follow through on their threats."

"They're probably watching us now," Gweneth spat.

"No doubt, but we'll manage." Ellard strode to the front of their cell and stared through the bars. Leeam and Sheera were both lying on the deck. "Stay still," he said in an undertone. "The man behind your capture has joined the ship. He knows how you feed and has ordered us to have sex in order to make sure you remain healthy. You'll have to look livelier soon because he's intending to inspect his merchandise."

"We hear and will follow your suggestion," Leeam replied, his voice a whisper.

Gweneth retreated to the far corner of their cell and sank to the floor. Ellard stalked over to join her.

"I don't like this."

"Me neither," he said. "But we're going to push aside our discomfort and do as we're told. But the longer we delay their plans, the better the chance we have of giving Ry and the others a chance to rescue us."

"It irks me that we need saving."

"I hear you. I'm in charge of security. How do you think that makes me feel?"

They stared at each other and Gweneth sighed.

"How are we going to do this? You're right. There is no alternative. That man meant business."

"We can leave our clothes on and work around them."

Gweneth scowled. "This is a horrible idea."

"On the plus side, it's never a hardship to touch you."

"You sweet talker."

"I try," Ellard said.

"You always know the right thing to say to make me feel safe."

The tension creasing his face eased and his eyes softened to a pretty leaf green.

"I like your eyes. They're so pretty. They remind me of the forest. Some men have long eyelashes. You have long lashes."

Ellard raised his hand to cup her cheek. "They're the same color as yours."

"No, they're not. Are we going to have our first argument?"

Ellard chuckled, and the dread in the pit of her stomach faded. If they could joke while incarcerated on a reiver ship, they could manage to have sex to order. "One cycle, I'd like to make love in an actual bed. A nice, comfortable bed with a sanitizer room attached. Food and maybe a beverage."

"I think we could arrange that. I have a suite at the castle. Big gel-bed."

"How big is your sanitizer room? Big enough for two?"

"I don't know."

Gweneth grinned. "Doesn't matter. We'll experiment once we get home."

Ellard leaned closer and pressed his lips against hers. He seemed so calm, and his demeanor helped to stuff down her panic. She could do this and retain her dignity, even if every reiver on board this ship lined up to watch.

Gweneth let her hands creep around Ellard's neck and wriggled closer. She scowled at the discomfort and pulled back. "Could we lie down?"

Ellard pulled back and nodded. "Lie against the wall and I'll take the side nearest the door."

If he rested with his back to the door, none of the reivers would see much of her or him either. She could do this.

"Take off your tunic," she suggested.

"Why?"

"I like looking at your sexy chest."

He eyed her with a steady gaze. "You'll see my arm stump."

"It won't scare me."

"It's not looking that good. Because my Stores ripped off, it hasn't healed in a nice way. The combination of my shift and the plant made a mess."

Gweneth made a choked sound. "I'm so sorry. I know your feline genes will have healed you, but you should see a medic. Ellard, what are we going to do?" Gweneth bit her lip. "No forget

I said that." She pressed a kiss to the base of his neck, drawing in his familiar scent.

"We're going to pretend we're in the privacy of my suite with an entire eve ahead of us. No drama. Nowhere else to be. We've just eaten a delicious meal—"

"What sort of meal?"

He stroked a finger across her lips. "A steak. A thick, juicy malpack steak and one of Keira's pies to finish. Keira makes good pie. That's how Jarlath and I met Keira. She was picking berries to make a pie."

"That sounds good." Gweneth lifted her chin to search his gaze. "Do you have anything against vegetables?"

"I can eat a few."

"Good to know." Cracks were beginning to appear in her brave front, her throat so tight with fear it had become difficult to squeeze out words.

"Hey, hold on to your confidence. We'll get out of this somehow."

"It's hard."

"I know. Back in the war, after I learned Marjo and Mareeka, the twin chameleon shifters, had duped me, I found it difficult to get my mind straight. I blamed myself and when I lost my arm..." He stared at her, passion swirling deep in his gaze. "I didn't want to live."

"I've heard bits and pieces about the war. The leader of the House of Cawdor was a nutter."

His brows rose. "What is a nutter?"

"His brain tripped its wiring. He had kangaroos in the top paddock." A loud giggle erupted at his expression and she clapped a hand over her mouth. "He was a sandwich short of a picnic and had bats in his belfry."

"You're poking fun at me."

"Earth speak. I learned it from my friend Olivia."

"The leader was a despot," Ellard said. "He wanted to rule Viros and take advantage of our mineral deposits."

"He failed," Gweneth said. "These people will fail too. We will get Leeam and Sheera back to their family."

A thud sounded on the door and Malasses strode into the area between the cells. "I expected the pair of you to be busy by now." He sniffed the air, his nostrils flaring and making an odd sucking noise. "You haven't finished because I should smell sex."

Gweneth froze and peered over Ellard's shoulder. "It's him."

"Ah!" The man had taken his attention from them to study Leeam and Sheera. "A young couple. You have done well, Captain."

"We put the collars on them like ya told us. The trap knocked the stuffin' outta 'em," the captain drawled. He stood apart from the horned man, his hand on his sword hilt.

"I can see that. They require food." The horned man turned to their cell, his face hard with determination. "Feed my possessions. I go to dine. On my return, I expect to see them looking healthier." He wheeled around and strode away.

"Is that... Does he have a tail?"

"Yes," Ellard said. "I've heard of the Kiraxes race, but I've never seen one in person. They're fierce fighters and very territorial."

"What do they use their tail for?"

"I don't know. He has horns and scaled skin too."

"Perhaps he grasps with his tail and then gores his victim," Gweneth said. "I don't feel like having sex."

Ellard ran his hand down her back, a slow, comforting slide. "We need to send them some energy."

"I know." Gweneth sighed and grasped his face so he glanced at her. "It's the situation, Ellard. Not you."

"I understand." He repeated her words then kissed her, his lips silky soft and tempting. "If I don't get a chance to tell you..."

She slapped a hand across his mouth and glared into his kind face. "Don't you dare speak now. We can say everything we need to say to one another once we return to Viros. Do you hear me?"

Ellard peeled her fingers away from his mouth. "I think Leeam and Sheera heard you."

"We did," a soft voice carried to them from the other cell.

"Not helping," Gweneth snapped.

"No more talking. The horned man means every word. Now close your eyes and pretend we're lying in your favorite place and we're all alone. You tell me where we are."

Gweneth racked her brain and smiled. "We're on Viros, and we're having a picnic on Keira's farm. We're at their swimming hole."

"The perfect place," Ellard whispered. "Have we gone swimming?"

The vision exploded in her mind and she started talking. "We arrived at the picnic spot on your cambeest. It's hot, and we wanted to refresh ourselves. After your cambeest has taken a drink, we remove his saddle and tether him. He's happy and busy snacking on the different plants. We're hot too, so we strip off all our clothes and go for a swim. The water is cold and I stop mid-thigh deep. You splash me and start a water war."

Ellard laughed against her temple, his warm breath feathering downward. "I bet I win."

"We both win. Once we're both wet, we relax in the shallow water. It's warmer and more comfortable. Your arm is around me, holding me tight, and I feel happy and secure."

"Give me two arms, kitten. Let me be whole in your dream."

Her eyes flicked open, and she frowned. "I'll do that but know this. To me, you are whole. You're strong and kind and a good man. I don't need two arms."

Sadness tinged his faint smile, and she made a mental note to reassure him another time. The truth—she didn't notice his missing arm, not when the male was so big and strong and managed to work around the disability most of the time.

"Shush, kitten. Tell me what we do next."

Obediently, she closed her eyes and sank back into her vision. Heat. Water. Naked bodies. Ellard.

"You start touching me. A phantom skim of fingers across my face." She felt the light touch of his fingers and smiled, releasing the tension she'd held in her body and relaxing against him. "You grasp my hip and hold me still while you explore my breasts. You pinch and tug and stir a longing inside me, an emptiness that only you can fill."

His hand slipped beneath her tunic and up to her breast. He stroked her nipple through the lacy cup of her bra, the friction sending the first stirrings of arousal to life.

"Your skin is soft. I love touching your skin."

Gweneth wriggled and tugged up her tunic to bare her bra.

"Tug it aside for me, so I can lick your nipples."

Gweneth wriggled again and unfastened the hooks so it fell away from her breasts.

"Beautiful," he whispered and dipped his head.

The instant heat around one nipple had her sighing. Something about Ellard felt so right. She was certain she loved him, even though it had happened so quickly. Love at first sight. Maybe. Almost. Definitely lust at first sight, which sounded weird because she'd always pictured someone like Ry. Understandable since he stood as her role model.

"Gweneth, where have you gone?"

"I was thinking I wanted you from the first moment I saw you."

She heard a swift intake of air and waited for his response. When it didn't come, she didn't push. Not the right time. Instead, she burrowed her hands under his tunic and stroked his flat belly and the ridges of his abdomen. Their mouths met, and she allowed herself to sink into the vision again—one of picnics and privacy, skinny-dipping and hot, fulfilling sex.

His muscles pressed against her, and his body surrounded her with heat and protection. Skinny-dipping, she reminded herself. Her fingers wandered, wriggling beneath his tight-fitting trews.

He lifted his hips. "Yank them down a bit. They can watch my butt."

"I do," she said primly. "Whenever I get a chance."

"What?" He stared at her, questions swirling in his green gaze.

She bit her lip, unwilling to reveal her innermost thoughts while incarcerated in a cell. Although, he couldn't get huffy and leave. A captive audience. "Because you belong to me," she blurted. She managed to keep her focus on his face, saw the way he froze, and held his breath.

"No one has ever wanted me in that way before." His words sounded hoarse as if she'd shocked him. "Not a woman."

She slipped her hand downward and curled it around his cock, tightening her fingers until she garnered his full attention. "I've told you about my father and how Ry offered me an escape from an arranged marriage. I have good role models and I know what I feel. This isn't a whim on my part."

"But—"

"Ellard Tetsu, if you tell me once more that you're ugly and handicapped, I will box your ears!"

His brows rose. "Pardon?"

"I will beat your face with my fists, and don't think I can't because a pissed woman can do anything."

"I know what it means." He stroked her face, the rough pads of his fingers leaving a tingly trail of awareness. "I can do without scars to add to my looks."

"Well," she said.

"You might have convinced me."

They stared at each other for a long sec, and Gweneth found her lips quirking. Ellard laughed softly, and she lapsed into a full-out grin.

"Well, good."

He kissed her, a tender exchange of promises and warmth cradled her heart. She thought she might have convinced him. Finally.

"Slip my trews down," he urged.

This time, she followed his suggestion. She wriggled down his body and took him in her mouth.

"No, I—"

"This one is for you, Ellard. I want to do this, and it might be enough."

"But—"

"Stop arguing." She bent to explore his shaft, delighting in the contrast in textures, the softness over rigidity, the way he expanded his length and size. He groaned, a low sound full of need and urgency, and she enjoyed that too.

Gweneth became aware of her feline part, the weight of tension exploding through her mind. A rumble squeezed up her throat and erupted free.

"You're purring," Ellard whispered.

She swiped her tongue over the head of his cock, savoring his wild, musky flavor so much she repeated the move.

"Your tongue feels rougher than normal."

She lifted her gaze. "What?"

His breath whooshed out, and he stared at her face. "Nothing."

Gweneth went back to her task, licking and manipulating his flesh, dragging grunts and groans from him as she took him inside her mouth. Kaya had told her about this, described the act and what to do. She remembered everything and sucked him as deep as she could.

His big body trembled, and the amount of pre-cum increased. She licked and teased, thrilled that he'd allowed her this intimacy. His hips shifted, pushing him deeper. Recalling Kaya's words, she used her hands at the base of his shaft for better control while she made free with her lips and tongue, teasing the head and giving him the friction he needed to orgasm.

His hand smoothed across her head, gripping and releasing her hair. His hips bucked, pushing his shaft deeper. He jerked back, allowing her respite before he thrust again.

He cried out, his cock pulsing, then he was coming, shooting his seed down her throat, his big body shaking with the force of his release.

Gradually, she pulled back. She wiped the back of her hand over her mouth and grinned at him. "Doing that makes me feel powerful."

Ellard yanked up his trews then reached for her, dragging her into his embrace. "It also brings out your feline. Did you feel her?"

"I felt something."

"You were purring and your tongue felt rougher than normal. For a sec there, your eyes shifted."

"Really? I wonder if I'll manage to shift one cycle. Watching Jannike and Camryn play with their mates in cat form... I suppose I shouldn't tell you this, but I get jealous. A bad character flaw."

Ellard slid his mouth over hers in a tender kiss that she felt clear to her toes. His eyes were bright as he smiled at her. "There is nothing flawed about your character, kitten, you're the nicest feline I know."

"Ellard."

The soft whisper had them both sitting up to stare around their cell. An almost transparent figure stood in their cell with them.

"Niran?" Ellard murmured.

"It is I. My apologies. I didn't mean to peep on your private moment."

"It's all right," Gweneth said.

"Thank you. The *Indefatigable* is close. I said I'd shimmer aboard to see what we're up against. Are Sheera and Leeam here?"

"Uncle?" Leeam's voice crossed between the cells.

Niran turned to face them, relief filling his expression. His shoulders slumped momentarily before he turned back to Ellard. "Report for Ry, Shiloh, and Ransom."

"Scothage reiver crew, not overly intelligent but they managed to set traps for Leeam and Sheera. Paid by a Kiraxes called Malasses to collect Incorporeal specimens. He has collared Sheera and Leeam to prevent them from using their full powers. Scothage consists of a captain and six crew. There could be more, but that is the number we can confirm. The Kiraxes is the dangerous one. He seems to know a lot about the Incorporeal race."

"He would," Niran said tersely. "Old foe. The ship's destination?"

"Destination is Kiraxes."

Niran nodded. "I'll tell them." He faded from sight.

Gweneth and Ellard stood and walked to their cell door. Sheera and Leeam had also stood and appeared healthier than earlier.

In the distance, a siren sounded.

"They know they've come for us," Ellard said.

Niran flashed back and presented two small blasters and two knives to Ellard. "Ry said to tuck these away. They might come in handy."

Ellard handed a knife and blaster to her and she tucked the knife in her boot, the blaster in the internal pocket of her trews. With her tunic pulled over the top, the Scothage reivers wouldn't notice the weapon during a quick visual.

He flashed into the other cell and handed Leeam and Sheera thin blades. "The Kiraxes is vulnerable to strikes in the gut. Wounds in this region are always fatal to them. Use the weapons wisely since you will have one chance. I will be back and attempt to shimmer you off the ship, but those collars are a problem. The Kiraxes will have the control on his person, and I fear the collar will prevent you leaving his vicinity."

"Yes, Uncle," Leeam said, but his uncle had already gone.

Running footsteps sounded, heading toward them and two breathless Scothage reivers appeared, weapons brandished, eyes wild while the sirens continued to wail. The Kiraxes arrived, expression angry yet determined.

"Ah, my property appears healthier."

The dull boom of an explosion sounded, the ship jerking violently. The Kiraxes lurched off balance, striking the cell doors. The two reivers squawked in alarm. One flew against the wall, bounced off and hit the Kiraxes, knocking them both off their feet.

Sluggishly, the ship righted and Malasses rose with a ferocious scowl. "If anyone comes near my property, you will shoot to kill. If you fail, I will skin you alive." His tone said this wasn't a threat. With one final, glare to reiterate his warning, he took off at a sprint.

"Attract their attention," a voice whispered against Ellard's ear.

"Hey," Ellard said. "What's going on? Is someone attacking? You need to let us out of the cell. We can help protect the ship."

"We not be stupid," a reiver said. "They be coming for you."

Another boom, closer this time made the entire ship shudder.

In the Incorporeals' cell, sparks flashed without warning. A pained groan filled the air, and a weird curse that came from the corner of the cell snared everyone's attention. Leeam and Sheera stood there, mouths open, then belatedly Leeam doubled over and groaned.

Gweneth caught the faint flicker, gone in a blink. Was Niran injured?

One of the reivers edged closer. "What be wrong?"

"Stomach," Leeam groaned. "Must be a reaction to the collar. You'll have to remove it."

"I no think so. The Kiraxes never make threats," the reiver said.

While Leeam had their guards' attention, Ellard pulled out his blaster.

"I'll take the one on the right," he murmured.

Gweneth nodded, cautiously removing her weapon. She pressed

the safety, the faint click loud in the cell area.

"They've got a—"

Twin blasts rang out, striking the reivers before they could draw their own weapons. They fell and didn't stir again.

Gweneth pulled out the knife Niran had given her and started to work on their lock. Niran flashed into sight, groaning as he attempted to rise from the floor.

"Those collars kick," he said. "I suspect he's built something into them to stop other Incorporeal beings flashing in and attempting a rescue. We need to get his control."

"If it's on his person, we'll have to kill him," Ellard said.

In the distance, weapon fire sounded.

"They must've boarded," Ellard said. "Kitten, how are you going with the lock?"

"Patience," Gweneth said, her expression intense with concentration. "Almost." A click and the cell door opened. "After you, sir."

"Smart arse," Ellard muttered. "I think we should stick together. Open the door for Leeam and Sheera. Niran, will you be all right?"

"Not full power after touching Leeam," he said. "Collar must suck from other Incorporeal somehow. Modified since last saw a Kiraxes. Can't shimmer back to ship."

"Can you stay invisible?"

"Yes."

Gweneth straightened from working the lock on Leeam and Sheera's cell and tugged the door open. "Practice makes perfect."

"I'll take point," Ellard said. "Niran, you stay behind me with Leeam and Sheera. Only act if necessary, since they aren't aware of your presence yet. Stay invisible. Gweneth, you protect our rear." He stooped to pick up the blaster from the nearest reiver while Gweneth stripped the other reiver of his weapons. 'Let's go kick reiver arse."

CHAPTER 14

E llard cast out his feline senses as he led them down the corridor, possibly into danger. Not that he could do anything else. None of them wanted the outcome portrayed by the reivers or Malasses, the Kiraxes male. As he approached the intersection where the gray corridor split into two, he slowed. They'd gone right last time. A metallic thump reverberated throughout the ship, and an instant later, the vessel shuddered. Hope rose in him. He prayed the sound truly was the big grappling hooks that bound ships together in deep space.

Shouts sounded to their right, and after a brief hesitation, Ellard headed in that direction. The reivers would be busy repelling the attack and wouldn't expect a sneaky rear strike. He padded cautiously along the gray corridor, blaster extended in his hand. The shouts increased, the captain barking out orders.

"Aye, hold her steady. Wait, wait...fire weapons!"

Boom. Boom. Boom.

The ship quaked, groaned.

"Bank," the captain ordered. "Come ye around and be readyin' weapons again."

"You assured me your ship came equipped with enough firepower to withstand an attack," Malasses snarled.

"Aye, one opponent in a fair dogfight, not two ships," the captain snapped, not cowed by the Kiraxes male, despite his ferocious appearance. "These be experienced pilots. They be knowin' our every move before we make the evasion."

"Outsmart them. That's what I'm paying you for," Malasses said.

The Kiraxes male's voice emerged quiet and even, and Ellard thought the captain should pay attention. This was a dangerous man. Unpredictable.

"I will go and check on my property. Make sure it is unharmed."

Grata!

Gweneth glided up beside him, blaster at the ready.

Footsteps sounded, coming closer. Hard. Confident.

Malasses appeared in the doorway of the bridge. His eyes widened, and he charged, head down, horns in the perfect position to gore an opponent.

Ellard fired.

Gweneth fired.

And Malasses kept coming, his enraged bellow roaring through the corridor. At the last sec, Ellard dodged and pushed Gweneth out of the way. Malasses caught Ellard's ribs on his right side and bellowed in triumph.

Something hit the ship, and Malasses lost his footing. He crashed to the floor and skidded into the wall, his horns and skull hitting the solid surface with a sickening thud. He groaned and shook his head.

Ellard struggled to get to his feet, scrabbling on the floor. Grata, his damn arm would be the death of him. He pushed up onto his knees, but Malasses kicked him in the gut before he got to his feet. He fell back with a curse. The bull man laughed and lowered his head, the light catching on his black curled horns.

A siren started to wail somewhere close, the piercing sound shredding Ellard's thoughts. *Get up. Get up! Before the gratason gores you.*

Ellard scrambled along the deck of the ship. It tilted without warning, knocking them all off their feet. He slid against the wall, his arm stump slamming hard against the solid surface. Pain rippled to phantom fingertips, and he grunted but managed to retain his blaster.

Malasses gave a roar of triumph.

Had he grabbed one of the Incorporeals?

Got to stop. Keep safe.

One of the women screamed. Gweneth? Panic roared through Ellard, his feline pushing past his control so fast he couldn't control the change. His tunic split with the force of the morph from humanoid to feline, and he wriggled free of the remnants. Experience had taught him, it would get in the way and hinder a fight. Tunic free, he struggled to right himself, a snarl of feline fury blasting free.

Gweneth had her weapon pointed at Malasses, but he advanced on her, his arrogant expression telling Ellard he thought he could best her.

He thought she wouldn't shoot.

Idiot gratason.

The ship listed in the opposite direction, flinging everyone off their feet, just as she fired her blaster. Malasses bellowed in pain. Gweneth struck the wall but retained her weapon.

His stomach. Good shot, kitten.

Malasses didn't try to stand again. Instead, the massive beast fumbled for something in his pocket. A small control, it fit in the center of his palm. He rolled, giving a pained snort. His jaw set in a determined line and pointed it at Sheera and Leeam. "Shimmer us to the ship's tender. In the hold."

"No," Leeam said, his voice defiant.

Immediately, his collar sparked a fiery blue. Leeam screamed, the sound high and freaky. A chill rippled over Ellard's fur. Where was Niran? Why couldn't he grab the control?

"Shimmer us now," Malasses bellowed as the ship leveled.

Ellard skidded into Malasses and swiped him with his claws.

Malasses bellowed like a male bull-deer in rut. He lowered his head and shoved his horns against Ellard's ribs. Without room to move, he didn't do much damage, but it still phrullin' hurt, the force enough to separate their straining bodies.

Gweneth fired at Malasses, the shot so close that Ellard smelled the charge.

Malasses pushed on the control clutched in his hand. Blue sparks shot from Sheera's and Leeam's collars.

"Shimmer," Malasses ordered.

Gweneth fired a third time, and Malasses groaned, his big body slumping against the wall while Leeam and Sheera shuddered, blue sparks spitting from their collars, pain racking their bodies.

"Not...going...to...lose." His trembling hand rose, still grasping the control. "Shimmer."

Sheera collapsed against a wall while Leeam fell to his hands and knees, his breath coming in hoarse pants.

"Can't," Sheera pushed out. "No power."

Malasses pressed his free hand against his belly, and Ellard saw fluid seeping from his wounds. Malasses's big shoulders drooped, but a crafty expression filled his eyes. He lifted the hand with the control to his mouth, shoved it inside, and swallowed it.

"No!" Gweneth shouted.

Malasses grunted, struggling to keep his head upright, his eyes open. "Not lose."

Ellard snarled and leaped at him, claws swiping, but it was too late.

"Ellard," Gweneth said. "Ellard! I think he's dead."

Some of his fury subsided, and Ellard backed away from the Kiraxes male.

"Leeam." Gweneth crouched beside the Incorporeals. "Are you all right?"

"Not dead," Leeam said in a faint voice.

"Sheera?" Gweneth checked on her next.

Sheera lifted her weighty head, her face shaded a delicate blue. "Hurts. Everything hurts."

"Where is Niran?"

"F-floor." Sheera had difficulty pushing the word out. "Hit head." Her chest rose and fell. "Not m-moving."

Ellard turned and couldn't see a thing.

"We need to get these collars off them," Gweneth said.

Voices shouted. "Ellard!"

Shiloh? Ellard gave a feline shriek, and running footsteps headed in their direction.

Ellard stared at his younger brother as he raced toward them, expression fierce, blaster at the ready. Ransom, ran behind him, equally ferocious.

"Everyone all right?" Shiloh demanded. "Who is that?" He kept advancing and tripped without warning, catching himself on his hands before he struck the floor. "What the phrull?"

"I think you found Niran," Gweneth said. "The ship has been moving around. Sheera said he hit his head. How can we check on him if we can't see him?"

"Me," Leeam said and attempted to move toward Shiloh. He groaned, the half a step he took taking more power than he had. He slumped.

"Let me help." Gweneth slipped her hand around his waist and supported most of his weight.

"Stop," Sheera said. "Niran is right in front of you."

Gweneth released Leeam, and he dropped to his knees, his trembling hands reaching for his invisible uncle. "He's alive," he said hoarsely. "I'll look after him."

"Good," Shiloh said. "Who is that?"

"That's Malasses, a wealthy trader from Kiraxes," Ransom said with distaste. "Where is the control for the collar? He must have it on him somewhere."

Ellard shifted and fingered his side where Malasses had got him with his horns. "He swallowed it. Need to secure the bridge."

"Ry has weapons locked on them." Shiloh felt the deck around him and carefully climbed to his feet. "They're not going anywhere."

"We need that control," Ransom said. "It's impossible to remove the collars without it."

Ellard grimaced. "Who is going to retrieve it?"

"Not me," Gweneth said. "I blasted him."

"You?" Shiloh glanced at Ellard and noticed the absence of his Stores for the first time. "Where is your arm?"

"Long story," Ellard said. "The bridge. I don't trust those Scothage reivers. The captain is crafty."

Ransom pulled out a knife. "I'll retrieve the control and guard the Incorporeals. The three of you should be able to secure the bridge."

"Which way?" Shiloh demanded.

Ellard scooped up his blaster. "This way."

He set a brisk pace down the corridor, aware of his brother and Gweneth trailing him. He wanted to tell her to stay with Ransom because it would be safer if the Scothage males attempted to resist. Yet, she had saved them from Malasses and kept her wits in a difficult situation. Gweneth had earned her place at his side, even if the feline part of him hated the idea of her in danger.

Ellard burst onto the bridge. The captain sat at the ship controls, his features grim, his attention on the *Indy*, visible through the viewport. The rest of his crew stood behind him.

"I'll check them for weapons," Shiloh said and rapidly conducted a search. He retrieved four blasters, two short swords, and six knives. "Here. Com Ry."

Gweneth accepted Shiloh's com unit and contacted the *Indy*. "Ry, it's Gweneth. We have control of the ship."

"Is Niran with you?"

With his feline hearing, Ellard could hear the conversation.

"Yes."

"Tell the captain to set course for Narenda," Ry said. "Lynx will disengage Ransom's ship and fly it back to Narenda. Tell Shiloh and Ransom to stay on board."

"Aye, Captain," Gweneth said.

"Is there anywhere to keep these reivers so they stay out of trouble?" Shiloh asked.

Ellard glanced at Gweneth and smiled. "We know just the place."

Planet Narenda, home of the dragon shifters

The *Indy*, the reiver's ship, and Ransom's ship kept close as they headed for the spaceport on Narenda. Gweneth watched the green-and-blue planet come into view as they angled into the atmosphere. Narenda had more water than Viros, hence the splashes of blue on the surface. As they neared the spaceport, the jagged mountain range where the reivers had captured them came into view in the distance. Between the mountains and the town, the forest and lakes took precedence. Then, they were coming in to land at the spaceport, and Gweneth noticed ten dragon shifters, heavily armed, waiting for their arrival.

The reivers' ship landed with pinpoint precision, and the captain powered down with competent ease. As the engines grew silent, she heard his sigh. Her blaster rose, and she nudged his shoulder to remind him of her weapon.

"No escape attempt. Aye, we had a good run," he said and shrugged as if he had not a care in the world. "We be eludin' capture for several rotations, made a good living from our pickin's."

"Silence," Gweneth ordered. Something about him, his easy attitude, the watchful eyes, the tilt of his chin, told her he was lying through his teeth and would seize the first opportunity to escape. The man had intended to sell her and Ellard for profit, and she didn't trust him for a sec.

He shifted his weight and made to stand.

"Stay," she barked. "Open the entrance to your ship."

"And if I say nay?" His gaze met hers in a challenge.

"I killed Malasses. I shot him in the gut three times. My hand didn't shake." She didn't attempt to break their visual connection, just stared back and prayed none of her inner turmoil leaked free. While she'd help save Leeam and Sheera, she took no pleasure in her first kill. Once, while Ry schooled her in the use of a blaster, he'd told her she shouldn't learn unless she planned to fire the weapon to save herself or others. Learning to operate a weapon came with responsibilities. She must never point a weapon unless danger lurked, and she needed to remember that taking a life came with a price. The faces haunted dreams, and a kill claimed a part of the shooter's soul. She hadn't understood his calm yet determined words and had merely nodded and agreed.

Now, almost two rotations later, she comprehended his lecture. She wouldn't sleep well this eve.

"You shot him?"

"Yes."

"Nay, don't believe you."

"It's the truth," Ellard said from behind them.

Shiloh stood at his brother's side, watchful, his feline close to the surface and ready to pounce.

"What you be doin' with me and my crew?" the captain asked.

"That is up to Ransom and his people," Ellard said. "Open your cargo hold to allow the dragon guards aboard."

Some of the confidence seeped from the captain, and he lost his easy insouciance. He pushed a button on his controls, raised his hands, and stood.

"Gweneth!" a masculine voice roared.

"Gweneth!" another voice shouted, this one female.

"You'd better go and reassure your friends before they do some damage," Shiloh said.

Gweneth smiled and went to the entrance of the bridge. "I'm here on the bridge."

Ry jogged around a corner, followed by Kaya. In three giant steps, Ry grabbed her, wrapping his arms around her in a hug. Just when she wondered if she'd manage another breath, he released her, a hand on each shoulder as he studied her face. "Are you all right?"

"Yes."

Kaya scrutinized her face for a long moment and finally nodded, her blue hair swinging to reveal her pointed ear. "You look different."

"It's been an adventure. I just want to go home." Gweneth wouldn't reveal personal details. Kaya's intense interest told her she required a distraction. "I managed to talk the dragon shifters into attending the festival. They'd like to exhibit their jewelry. How did everyone else go? Are there enough of our neighbors interested to bring extra visitors to Viros?"

"Everyone we approached agreed," Ry said. "You had a good idea. Everyone thinks so."

Pleasure rose in Gweneth, and she clapped her hands together and wriggled happily. "I can't wait."

"Do you need Mogens to treat any injuries?" Ry asked.

"No, but Ellard might need some treatment. He lost his Stores arm, and Malasses got him in the ribs with his horns."

"A man with horns? A Kiraxes?" Kaya demanded.

223

"Yes."

Kaya's blue eyes narrowed to slits, her curiosity roused again. "The Kiraxes people are known as hard-arses. They mean business."

Nothing less than the truth. "No, they don't muck around."

"How come you're still alive? How come he didn't thrust you out into deep space?"

"He needed us."

"Why?"

Ellard walked up behind them and slipped his good arm around Gweneth's waist. "Can't you save your questions for later?"

Kaya looked from him to Gweneth and back, then focused on the physical contact between the two, her eyes shining with curiosity. "But I need answers now."

"And I have questions for you and Nanu." Gweneth narrowed her gaze on her friend and caught the slight ear twitch. A tell for Kaya. "I wanted to thank you."

"Why?" Kaya backed up a step.

"The ship maintenance you and Nanu taught me came in useful. Someone screwed around with the wiring in the *Gallant*."

"No! Why would they do that? Do you think one of those radicals who want to oust Lynx and Shiloh managed to get on board?" She had her innocent tone down pat but her right ear twitched again.

Definitely guilty.

"I don't know," Shiloh snapped. "But if I catch the culprits, I'll toss them in the dungeon without a trial. Ellard and Gweneth could have died." He shot a glance at his older brother, some of his anger dropping to the level of a worried frown. "Ellard needs a medic."

"How are Sheera and Leeam? Has Niran woken?" Gweneth asked.

"They managed to shimmer from the ship," Ransom said from

the end of the corridor. "You are welcome to rest and recuperate at my home."

"Thank you," Ry said. "But my mate is about to deliver our child. We'll fly back to Viros. Mogens can treat Ellard and Gweneth on the flight back to Viros."

Kaya eyed Ransom and tucked a strand of hair behind her ear. "Pity we're not staying longer."

"What about my ship?" Shiloh asked.

"It is repaired and ready for you," Ransom said. "Ellard, I will arrange for your luggage delivery to the spaceport. It won't take long."

Gweneth went to Ransom and hugged him. "Thank you. We will contact you with more details about the festival."

Ellard growled, and Ransom smiled and placed distance between him and Gweneth. "I would like that. We will enjoy our visit to Viros."

Shiloh offered his hand to Ransom. "The king of Viros bid me to extend an invitation to stay with us at the castle during your visit. We can place a suite of rooms at your disposal."

"And the other dragons in my party?"

"We can discuss that, but most of the other visitors will stay at the Feline Inn, which is not far from the castle. You are welcome to have guards at the castle if you wish."

The tenseness in Ransom dissipated. "That is acceptable. Thank you. I will escort you to your ship."

"Everyone to the *Indy*," Ry said. "We'll depart as soon as the luggage arrives."

"The males on this planet are prime," Kaya said.

"We don't have time for you to play with them," Ry informed her. "I want to get back to Camryn."

Less than a cycle portion later, the green-and-blue planet grew smaller and smaller and disappeared from vision with the naked eye.

Gweneth unstrapped her safety harness and stood. "I'm going to my cabin to sanitize and change."

Mogens stood too, his face a pearly gray, an indication his mood hovered midway between happy and angry or disturbed. "Do you require any medical attention?"

"I have a few scratches and grazes. Nothing serious. Ellard is the one who requires your aid," she said.

Mogens regarded her and tilted his head in acknowledgment. "Come with me," he said to Ellard. "You can sanitize in my cabin."

"I don't—"

"I can smell your blood. You wear a wound on your side. Go with him," Ry said and his voice held a snap of tension. "Mogens is skilled and will help."

"Ellard, Mogens will help you," Gweneth said, her tone imperious. "Don't make me hold you down for him."

Kaya coughed, her head cocking like a curious bird.

"Check on Gweneth first," Ellard said after a lengthy silence.

"My cabin is near Gweneth's," Mogens said, a ribbon of black dissecting his face. "I don't need to read the clouds to learn of your stubbornness." Mogens issued a heavy sigh. "All felines are stubborn." He glanced at Gweneth. "Half-felines too."

"Very well." Ellard stood and followed her and Mogens off the bridge.

"I wonder what happened between them." Kaya's nosiness trailed them, as did Ry's comment about this being none of their business. Gweneth and Ellard would tell them what they wished them to know.

"But aren't you curious?" Kaya demanded.

"No, I want to get back to—"

Gweneth didn't hear any more but guessed Ry wanted to be with his mate. They passed their mess room and the galley and headed into the accommodation corridor, where they all had cabins. Their corridor wasn't gray. She and the others had painted a colorful mural of the different things they'd seen during their travels and her residual tension seeped away. *Home.*

"I am not badly injured." Gweneth came to a halt outside her cabin door. "Please, I'm telling the truth. I have bruises from when the ship jumped around. A couple of shallow cuts. Nothing is painful, and I'm healing rapidly."

"Go and sanitize, child," Mogens said. "I will deal with this stubborn feline first."

Gweneth pressed her palm to a decoder. Her cabin door slid open. "I'll come to your cabin once I'm finished."

Alone in her cabin, Gweneth sighed, feeling more tired than she'd ever felt before. Although she'd told the truth about her injuries, her body ached. Bone-deep. For a sec, she studied her image in a looking glass. A wild woman stared back. Hair loose and fluffy. A scratch on her cheek and a dirty smudge on the other. Her tunic bore three rips, and her trews had a hole in the knee. Her mud-splattered boots needed a good cleaning.

She forced her arms upward and managed to pull off her tunic. A big bruise covered her left side plus a few minor scratches. The faint bruises on the upper curves of her breasts made her smile. Ellard. She didn't mind those ones.

Gweneth turned away, tugged off her boots and trews. Her underwear hit the floor, and she stepped into her sanitizer. Warm spray pummeled her aching torso, and she sighed again. Luxury. The scents of lime and basil filled the air, and her mind shifted to Ellard again.

He'd become quiet, his thoughts turning inward. He'd decided he wasn't worthy of her or some such idiocy. Maybe he worried about his handicap, but she refused to let him get away with a retreat. They were good together, and she wanted him. She loved the big idiot. She, more than anyone, knew what it was like to get judged on appearance, so that excuse meant nothing to her.

Gweneth turned on the drying function and let the warm air

soothe her aching muscles while she formulated a plan.

Two cycles. She'd give him two cycles to clear his thinking before she acted.

She'd beat down his objections once.

She could do it again.

CHAPTER 15

M ogens led Ellard into a large cabin. The gel-bed sat against the far wall, bolted in place in case of space mayhem. An herbal scent perfumed the cabin, no doubt wafting from the bunches of dried flowers and plants hanging from a drying rack. A series of cupboards and drawers—of different sizes—covered the other wall, all fixed and guarded against movement from the ship.

Ellard knew his arm was bad. Yes, the stump had healed after the plant incident, thanks to the rapid healing powers that came from his feline heritage but it appeared ugly. He knew they couldn't attach another Stores and had doubts about alternatives. Then he needed to consider the cost. The installation of his Stores had wiped out his savings.

"Sanitize first," Mogens instructed.

Ellard gave a clipped nod. Since their arrival, he'd become friends with Ry Coppersmith's crew, but Mogens always held himself aloof. He spent his cycles in his medical lab or out in the forest collecting herbs and berries and visiting Kelvin, the tremin shifter in mourning and stasis, not far from Jarlath and Keira's farm. And when necessary, he treated Ry's crew and, more recently, the castle residents, both royal and staff.

"Hurry or I will bite you." A ribbon of white twirled across Mogens face, dissolving into the dove-gray.

Ellard felt his mouth dropping open as he gaped at Mogens. "Your teeth aren't sharp enough to do real damage."

Mogens chuckled, the sound resembling a fly-mo in need of maintenance. "You should see your face. Please sanitize, and I will do my best to aid you."

"I should be used to Ry's crew by now."

"We do our best to entertain." Another streak of white turned Mogens's face paler. Ellard recalled Gweneth telling him a pale Mogens indicated happiness. If his face turned charcoal gray or black, things in his world had taken a turn for the worse.

Ellard stripped off the tunic he'd pilfered on the reiver ship, awkward and resigned. He'd allowed himself to believe he could have a life with Gweneth, but he hadn't been able to deal with Malasses. Gweneth had managed to save them all. His lack of an arm presented difficulties in his everyday life. He couldn't...

He broke off the thought to struggle from his boots and the rest of his clothing. He stepped into the sanitizer, the warmth and pressure from the cleanser nozzles easing the tenseness in his muscles. He stood there for several mins, letting his mind drift while he enjoyed the sensation of being clean and safe. Then, aware Mogens waited for him, he switched on the drying function.

"Finished?" Mogens called.

"Yes." Naked, Ellard padded into the main cabin and came to a halt in the middle of the floor space. A satchel sat on the corner of the gel-bed, the contents open to his view. Small vials and bottles glinted under the light.

"Ah," Mogens said, and he circled Ellard. "Bruises. This cut appears infected." He traced the cut along Ellard's ribs, one Malasses inflicted with his horns.

"The Kiraxes attempted to gore me."

"Their horns have poison. I can treat that. Sit on the corner of my gel-bed. I'll treat the cut, then take a look at your stump."

"It's not good."

Mogens met his gaze. "No, the arm will be problematical."

Ellard dipped his head in acknowledgment, glad the medic didn't attempt to lie. The foul-smelling salve Mogens placed on the cut made him sneeze, but the instant it contacted his skin, the faint burning that had plagued him ceased.

"Your feline genes will heal the rest," Mogens said. "Now let me take a look at your arm."

Ellard gritted his teeth while the medic probed his stump.

"Fascinating," Mogens said. "I can see the replacement medics' attachments, but your feline has healed over them. They sit below the skin. How did this happen?"

"I got caught in a plant. It attempted to eat me, and between that and my shift to feline, I lost my Stores. The plant produced this sap stuff that burned skin, and my Stores didn't stand up well to it either. The sap pitted the surface from what I saw."

"Your feline genes saved your life," Mogens said. "If the dissolving had continued upward as far as the stump, you might have died."

"They told me the chances of the Stores failing were low."

"And the installation could never be duplicated," Mogens added. "I did some research."

"No, it's something to do with the way they fit the arm." A lump grew in his throat and he had to swallow when he wanted to hit something. The Stores had given him mobility and made him feel more normal. Once he'd had the Stores installed, most people didn't notice his lack of an arm. Now, he'd have an empty sleeve, and for the rest of his life, he'd have to struggle with his handicap.

"I will do more research," Mogens promised. "There must be something we can do for you. Meanwhile, I can make a salve for your stump. Although it has healed over, the surface is jagged, and I suspect it is tender."

Ellard nodded at his questioning look.

"My salve will help with that. Apply each eve before you retire."

"Thank you."

"I'm afraid I don't have trews that will fit you, but I can give you a robe."

"Thanks," Ellard said.

A tap sounded on the door, and it opened.

Ry stuck his head inside the cabin. "Shiloh commed. Said he had some clothes in Jannike's cabin." He handed over a pile of clothes.

"Thanks." Ellard stepped closer and awkwardly accepted the pile of clothing.

Ry hesitated, then nodded and retreated, the door closing with a faint click.

"Do you require my help?" Mogens asked.

"No." Ellard regretted his sharp tone when he uttered the word, but Mogens didn't react.

"I will blend the salve. We'll apply some before we arrive at Viros."

Ellard struggled with the clothes, dressing taking him much longer than usual—a return to his time before the Stores installation. A heavy pressure slumped his shoulders and pushed against his mind. He'd been fooling himself. This was his future and he couldn't inflict it on Gweneth.

Castle, Viros City

Gweneth strode into the castle with Ry, Nanu, Kaya, and Mogens, her mood one of anger and frustration. Ellard had ignored her once the *Indy* landed, and it had hurt. His stiff attitude had hurled her back to the horrid days at her father's mansion on Ornum. The pain. The confusion. The humiliation.

Except this time, she didn't have to accept the behavior.

No, she'd give him space, recuperate herself since her bones ached still, and she craved sleep. The next cycle, she'd run him to ground and give the stubborn, mule-headed male an ultimatum. She was not a toy or a convenience. Nor was she promiscuous or an idiot. She was, however, pissed and once she felt more herself, she'd hunt down the stubborn feline and give him her version of the truth.

Jannike hurried up to them, her hand cupped over her rounded stomach. Gweneth smiled inwardly at the protective gesture. Jannike might stomp and mutter about her pregnancy but she wanted this child. "Hurry," she gasped out. "Camryn is having her baby."

Ry cursed and went Incorporeal white. "Where?"

"The medical suite."

Ry took off at a sprint, the rest of them hurrying after him.

"Why didn't someone contact us?" Ry demanded.

"Camryn knew you were on the way, said it would take a while, and threatened to bite anyone who told you before you stepped foot in the castle," Jannike said, her words coming out between puffs.

Gweneth forced herself to follow, excited about the impending arrival, yet her aching body and extreme fatigue stopped her from enjoying the occasion. The winding corridors, lined with tapestries and artwork, blurred, her focus on each footstep, the *slap, slap, slap* of her boots the one thing keeping her moving.

Finally, they arrived at the medical suite, a modern affair with pristine white walls. To the right, a small reception room, full of comfortable gel-chairs, a com unit, and a meal station waited for friends and relatives—in this case, the royal family or staff now that Lynx had stepped into the shoes of king. To the left, several males and females surrounded a surgical gel-bed.

A scream rippled through the air. Gweneth felt the pain, the anguish in the sound. Her nostrils flared, and she smelled the acrid scent of cleanser and medicines. She smelled fear and frowned at the unfamiliar scent—the heavy metallic weight of it as it coated her senses.

"Camryn," Ry said, and he strode to the bed, pushing past the medical staff.

As one, they squawked, pointing at his clothes and their pristine masks and apparel.

Mogens hustled over to Ry, spoke in an undertone, and Ry reluctantly retreated. Both he and Mogens disappeared into a small alcove.

Unable to stand an instant longer, Gweneth wobbled to the nearest gel-chair and dropped onto it.

"Tired?" Jannike asked.

"Yes."

Jannike sat with a heavy sigh. "Me too."

Mogens and Ry reappeared, appropriately gowned in medical white. Ry pushed past the medical staff to get to Camryn while Mogens approached them. A stripe of black raced across his face when his gaze came to rest on Jannike.

"Gweneth, please escort Jannike to her suite. Both of you look exhausted. The babies will not arrive before morn."

"Babies?" Gweneth demanded, her words echoed by her friends.

"Two," Mogens said. "I have seen the signs in the clouds, and the medic has just confirmed. Jannike, you require your rest. Gweneth, you will see she gets back to her suite, com either Lynx or Shiloh and once they arrive, you will sleep too."

"All right," Jannike said without argument. "I am tired." She rubbed her belly. "The babe likes to kick."

Gweneth forced herself to stand, wincing at the sharp aches in her bones. Yes, she required sleep. "Call us if the babies arrive."

"I promise," Mogens said.

With nothing but willpower, Gweneth walked Jannike to the royal suite, thankful of Shiloh's presence when they arrived.

"Camryn is having two babies," Jannike said. "By Jupo's teeth, I'm glad I am only having one. She bounces and kicks inside me. Never still. I need to pee."

Shiloh smiled after his mate. "Thank you for saving my brother."

"We saved each other." Gweneth's mouth opened in a yawn she couldn't control. "Sorry. Mogens will contact us when the babies arrive."

Shiloh nodded. "Go. You need rest."

"Yes," she said, and with a tired wave, she pushed her feet into motion.

The short journey down another corridor—the castle layout confused many visitors and Camryn called it a rabbit warren—past a suit of Peravian battle armor that glinted an unlikely pink under a spotlight and around a corner, she arrived at her suite. The door slid open to her palm print and Gweneth headed directly to her gel-bed. As she passed a looking glass, she paused to study her face. The cuts had almost healed, but that wasn't what made her stare. She leaned closer to peer through blurry eyes. The cat tattoo that had caused so many problems with her father had disappeared, leaving her cheek bare.

She blinked. Once. Twice.

The tattoo didn't reappear.

She shrugged, the lift and fall of her shoulders squeezing a groan free. Grata, that had hurt. Deciding to ponder the peculiarity the next cycle, she dropped onto the corner of her gel-bed and struggled to remove her boots.

Each boot clumped to the floor, followed by her inner linings. Too exhausted to remove her clothes, she crawled into the middle of her gel-bed and sighed at the relief of not having to hold her body upright. Her eyes closed and she sank into sleep.

She dreamed of a cat. A lone black leopard—a male—stepped his way confidently through a forest. Gweneth didn't know how she knew the leopard was a male, but she sensed it, smelled it, and accepted the instinctive knowledge.

Gweneth followed, slinking low, trying to follow without detection. The leopard stopped and turned to face her. Detected. Undeterred, she rose from her dropped position and stepped daintily across the forest floor to join him. She rubbed against his flanks, marking him with her scent.

Mine.

Mine.

A sharp pain cut across her awareness, making her freeze in the action of rubbing noses with the leopard.

Gweneth's eyes flicked open, her vision wavering. Something burst within her chest, pushing, pushing, pushing while the ache and throb of her bones increased until she cried out with the pain of it. She groaned, too fatigued to resist the force that seemed determined to detonate her weak body.

She closed her eyes against the burst of brightness, the intensity of the colors and textures. Every one of her senses—smell, sight, touch, sound, and taste—cataloged impressions, bombarding her brain with information. So much information.

Intense pain burst through her arms, her legs, her torso, and she cried out, but that sharp jolt had done something, eased the pressure. The discomfort faded, and Gweneth took a deep breath. She opened her eyes and squeaked, instantly squeezing them shut again.

The squeak emerged as a throaty growl, and she froze.

Her throat worked in a swallow as she sought the courage to confront the truth.

She'd morphed into a feline.

That was what every clue told her.

Gweneth took a deep breath and opened her eyes. She jumped off the bed. *Jumped*.

Four legs. Paws. Black fur. A tail.

Cat.

The remnants of her tunic and bra draped around her chest and ribs. Ah, yes. The clothes on the top half of a feline body didn't survive a shift, while any clothing or footwear below the waist somehow melted into the skin. She managed to wriggle free of the shredded clothing, irked because that had been her favorite bra. At least the matching panties would reappear once she morphed back to humanoid.

The feline part of her ordered her to explore, to check her suite for safety. Since she couldn't fathom an argument, she padded a slow lap of her sleeping chamber, filling her nostrils with familiar scents and the underlying ones her humanoid nose didn't catch. She caught faint laughter coming from the public square outside the castle walls. Gweneth padded to her reception room window and jumped to place her paws on the window to take a look.

The restaurant at the far end glinted under the whitelight. Wow, she must have slept through the blacklight. Several feline males sat around a table, relaxing with tankards of reeb. At another table a Redd couple, their cinnabar skins gleaming beneath the whitelight, sat with a snack. She stood too far away to see what they ate, but suspected their meal consisted of sticks of roasted meats, a specialty of the house.

Satisfied she wasn't dreaming, and she'd truly turned feline, she pondered what to do next. No one would come to investigate while the focus shined on Camryn and her babies. Gweneth would need to shift back to humanoid on her own if she wanted to leave her suite.

Now, what had Shiloh and Lynx told Jannike? Picture her humanoid form in her mind. Hold it there and concentrate.

With a raspy feline breath, she closed her eyes and pictured herself, plucking the memory of her reflection in the mirror from her mind. For an instant, nothing happened, and a flash of panic caused hesitation. The image faded, and she plonked her butt on the floor.

No.

No, she could do this. Camryn and Jannike managed. So would she.

Gweneth tried again and a prickling sensation tickled across her skin. She focused harder on her humanoid self and a dart of pain speared her ribs. She cried out, the picture popping like an Earth balloon. The pain—no, she thought. Not pain. More discomfort and bearable if she kept her breathing even and didn't fight or tense her muscles.

With a whoosh, the black fur melted back into her skin, and secs later, she stood on wobbly legs, garbed in her trews, her chest bare.

"Yes!" She fist-pumped into the air.

Her com buzzed and she strode to answer the summons. The rest and the shift had done her good since the weird fatigue she'd labored with had faded.

"Yes."

"Camryn and Ry have two babies, a boy and a girl," Mogens said.

"That's great. Are they all right?"

"Camryn is weak," Mogens said. "I pray she will survive. The babes are healthy and vigorous."

"I'll come now," Gweneth said.

Two cycles later

Gweneth waited for Mogens in the reception room of the medical suite. The rest of the *Indy* crew, plus Shiloh and Lynx, waited with her. A heavy silence filled the room, no one verbalizing their thoughts.

Things weren't looking good for Camryn.

After three cycle portions passed, Mogens entered the reception room. His color hovered between charcoal gray and black. Everyone stood, silent, waiting for his announcement.

"Camryn is no worse. She is very weak and has woken just now."

"Will she be all right?" Kaya demanded, her vibrant face pale.

"I will know more this eve," Mogens said. "If she struggles through this cycle, I think she will recover, although she is exhausted. I go to rest. Ry will com me if he requires my aid."

"Mogens, I will walk with you," Gweneth said.

He offered a quizzical look but no comment, and she fell into step with him as he turned toward the exit. Once they were out of earshot, he glanced at her again. "Do you have a problem?"

"Two eves ago, I shifted to feline."

Mogens stopped walking. "Your facial tattoo is gone. I thought you'd applied makeup to hide it as you sometimes do."

"No, it's vanished."

"You have mated with Ellard?"

"No. We didn't mate."

Mogens frowned. "Another anomaly. The process varies with each feline. The Virosian felines are consistent in their behavior but none of the *Indy* crew reacts in the same way. Have you a tattoo on your back like Camryn and Jannike?"

"No." She'd checked in the looking glass and seen nothing but bare skin.

He nodded. "Nothing else is amiss?"

"I feel fine and managed to change from feline to human on my own."

They halted outside Mogens's suite. "Com me if you feel unwell or anything else seems amiss."

"I will. Mogens, do you...will Camryn recover?"

"I pray it so. A cloud reading will help, I think."

Gweneth nodded and pressed an impulsive kiss to his cheek. A white swirl diluted the darkness from his features. "Rest well,

Mogens. I will try and persuade Ry to take a rest."

"Good luck." His eyes crinkled at the corners. "Good luck with your intentions, child."

Planet Narenda, Chieftain's office
"What do you think?" Niran asked.

Ransom pushed away from his desk and stood to join Niran by the window. The vibrant flowers in the gardens glowed like jewels in the foreground, the wild forest flora beyond another sea of color. Predominantly green, but tinges of pink and red dotted several of the trees. And beyond that, the terrain shifted to rolling hills, the very start of the mountain range where they found the raw materials to make their jewelry.

As a youngster, he and his brothers and friends had practiced flying in the fields on the other side of the trees and to prove their bravery, they'd flown close to the start of the chain of mountains—just to show they could withstand the resonance. He snorted under his breath. Young fools. A small hit of resonance in the form of stones didn't hold much danger. In some dragon shifters, the resonance caused drunken symptoms. An entire mountain range, however, could kill, sending them mad with the ringing in their ears.

Only a few of the much older dragon shifters ventured near the mountain range, and they never managed to stay long.

The dangers Leeam and Sheera had faced meant Niran was reluctant to allow his people to venture into the area again. Not that Ransom blamed him. Luckily, their stocks of stones were sufficient. For now.

"It is a good idea." Ransom tore his gaze from the view outside his window and turned to the Incorporeal leader. "I will com the king and request a meeting, ask if they will allow you to shimmer into their territory."

"Please request Ellard's and Gweneth's presence."

Ransom nodded. "I will do as you ask. It is time."

"Yes," Niran said. "As much as I will miss them, it is time for a change."

Ellard's suite, House of the Cat castle, Viros

The determined thump on Ellard's suite door echoed in time with his head. *Bang. Bang. Bang!*

"What do you want?" The black mood that hovered over Ellard burst free in a feline snarl. "Go away."

"I order you to open the door." His younger brother. Determined, judging by his crisp words.

"And I order you to open the door," Lynx said in a quieter yet implacable tone. "Don't make me order your soldiers to break down the door."

Ellard stomped to the door and wrenched it open. His empty tunic sleeve flapped at his other side in silent mockery. "Say your piece and go."

"Niran, the Incorporeal leader, has requested a meeting. He asks that you be present. The meeting takes place at one portion cycle." Lynx looked him up and down. "Enough time for you to apply stop-beard and sanitize."

Shiloh's nose wrinkled in a fastidious manner. "You reek."

Ellard opened his mouth to tell them to phrull off, but Lynx held up an imperious hand. His brother's friend hadn't taken long to get a king attitude. He snapped his mouth shut.

"You will attend. This is a chance to advance trade and public relations. We need to establish good relations with our neighbors."

"Fine," Ellard bit out. "Where is the meeting?"

"The morning room," Shiloh said. "One portion cycle. Don't be late."

His brother and the king left, closing the door behind them. Ellard took a sec to mentally curse then headed for his sanitizer.

Two mins past the portion cycle mark, Ellard presented himself at the morning room door. He knocked, and Lynx answered, ushering him inside. Jannike and her friends had changed the furnishings, and the room no longer appeared cluttered. Instead, the sparseness of it, the new warmth and richness of the red-jewel tones, the comfortable gel-seating made it a suitable, if informal, place to host a meeting. Ellard took two steps and came to an abrupt halt, his nostrils flaring. His head snapped up, his gaze sweeping the rest of the light-filled room.

"Gweneth," he said and was proud of his even tone. "I didn't realize you would be here."

"Niran requested her presence too," Lynx said.

Ellard gave a curt nod and walked over to the window, an excuse to rip his gaze off her enticing figure. The city spread out below and beyond the vivid greens of the forest, but nothing about the view diverted him from Gweneth. She looked good. Beautiful. His pulse jumped into a racy beat, and his feline stirred beneath his skin—a ripple of protest at the distance between them. His cat didn't understand. His handicap would drag Gweneth down, and she deserved so much more.

Unable to resist, he turned and caught the arrival of Niran as he shimmered into view. He wore his long white hair loose apart from two thin braids on either side of his face. Dressed in a frilly white shirt and tight black trews with boots, his white eyes scanned the room in a trice. An instant later, Leeam and Sheera appeared, their hands clasped. The couple wore color, so much color that Ellard blinked. However, their smiles eclipsed the bright reds, pinks, and blues of their garments.

"Greetings." Lynx flashed a grin of greeting. "Welcome to Viros."

"Thank you," Niran said. "It is good to meet you in person. This is my nephew Leeam and his mate Sheera."

"I am pleased to meet you. We have made a point of meeting our neighbors," Lynx said. "Closer relations benefit us all. Please, have a seat."

"Thank you."

While Lynx and Niran completed the polite courtesies, Ellard watched Gweneth. She didn't watch him back. Instead, she said something to Leeam and Sheera and the three were soon in animated discussion.

"Ellard," Shiloh said in a sharp tone.

Ellard blinked and realized Lynx wanted him to join the discussion. He stalked over to the three men and sat.

"Ransom and I were both impressed by the way Ellard and Gweneth protected Leeam and Sheera. You joined the search and ultimately found them, facing danger to keep them safe."

"I'm a soldier," Ellard said.

"No," Niran said. "Not everyone would do what you and Gweneth did. My family and friends have prospered on Narenda with Ransom and his people. We have multiplied to such an extent it is now necessary to splinter and find a new home. Now that Leeam and Sheera have officially mated, I seek your permission to allow them to live on Viros. I requested Ellard's and Gweneth's presence because I would like them to be our liaison."

Ellard glanced at Lynx and Shiloh and saw they didn't fully understand what Niran was asking. He swallowed and led with the truth. "Gweneth and I aren't together. We can't—couldn't—provide sustenance for Leeam and Sheera."

"I see," Niran said, his pinprick glacier-blue pupils increasing in size as he scrutinized Ellard. "The Incorporeal race requires sexual energy to survive," he said to Lynx and Shiloh.

"So Ellard and Gweneth kept Leeam and Sheera alive," Lynx said with interest, finally understanding.

"Fascinating," Shiloh murmured.

"If Leeam and Sheera came to live here, what would be involved?" Lynx asked. "Would they need to live in the castle?"

"That would be best, but they need to live near sexually active couples."

Shiloh grinned. "I guess a triad would work."

"Even better," Niran said.

Lynx frowned. "How does this work? Do they need to be in the same room?"

"No. We are not peepers or voyeurs, but we are aware when lovers are active. We can absorb the energy from the room next door or a corridor. The lovers who feed us never know of our presence. We do not require feeding every cycle and can stockpile the energy. We can also share the energy, which is how we feed our youngsters until they're mature enough to collect their sustenance."

"Shiloh and I are mated to Jannike. We have another mated couple who live in the castle, plus several other friends who sometimes bring partners back to their suites—as long as the partners can pass security checks. My brother and his mate also reside here at times. If that is acceptable, we can offer Leeam and Sheera a suite of rooms within the castle for their accommodation."

"You would do that?" Niran asked.

Lynx nodded. "The castle was a lonely place during my childhood. I like having more inhabitants. If you are unsure, you are welcome to stay on a trial basis."

"Your charges?" Niran asked.

"All we ask of our friends is that they help with anything that requires aid. For example, Gweneth had the idea of holding a festival. We have split the tasks and are all helping to make it a success."

"Ellard, you haven't told your king of our powers," Niran said.

"No, I thought it best to keep it quiet. Not that they would spread the news or take advantage, but—" Ellard shrugged. "I didn't want to endanger you by telling your secrets."

Niran beamed. "I knew Viros would be a good place." He

turned to Lynx. "The Incorporeal people feed on the sexual energy, but we are also able to conjure physical things from the same source." He waved his hand, and a drink appeared. He handed it to Lynx and conjured three more, plus a float table to place them on. He lifted one in a toast. "To your good health."

Lynx and Shiloh eyed the drinks suspiciously, but Ellard sipped his without hesitation.

"We can conjure anything, even spaceships. The items we conjure last for as long as the recipient requires them. Once they are no longer required, they will vanish. For example, if someone stole your clothes, leaving you naked, I could conjure you a suit of clothes. The clothes would remain until you reached your accommodation and took them off to replace them with another set of your own clothing. A spaceship will remain until the destination is reached. The food and drink we conjure nourishes."

"What happens if the Incorporeal dies or is killed suddenly?" Shiloh asked.

"The item remains until it is no longer needed. We offer useful gifts in exchange for sexual energy, but we are not bottomless pits of riches," Niran said, his tone becoming somber. "We reserve the right to conjure items as we see fit. No one may demand or order. It does not work that way."

Lynx took a sip of his drink, then another, his shoulders relaxing. "Leeam and Sheera are welcome to stay at the castle. I suggest a short stay—maybe seven or ten cycles—first to see if they enjoy it here. We do not require anything in return. If Leeam and Sheera want to help us organize the festival, they may do that."

Niran stood. "Leeam. Sheera."

The couple turned with broad smiles and approached.

"King Lynx has invited you to visit," Niran said.

"With a view to see if you would like to live at the castle full-time," Lynx said.

Sheera clapped her hands together. "We would like that very

much. We have missed Ellard and Gweneth."

"Ellard and Gweneth will give you a city tour," Lynx said. "Is there any reason the stay cannot start immediately?"

"Leeam?" Niran asked.

"We would like that," Leeam said.

"Very well," Niran said. "May I return in ten cycles?"

"Come at the same time to this room," Lynx said. "We will await your arrival."

Niran inclined his head. "Thank you. In ten cycles."

"Can we do the tour now?" Leeam asked, beaming with excitement.

Ellard glanced at Gweneth and away, a tight band of emotion forcing him to struggle for breath. "Of course," he said. The sooner they did the tour, the sooner he could lose himself in work. It was time to check the fitness of his soldiers and guards. That would help keep his mind off Gweneth.

CHAPTER 16

EIGHT CYCLES LATER, GWENETH'S SUITE

Sheera shimmered into Gweneth's suite, startling a squeak from Gweneth. She pressed her palm against her pounding heart and glared at the Incorporeal woman.

"New rule," she said with a distinct edge to her tone. "You and Leeam are welcome to visit me at any time, but you must shimmer your arrival outside my door and knock for admittance. This is my private space. You must do the same for all of us. Knock for admittance, and if we come to visit you in your suite, we will do the same. Clear?"

Some of Sheera's good humor faded and she started to vanish.

Gweneth grabbed her arm. "Stay. I am not feeling well, and I'm grumpy."

Sheera solidified again. "I'm sorry. You're right of course. Leeam and I will remember our manners in the future. What is wrong with you? Can I help?"

"Keep me company until Mogens arrives. I commed him, and he said he'd drop by after he checks on Camryn."

Sheera gave a wide smile. "The babies are beautiful."

"I know. They are healthy. I hope Camryn recovers soon. Ry is worried and snapping at everyone." She made a moue with her lips. "It must be catchy." Her stomach roiled without warning and she made a run for the sanitizer room.

The small amount of food she'd managed to eat after rising came back up. Her stomach muscles heaved, her throat burned as she lost her breakfast. Gweneth wiped her mouth with the back of her hand and straightened with a sigh. Even that hurt.

"Mogens is here," Sheera sang out.

"Let him inside," Gweneth croaked. "I won't be a min."

Gweneth gripped the hard edge of the sanitizer unit and stared into the looking glass. The paleness of her features brought to mind a healthy Incorporeal. Pale with an underlying pinkness.

Her stomach did a shimmery dance again, and she froze, wondering if she should dare move.

"Gweneth?" Mogens' footsteps approached. "Sheera said you aren't well."

"Is Sheera still here?"

"No, she shimmered out to meet Leeam in the gardens once I arrived." He shook his head, his pale gray features alive with good cheer. "They are so young and full of enthusiasm. I am glad you were able to save them."

"Me too," Gweneth croaked, the writhing of her stomach too much for her. She vomited again.

"Ah," said Mogens. "I begin to suspect the nature of your illness."

"Can you fix me? This is the third morn I've been sick. It's weird because I only get sick in the morn. By eve, I'm hungry and able to eat."

"'Tis as I expected, child. Wash your face and rinse out your mouth. I'll be in your relaxation room when you're ready, and we will talk."

Gweneth sucked in a deep breath and followed Mogens's instructions. "Is it something serious?"

"I suspect you are pregnant."

The verbal punch had her clutching her chest, struggling to breathe. He...he... Pregnant? She couldn't be. "I used your birth control tonics. You know that."

"Yes, but you and Ellard created sexual energy to keep Leeam and Sheera alive."

Gweneth swallowed, Ellard's recent behavior another hard slap to her equilibrium. "Um, yes? But that wasn't long ago. Should I be having this sickness already?"

"Let me analyze a blood sample to confirm, but I'm fairly certain. The morning sickness is another feline shifter peculiarity, since it occurs almost straightaway. I believe the sickness doesn't occur until at least week six in humans. That is what Camryn's sister-in-law told me during our Earth visit." Mogens opened his satchel and competently took the sample. He placed the vial containing her blood inside a protective vessel and closed his satchel. "I will have confirmation in two cycle portions."

Gweneth nodded and sank onto her favorite gel-chair, no longer able to support her weight on her shaky legs.

"It will be all right, child." Mogens patted her shoulder.

"Ellard has distanced himself. I-I don't know how he'll react to the news."

"Let me get confirmation, and we can go from there." Mogens squeezed her shoulder, a ribbon of black bleeding into the gray of his countenance. "You have family, friends. No matter what happens, Gweneth, you will have our support."

She nodded dumbly, her mind full of shock, disbelief, and if she was honest, a trace of excitement because she didn't doubt

Mogens's diagnosis. He seldom made mistakes.

A baby.

She watched Mogens depart, her vision focused on the solid door as he closed it with a soft click.

A baby.

Her hand went to her flat belly, and she rubbed lightly. "I wonder how your father will react."

Two cycles later.

Ellard arrived in the communal dining room to find his brother and Ry.

"How is Camryn?" he asked.

Ry yawned and rubbed his blood-shot eyes. "Mogens says she's improving, but she sleeps most of the time. She lost so much blood."

"The kittens?" Shiloh asked.

Ry smiled briefly. "My son and daughter are thriving."

Lynx arrived with a pregnant Jannike. Nanu and Kaya strode in a few secs later.

"I'm starving." Kaya sat at the table and helped herself to a wedge of Polis melon. Cubes of the delicate pink flesh disappeared into her mouth with rapid efficiency.

Mogens arrived, his black satchel clasped in his left hand.

Everyone grabbed their normal seats and started to break their fasts.

Gweneth didn't come, and the lump of unease sitting in the pit of Ellard's stomach grew. He hadn't seen Gweneth for cycles. She didn't join them for meals, and he hadn't seen her around the castle. Not that he'd been around much. He'd spent three cycles out at Jarlath and Keira's farm, and the rest of the time, he'd kept busy putting his soldiers through rigorous training and tests.

Still, he would have expected to catch glimpses of her throughout his cycle.

His conscience urged him to talk to her again, to explain why it would be best for her to move on with her life without him. Tension bled through his limbs, bringing his feline to the surface. His hand tightened around his vessel of tay, claws protruding from beneath his fingernails.

This cycle, he decided.

Putting this meeting off was cruel to both of them.

"Does anyone know where Gweneth is?" he asked.

"She isn't feeling well," Mogens said. "She is in her suite."

Ellard stood.

"Take her this," Mogens said, handing him a plate bearing two slices of hardtack biscuit.

Ellard started to add quigly spread, a fruity green concoction, and the traditional accompaniment, but Mogens shook his head.

"No, just the hardtack. Tell her to nibble on it," Mogens instructed and calmly returned to his meal.

Ellard frowned at Mogens, frowned at the squares of crisp hardtack, and shrugged. Mogens was the medic. He supposedly knew his art.

At Gweneth's suite door, he paused, hampered by the plate in his one hand. In the end, he kicked the door. Soft voices came from within and an instant later, Leeam opened the door, a vision in green and red.

He beamed, his pale face glinting with undertones of pink. "Ellard. Just in time. Sheera and I have a com-meeting with Uncle Niran."

Ellard stepped into Gweneth's suite, his gaze going straight to Gweneth. She sat curled up on her favorite gel-chair, her features wan yet beautiful.

His breath caught as he stared at her.

"Hello, Ellard. Did you enjoy your stay with Jarlath and Keira?"

"Yes." He thrust the plate at her. "Mogens told me to bring you these. He said you should nibble on them."

"Thanks. Why are you here? I thought you'd said everything when you rejected me on the journey from Narenda."

Ellard flinched at the harsh words even though he deserved them. He sighed and decided to lead with the truth. He owed her that at least. "I love you, Gweneth. From the moment I saw you I wanted you."

"You have a funny way of showing it."

"Please, let me finish."

She sniffed and bit off the end of a hardtack.

Unable to stand in one place, Ellard started to pace. "You know my history. Because of me, the House of Cawdor got a foothold here on Viros. No woman had ever paid such close attention to me before, and I fell for it. I'm not pretty like Shiloh, and now I have one arm."

"You can get another."

"No, I can't. Not only was it expensive, but the way they installed it meant it was a one-time proposition. They warned me of this, and I accepted the risks. Most beings who have a Stores go through their lives without mishap. I had bad luck." He squeezed his eyes shut, trying not to let self-pity take over. Jarlath had lectured him, told him he was unique, and he felt proud to call him a friend. He'd also threatened to kick his butt if he fell into despondency again. Ellard accepted he was a work-in-progress in the self-pity stakes. While he struggled, Gweneth didn't need the weight of his problems on her shoulders.

"I'm sorry. I didn't realize." She leapt out of her gel-chair so fast the impression of her butt remained for secs after she'd disappeared into her sanitizer room.

With his acute feline hearing, Ellard caught the loud noises she made as she vomited.

His footsteps took him to the doorway.

"Go away."

"No, you're not well. Let me call Mogens."

"He can't help me." Gweneth straightened. "Wait for me out there. I have something to tell you."

Indecisive, Ellard hovered.

"Wait for me." Gweneth slammed the door in his face.

Unable to sit because of his worry, Ellard paced back and forward in front of a window. Not even the view of the square and the forest beyond, one of his favorite places, snagged his attention. Instead, he worried about Gweneth. Mogens knew of her symptoms, yet he hadn't seemed overly concerned.

The click of the door drew his attention, and he spun around to face her.

"Have a seat."

Ellard studied her impassive features. "I prefer to stand."

"So it's easier for you to get a running start?"

He gaped at her. "What?"

"The reason I keep throwing up each morn is because I'm pregnant."

Her words pierced the silence like blaster fire. Ellard's knees wilted, and he dropped, a gel-couch breaking his fall.

"Did you hear me?" Spots of color highlighted her cheeks.

"Pregnant?" He swallowed, certain his hearing deceived him.

She sighed. "Yes."

"You...pregnant?"

"Yes," she snapped, her chin lifting in challenge. "And before you ask, Mogens is sure."

Panic, like he'd never felt before, blasted through him. Thoughts roared through his head, and his feline took over. Flight. He traveled halfway down the corridor before his humanoid self thought better of the action.

Unwilling footsteps took him back, and he found Gweneth curled up on her gel-seat, silent tears running down her cheeks.

Something twisted inside him. She was his mate. He knew this even as he knew that tying herself to him wasn't her best option.

"We're having a kitten?" Even in his state of shock, he didn't doubt her words as truth. If she expected a child, then he was the father.

"Yes."

"All right. What do you want me to do?"

Her mouth tightened. "You don't have to do anything. I just thought you should know."

"Gweneth, I'm no catch. I'd be loyal. I'd love you and our kitten, but I could never hold them. Not safely."

"I don't want you to take responsibility for me and our kitten because you feel guilty. I need love like Camryn and Jannike have. I won't settle for less."

"I understand. Let me help you as a friend."

"I-I don't think that's a good idea. Ellard, you don't understand. I love you. I have loved you since I first saw you. When I look at you, I don't see a handicap. I see a strong, loyal man who would do anything for his friends. I don't want you to commit to me because you think it is the right thing to do. I deserve a male who loves me without reservation. If I say yes to you now, what is to stop you from changing your mind later? We wouldn't be proper mates. Nothing would hold us together."

"Our kitten would—"

"No. I won't allow my child to be put in that position."

"Our child," Ellard countered. "Nothing has changed since we were on Narenda."

"Not true." Gweneth faced him without flinching. "You rejected me. I'm telling you about my pregnancy because it's the right thing to do. You should know you're going to be a father."

Ellard stared at her, attempting to read her mind. Despite engaging his feline senses, he discovered nothing of use, no clue as to how he could fix this breach between them.

"You should go now," Gweneth said.

Ellard stared at her for a fraction longer and realized he needed to regroup. Nothing he said now would help the situation, one of his own making he had to admit. She needed time. He needed time.

"Com me if you need anything."

"I don't need you."

"Com me," he insisted.

After a brief pause, she gave a grudging nod.

"Thank you." Ellard turned away, confident she would com him, but the knowledge didn't halt the turmoil rising in his gut. His feline snarled, the cry of displeasure echoing through his head. *Mate. Mate. Mate.*

The word, the thought repeated over and over until he wanted to growl and roar at the accompanying pain. This wasn't how he'd imagined this meeting. Ellard headed along the corridor, flinching at the close of the door behind him. It sounded like a full stop on the problem. Pregnant. He was going to be a father. Dizziness assailed him, his stomach pitching as shock did a dance through his mind yet again. A father.

Without knowing how he got there, he found himself in the rear garden, striding amongst the formal floral beds toward the stand of trees at the rear. The clash of swords came from the practice area, and Ellard headed in that direction. Lynx and Ry practicing together. Shiloh stood watching and offering words of encouragement to both feline shifters.

Shiloh glanced at him, frowned. "What's wrong?"

"Gweneth is pregnant."

"What? How?"

Ellard barked out a laugh. "The usual way."

"Birth control?"

"She took birth control," Ellard said. "At least, that is what she told me."

"What's the problem? You love her. Even I can see you love her. I saw the two of you together." Shiloh's brows drew together. "Wait. What did you do?"

"I told her I held no interest in pursuing a relationship with her."

"What?" Shiloh shut his mouth with a click. "Why would you do that? She's been chasing after you since she first arrived on Viros. I've seen you looking back."

Ellard swallowed to rid himself of the lump that had taken up residence in his throat. "Look at me. I'm nothing to look at, and I've lost my arm. I can't hold a kitten—not easily. It takes me longer to get things done. I'm handicapped, and I don't want to put that extra pressure on a relationship. When I had my Stores it wasn't so bad, but now..."

"Rotten luck losing your Stores." Shiloh clapped him over the back. "But you're still alive. Don't let Father's prophecy become true."

Ellard pulled his face. The instant he'd lost his arm, his father had wanted Jarlath to replace him with an able-bodied soldier. Jarlath had refused and forced Ellard back to the land of the living. Ellard snorted inwardly. He'd become stubborn and believed his life over, but Jarlath hadn't put up with his sorry-for-me attitude. "I did save the girl. That has to count for something."

Shiloh grinned, and for an instant, Ellard felt transported back to their childhood. He'd been the sensible one while Shiloh, aided by Lynx, had created trouble and chaos. "You helped the girl become pregnant. What are you going to do?"

"I want—she's my mate. I know this, but how can I saddle her with my problems?"

"Look at it this way, Ellard. What would you do if another male came along and wanted her?"

A savage growl escaped him, shocking him with its intensity.

"Your answer," Shiloh said lightly. "You want the child?"

"Yes." He never hesitated, which gave him pause.

"You need to woo her. Apologize and become her mate."

Ellard snorted. "You make it sound easy."

"Wooing a mate is never easy, but the heartache and uncertainty is worth every stressful sec."

Ellard turned and stalked back toward the castle.

"Where are you going?"

"To start my wooing."

"Women like flowers," Shiloh called after him. "You could pick some before you go back inside."

Ellard halted. "I might need help."

Shiloh sketched a bow. "At your service, brother."

Flowers picked, Ellard caught his breath as he knocked on Gweneth's suite door. The scent of the brocken flowers filled the air, sweet and fragrant, their white petals and red throats contrasting against the pale pink fern leaves. He hoped Gweneth would enjoy them. He juggled the flowers and awkwardly knocked with his foot again.

Sheera opened the door. "Come in. What pretty flowers."

"They're for Gweneth."

"A good start." Sheera's voice held approval.

"Ellard, what are you doing here?" Gweneth asked, and her tone sounded distinctly cool.

"I was wrong. Thickheaded and stubborn. I want to make it up to you." Ellard handed her the flowers.

She accepted them, pausing to sniff them before handing them to Sheera. "Why should I let you do that? What is to stop you from changing your mind again?"

"I deserve that." Ellard took a deep breath and dredged for the right words to persuade Gweneth to his way of thinking. "I think of you all the time. You're the first person I think of when I wake in the morn. You're the last person I think of in the eve. I dream of you." He paused. *What else?* "I can't promise not to make mistakes in the future, but know I'll try hard to always do the right thing."

Gweneth's dark brows rose. "I see. Anything else?"

"I will love you and our kitten. I will support you—"

"Will you allow me to continue working with the *Indy* crew?"

Ellard paused, aware of the silent dare in her words. They both knew Jannike struggled with her mates on this point, especially since her pregnancy. Gweneth was already pregnant. He forced himself to nod and made a mental note to offer his services to Ry. Where Gweneth went, so did he. "You're part of the crew. That doesn't need to change."

She nodded, her green eyes without expression. "Good."

His gaze wandered her face, coming to an abrupt halt when he reached the spot of her facial tattoo. It had disappeared, and he could see her face was free of the paint she and the other female crew sometimes wore. "What happened to your tattoo?"

"The strangest thing. I shifted the other night."

"Why didn't you say something?"

"I don't know if I can do it again, and I didn't try because I haven't been feeling well. Mogens said I should wait until I felt ready. He also suggests that pregnant felines try not to shift too often—for the good of the baby."

"Has the tattoo reappeared on your back?"

"No."

"I see."

An uncomfortable silence bloomed between them, and Ellard wanted to move. He fought the urge. Finally, when he could bear the hush no longer, he said, "I want you, Gweneth. You and our child. Will you give me another chance?"

"I'll think about it," Gweneth said. "Sheera, please show out Ellard. I wish to have a rest." And she turned away, disappearing into her chamber.

Once the door closed behind Ellard, Gweneth strolled back out to her reception room to spend time with Sheera.

"Ellard is sorry. I can see he loves you." Sheera dropped onto a gel-chair, her red jumper and black trews a contrast with the cream syn-leather of the chair. She flicked her wrist and a float table appeared along with two glasses of juice. "Why didn't you tell him you forgive him?"

"He hasn't groveled enough," Gweneth said.

"Groveled?"

"He needs to prove his intent. His love. My father spent rotations making me feel worthless because my feline half made me different from the other people on Ornum. I'm not going to let anyone treat me as inferior. If Ellard wants me, he'll fight for the honor. I want him to realize I don't care about his exterior. That's not important to me. It's what inside that counts. I want Ellard to realize he doesn't need to worry about other felines, other beings and what they think. He's a good feline. Loyal. He has a big heart, but he needs to trust that I have the same traits, that I can be his best friend. Ellard needs to trust me."

CHAPTER 17

ONE CYCLE LATER

G weneth walked into the reception room with Leeam and Sheera to find Ellard waiting with Niran, Lynx, and Shiloh to hold their meeting regarding Leeam and Sheera. It had been postponed one cycle after Niran had needed to take care of some business on Narenda.

"Good timing," Shiloh said, and he walked over to hug her. "Congratulations," he murmured. "I understand I'm going to be an uncle."

"Maybe."

"Be gentle with him. He's a male, and we can be thick at times."

A growl from behind them had Shiloh chuckling. After a quick squeeze, he pulled back and led her to a comfy chair.

Her gaze went directly to Ellard, and she found him watching her. Her breath caught at the emotion on his face, the open love and affection. She had to force herself to take a seat beside Leeam and Sheera.

Niran cleared his throat. "Leeam and Sheera have enjoyed their stay very much. They tell me you have made them feel at home and have fed them well."

Leeam grinned. "Very well."

"We would be honored if you would consider making this a permanent arrangement," Niran said. "We would, of course, compensate you."

"No," Lynx said. "All we require is for them to participate in life around here."

Shiloh nodded. "If Leeam and Sheera would agree to help in the same way all our friends do. That is all we require."

"You mean to physically labor rather than conjure?" Niran asked for clarification.

"That is correct," Lynx said. "None of us expect Leeam or Sheera to give us gifts or provide items. Shiloh and I prefer to do things ourselves rather than have people wait on us. Our friends are the same. We have all worked to better our lives. Conjuring items is all very well, but there is no satisfaction in things that come easy."

"Very well," Niran said, although Gweneth gained the impression something about this situation made him unhappy. "If you ever change your minds, please let me know."

"Leeam and I would like to reward Gweneth and Ellard for saving us," Sheera burst out.

"No," Ellard said. "We don't need anything. Gweneth, tell them. A reward isn't necessary."

Gweneth frowned. "Actually, there is one thing you could do for me. Ellard lost his Stores arm and because of the way it was attached, he can't have another, even if he could afford it. Is there any way you could provide him with an arm?"

"No. It's fine," Ellard said.

"It's not fine," Gweneth snapped. "Not when you're using your arm as an excuse to avoid happiness."

"I don't think—"

Lynx's gaze sharpened. "Niran, is this something you could do?"

"An arm would require a steady amount of energy expenditure," Niran said. "We could do this for you. The arm would be viable as long as Sheera and Leeam stay nearby."

"And if they weren't nearby?" Shiloh asked.

"The arm would remain as long as Ellard requires it, but in reality, it would be better if Leeam and Sheera were in the vicinity."

Gweneth's heart thudded so loud it deafened all other sound. She watched Shiloh and Lynx exchange a glance, a nod of acknowledgment.

"We've changed our mind," Lynx said. "Our fee is an arm for Ellard."

"No, I—" Ellard broke off as an arm formed and filled out his empty tunic sleeve. He stared at the pale, almost ghostly fingers and wriggled them. Then, he lifted his head and stared straight at her, his smile of wonder making her eyes well up.

"Hand me a drink," Lynx ordered.

Ellard stood and strode to a large float table. A large pot of tay sat beside a tray of empty goblets. He picked up the pot with his left hand out of habit.

"No, the other one," Shiloh said, hands crossed over his massive chest.

Ellard sent her another quick glance, this one with a trace of panic. Some of her irritation with him softened, and she circled Lynx and Shiloh to join Ellard.

"Put the pot down, Ellard. Try your new hand."

He stared at his ghostly fingers and wriggled them again. "What..." He paused to clear his throat. "What if I can't do it? What if I drop it?"

Gweneth reached out and squeezed those ghostly fingers. They were cool to the touch. "If you drop it, we'll pick it up and try again." When he met her gaze again, she gave a small nod.

He turned his attention to the taypot, flexed the fingers of the ghostly hand. She stood close enough to feel his rigid muscles and smell his apprehension. Weird, but she knew it was fear. Her feline stretched beneath her skin, making her smile. She would shift again. She knew it with every particle of her being, and that made her happy.

"Ellard, you can do this."

A rusty sound, almost a laugh came from deep in his throat. He reached for the pot, curled pale fingers around the handle and lifted it. A grunt of satisfaction came from him and with growing confidence, he poured tay into goblets. He set down the pot and picked up two goblets, one in each hand. A big grin wreathed his face as he handed the goblets to Lynx and Shiloh.

Gweneth's heart went pitter-patter as Ellard returned to pick up more goblets. He handed them to Niran, to Leeam and Sheera. The last two, he carried to her then he stood beside her, sipping the delicate green liquid, his wide grin still intact.

"Will the hand shift with him to feline?" Shiloh asked.

"Yes," Niran said. "It will do everything his other hand does."

Ellard beamed at Niran. No other word for it, and he instantly appeared years younger. "Thank you. Thank you so much."

"You're welcome. It's a small thing in exchange for what you've done for us. Ellard's arm will remain for as long as he requires it, but I will see to it that there is enough power to keep it in position."

Lynx smiled at Niran and slung his arm around Shiloh's shoulders, pulling his mate close. "Thank you for this amazing gift."

"If you have any problems, please contact us. We can have someone here in an instant," Niran said. "Leeam, Sheera, I believe you will enjoy living here."

"Thank you, Uncle," Leeam said.

Sheera hugged Niran. "We have loved our stay here. I can't

believe it will be our home."

"Make me proud, child." Niran blew a kiss and shimmered from sight.

"Wait," Leeam called and Niran shimmered back into the room.

Leeam grinned at Sheera. "Uncle, we would like you here when we present our gift to our benefactors."

Niran inclined his head.

"We have a gift already," Lynx said. "We don't require anything else."

Leeam conjured a small wooden box. "This is for Ellard and Gweneth, a special thank you. It is tradition, and Ransom received the same gift from Uncle Niran."

He opened the box and plucked out a ring. He gave it to Sheera and pulled out a second ring, which he kept.

Sheera approached her, happiness blazing on her pale features. "This is a special ring. It will shift with a feline and become invisible to all but an Incorporeal if you will it. This is a thank you for saving us and for being our friends. Let me put it on your right hand."

Gweneth gave a faint nod and held out her hand. Secs later, a golden band with inset green stones sparkled on her fingers. She glanced at Ellard and saw a matching but more masculine version of the ring glinting on his ghostly hand.

"Thank you," Gweneth whispered. "I didn't...we didn't expect a gift."

"I know." Sheera beamed and bounced up and down on her toes. "That's what makes it so perfect."

Ellard cleared his throat. "Thank you."

"You're very welcome," Niran said. "Ransom's workmanship is superior, and combined with our magic, the rings can never be lost or stolen." With a final wave, he vanished.

"You have an arm and a ring," Lynx said and grinned. "How does it feel?"

"A bit cold, but it works. It's amazing," Ellard said. "Gweneth, thank you for thinking of this."

"Maybe now you might believe in the future." She thought her snippy tone might drive him away.

"I deserve that. Can we talk? Walk with me in the gardens?" He offered his ghostly arm, and she bit her lip, trying not to smile.

She took his arm, the coolness making it feel more real, and they walked in silence from the room and out into the corridor. Meanwhile she could still hear Lynx and Shiloh talking.

"Why couldn't they have their discussion here?" Shiloh demanded. "We'll miss everything."

"Shush, they need to work things out for themselves. We can't interfere," Lynx said.

"I'm going to be an uncle."

"We're going to be an uncle," Lynx said. "As well as fathers. It's good all our children will play together."

"It *is* a good thing all our children will have each other to play with," Ellard said.

"Yes." It was still hard to believe she would be having a baby. "I will get big and ungainly."

"Beautiful," he countered as he led her from the castle out into the heat of the solar star.

A breeze tugged at her hair. Over to their right, a bird of some sort chortled from the depth of the trees. She couldn't see it but its happy sound had her smiling.

"Are you still feeling unwell?"

"Just in the morn," she said. "Mogens said it is normal."

"I hope you don't mind I told Shiloh about our child. I was excited."

"I don't mind, but I'd better tell Ry and the crew soon."

The sound of weapons came from the far end of the grounds.

"Would you like to do it now?"

"Yes."

They headed in that direction.

"How is the arm?"

"It works just like my other one. There's no pain and it doesn't feel heavy like the Stores."

"You never told me that."

"No, I was glad to have a functioning arm. This is so much better. It feels a bit cold, but that is a small price to pay for such a gift. And to be able to shift again without thinking, and to move freely."

Temptation sprang upon Gweneth—the idea of running with Ellard in feline form. If she could shift again...

"Ellard, could we try shifting now? Instead of going straight to see Ry and the others."

"I'm a bit nervous," he confessed.

"I don't even know if I can shift again. At least you know you can."

He halted and turned to face her. "There is a private area over to the right there, just past those trees. Why don't we disrobe and attempt our shifts where no one else can see?"

"Yes."

Secs later, she found herself in a clearing surrounded by trees. A fountain splashed into a shallow pond, the musical sound competing with the still invisible chortling bird.

"Do you remember how you did it?"

Gweneth frowned. "Sort of. Changing back seemed easier. I pictured my human self and concentrated on how my limbs felt."

"Perfect. You'd better take off your tunic. It's too pretty to rip during the shift."

Gweneth had worn her favorite set of underwear for the meeting too, because she'd wanted to feel good about herself. Confident. He'd noticed. Job done. "Good idea. Turn around."

"I've seen you before. You're beautiful."

His pretty green eyes glowed with truth and memories.

"Turn around." She gestured with her hand—a circle of

sorts—and caught the flash of disappointment that dampened his expression. "You distract me."

"Oh." He sounded much happier. Male smugness, and she couldn't find it in her to puncture his ego. She loved this shifter, even if he took his time to get with her program. While she didn't doubt his depth of feelings for her, he needed to learn to love himself. "Take off your tunic. I want to see your arm."

"You'll have to turn around for that." There went that smugness again. She found herself grinning.

"I'm still wearing my bra." She turned to face him and met his male appreciation.

"Still a pretty view."

"Thank you. Can I touch?"

"It doesn't hurt."

She stroked her hand over the cap of his shoulder and down the stump. Warm flesh beneath her fingertips. His normal flesh merged with the ghostly arm. Almost transparent yet perfect, with no visible joint. The skin of his Incorporeal arm felt much cooler and more solid than she'd expected, given its ghostly appearance. "Amazing. I can't see where it links. Scratch the back of your head. Touch the tip of your nose."

He followed her directions, mirth shining in his eyes. "Anything else?"

"Yes, I'm going to try to shift. Will my bones hurt in the same way?"

"Yes. You get used to it."

"You could have lied."

"You don't like lies. You've told me so."

Gweneth sighed. "True. At least I know you're listening to me."

"I've listened to everything you've told me. I'm trying to be the man you need."

"Ellard, you are the man I need. You just need to believe it yourself."

He stared at her for an extended sec then nodded. "Picture your feline in your mind and focus on running with me in feline form."

Without taking her gaze from him, Gweneth unclipped her bra and let it fall to the ground. She caught his open admiration as she shut her eyes, and it took a while to gather her thoughts. Slowly, she painted the picture of a sleek black feline in her mind. She willed herself to shift but nothing happened.

"Take it easy. It's hardest the first few times."

Ellard's soft words and encouragement flowed over her and the tension in her shoulders faded. Her skin started to tingle, her bones throbbed. Her mind wanted her to stop but the feline part of her rejoiced in this opportunity. Her skin prickled with greater intensity and her breath caught at the jagged pain that leapt over her body. She cried out, panic pushing her pulse rate to a gallop.

"Good job, kitten. Just a little more," came Ellard's calming voice.

The last part of the shift happened with a rush. Fur rippled over her torso, her bones lengthened, reshaped. Sharp teeth sprang into prominence, and she fell forward onto all fours. The pain ceased, the rush of senses taking her by surprise. Color popped and everything appeared sharper. Her sight. Her hearing.

Beside her, Ellard shifted with what appeared little effort, his ghostly arm morphing smoothly as Niran had promised. He stalked over to her and rubbed his head against hers. His shifted form dwarfed hers, yet she felt not a scrap of fear, especially when he purred. Then, he threw back his head and roared, a sound of victory and celebration.

The *thud-thud-thud* of running feet had them both turning, Ellard slightly in front of her in a protective stance.

Ry came to a skidding halt with Nanu and Kaya behind him. Lynx and Shiloh appeared secs later, and everyone stared at them.

"Who is that?" Kaya demanded. "I can see through—Ellard, is that you? Who is with you? If you've been playing around on

Gweneth, I'm gonna flatten you." She took two steps forward, halting when Ry seized her.

Shiloh folded his arms across his chest and broke into a grin. "Gweneth, have you been holding out on us?"

"That's Gweneth?" Ry demanded.

"Pretty sure," Lynx said. "Gweneth and Ellard came out here to talk, and that's Ellard."

Gweneth padded up to Ry and sat on her haunches before him. Ry hauled off his black tunic and tossed it aside. "Anyone else want a run?"

Lynx let out a whoop and flung off his tunic. Secs later, both he and Shiloh were in feline form, running through the trees.

"Not fair," Kaya huffed, her nose lifting.

"We'll go for a drink instead," Nanu said.

Gweneth went to them and rubbed against their legs. A purr emerged as they petted her while Ellard waited for her. A purr! Then she bounded off, tearing after Ellard and the others for a game of chase. Exhilaration roared through her with each leap and jump. Best game ever.

"Did you enjoy that?" Ellard asked.

Gweneth placed her palm on the keypad at the entrance to her suite. "I loved it. Everything seems so much more. I could hear small animals scurrying through the forest, and I could see more and the colors. So vibrant."

"Some felines see in color," Ellard said as they entered. "Others in black and white. That seems to run in families."

"I'm going to sanitize." Gweneth hesitated then nodded as she came to a decision. "Would you like to join me?"

"Yes."

The immediate agreement suffused her with pleasure, and she took his hand and led him straight to the sanitizer room. "We haven't finished our talk."

"Sounds ominous."

"It's not, but I want you to understand what I need from you. Love isn't enough."

"It's not?"

Gweneth turned on the sanitizer and started to strip. "I need to be able to count on you. If, for example, something happens to your arm, you can't decide you're not good enough for me again. This is the last time I'm going to tell you. I like what is in here." She tapped on his head. "And here." She placed her hand over his heart. "Physical appearance doesn't matter to me."

Ellard hesitated. "I promise to try. I can't guarantee I won't make mistakes, but I will try hard to remain positive." He stared at his arm. "Missing an arm—it makes me vulnerable. I can't protect you."

"I don't need protection. I need a man who will stand and fight at my side."

"We've already done that."

"And we were good at it." The twinkle in his eyes abraded some of her determination, and she castigated herself, bolstering her reserves. It was important that he understood and accepted her conditions. She stepped inside the sanitizer and held out her hand again. He whisked his tunic over his head and stripped off his remaining clothes and footwear with quick efficiency. "I love you, Ellard."

"I don't know why I fought so hard," Ellard whispered and tugged her against his chest. "I found it hard to believe my luck."

"Not luck. Design," Gweneth said.

"I love you too. I do."

"I know it," Gweneth said. "That part was never an issue."

"I want a proper mating."

Gweneth pulled away. "If we do that, there is no going back."

"I know. Do you love me enough to take a leap of faith?"

Gweneth stared at his plain face, his pretty green eyes, his ghostly arm, and the glint of the green jewels from his new ring. She thought of how she'd feel if something happened to Ellard, if he turned to another woman.

A feline growl escaped her and his eyes widened. "What?"

"Yes, but I'm warning you if I find you slipping and behaving as if—"

He blocked the rest of her words with a kiss. A soft kiss. A tender kiss. A kiss that said so much more than mere words. She wound her arms around his neck and leaned into his strength. Gradually, the kiss went from sweet to demanding, and his hands—both his hands skimmed down her back, pulling her even closer.

"Gweneth," he whispered.

She pulled away and briskly washed. "Ready to dry."

He followed suit and nodded. She hit the dry control. The dry cycle clicked off.

"I'm tired. I need a rest," she said.

"I find myself in need of a break too. My second-in-charge is capable of conducting the training this cycle." His gaze caressed her face and body and slid back to focus on her hair. A rash of goose bumps broke out on her skin—the good type that spelled excitement and eagerness for the coming cycle portions. "Could you take your hair down for me?"

"Of course." Naked, she padded to her sleep chamber, her fingers busily working through her braid and loosening the strands. She hadn't thought about her hair while she shifted. A fascinating process since her braid had remained intact. She'd bet makeup would stay in place too. A happy thing since she wanted to look her best, not only for Ellard but for herself. A snort emerged. Well, maybe she did put some stock in appearances after all. She tested the thought and nodded. It was more a fastidious cat thing to do with cleanliness and grooming.

Soft solar light poured through the windows, the storm-blue window screeners open to full. The faint scent of a floral perfume floated in the air—lavender with a hint of green herbs. Gweneth pulled back the pale blue covers of her gel-bed and slid into comfort. She could hear Ellard talking on his com in the main reception room. He finished and strode into her chamber to join her.

"I like your arm."

He glanced down and lifted his arm, then clenched his fingers into a fist. A sense of wonder etched into his expression. "I *love* my new arm."

"Can you feel textures in the same way you used to?"

He crossed the distance between him and her gel-bed. "May I?"

"Yes."

He rolled toward her and skimmed ghostly fingers over her cheek, down her neck, and came to rest on her breast. "I feel the softness of your skin, the beat of your heart, the fullness of your breast. I'd call that a big win." He pressed his mouth to her brow and pulled back to regard her with a serious mien. "I love you, Gweneth. I want you and our child more than anything. I know my behavior and my attitude haven't been the best, and I'm sorry I've hurt you."

"Ah, Ellard." Her feline stirred beneath her skin, the restless movement a reminder of her twin nature. "I have loved you for a long time. I watched you go about your job, trying to ignore me. I watched the way you trained your men and interacted with your brother, and every time, you claimed a bit more of my heart."

"I never thought I'd meet a woman who made me feel this way. A mate."

Happiness curled through Gweneth, warming her from the inside out. The corners of her mouth lifted, an outward expression of her mood. "Enough talk. Kiss me."

Their lips met with urgency, their bodies melting into each other. She explored his spectacular chest, his ridged abs and bulging pectorals, his flat stomach, the contrast of hard and smooth tantalizing and satisfying. Hers to fondle and pinch and stroke. When he went to flip her over onto her back, she resisted.

"No, let me go on top."

"Anything you want, kitten."

"Huh! I'll remind you of your words if we argue or have a loud discussion."

"Am I going to regret this?" The corners of his eyes crinkled, the amusement in him taking flight and gifting her with a sensual smile. Her toes curled.

"No." She settled herself on top, straddling his hips and grinning down at him. "I don't think so." She shifted toward his toes, her butt coming into contact with his erection. "I don't think either of us will regret this."

"You're beautiful, kitten."

"Thanks." She leaned closer to kiss him, and he sucked one nipple into his mouth. Heat and need roared through her as fast as a spaceship at full speed. She gasped at the sensations, at the ache that settled in her pussy, but was determined to take this at her pace. She traced her fingers over his cheekbones and brushed soft kisses to his eyelids. His eyes remained closed, and a smile curved his lips. Firm lips. Sensual lips. She traced them with the tip of one finger, and the curve deepened. Black hair framed his solid features. Taken separately, they were good features, but for some reason, they didn't combine with the perfection of his younger brother's. Gweneth pressed a kiss to the bridge of his broad nose. Some people might worry about their children inheriting his plain features. Not her. She would teach their children true values and be the loving parent she had lacked.

Now that she'd tested the idea, excitement expanded inside her. Ellard would make a great parent. He was patient and steady and loyal with a good heart. All excellent characteristics.

"You've stopped kissing me."

She glanced up to find him watching her, the curve still shaping his lips.

"You'll make a good father."

"I'm going to do my best."

The right words. She melted inside. "That is all I ever ask." She kissed him, a tender kiss and one she hoped would say everything that lay in her heart.

He lifted his hands to cup her face. "Please move a little faster. You're killing me here."

Velvet tension slid through her at his intent expression and the chill from his ghostly hand contrasted with the warmth from the other. Flaming stars, she wanted him. Raw need slid through her at the thought of sliding his cock inside her. His fingers trailed across her shoulders and slipped down her back to her hips.

"I missed you."

"I dreamed of you," he whispered, his breath hot against her ear. His hands kept stroking, stroking, stroking, hands never stopping in one place for long. Gweneth swallowed, her heart beating extra fast. The fingers of his ghostly hand slid between her legs—she knew because of the extra coolness of his touch. A quick punch of heat stole her breath as he delved between her legs. He hit a sweet spot, and she cried out, every nerve ending vibrating with the pleasure.

"Are you ready for me?"

"Always," she whispered.

She lifted and guided him to her entrance. Secs later, she pushed down without haste. His cock stretched her in a decadent manner, and she lifted a fraction, sinking back down with an easy glide. Gweneth experimented with the pace, with the angle, seeking the special spot that would detonate her senses.

"Touch yourself," Ellard said. "You know what to do."

He lifted his hands to cup her breasts, the contrast of warm and cold shooting pleasure through her.

Gweneth feathered her fingers over her clit and combined the caress with a slow up and down. An abrupt pinch of one nipple twisted sensation downward. The arrow of pain swelled and combined with the curl of heat in her pussy. A blissful agony, she thought.

"Do that again," she whispered as she rose and sank down on his cock. "Please."

He didn't. Not straight away. Instead, he teased her with words and actions.

"You are beautiful, Gweneth. I don't know what I've done to deserve you, but I won't fail you again." Tug. Caress. Tug. Tug. "I will love you and our kitten and make you both happy." Caress.

Gweneth trembled, his words as much as his actions driving her pleasure. She lifted and descended, going faster now as heat blossomed and settled at her clit.

Tug. Tug. Tug.

A whimper she couldn't contain filled the room and Ellard laughed, a joyous sound. The tug turned to a sharp pinch and sensual energy soared to life, burning her in a white-hot conflagration. Her orgasm consumed her, the walls of her sex pulsating for long moments. She sucked in lifeforce then leaned down to kiss him, a kiss designed to inflame with the same heat that filled her, to consume him.

He growled against her lips and rolled until she lay beneath him. Gweneth wrapped her arms around him and moved with him, with each thrust and retreat. He kept his gaze meshed with hers, his eyes smoldering with suppressed tension.

"I want to bite you."

She bared her neck.

"No, Gweneth. Not just a nibble. I want to create the mate bond."

"Yes," she murmured and moved with a speed she hadn't known herself capable of. Her teeth sank into his mating spot—the fleshy part where neck and shoulder met. They sank deep, and she tasted his blood in her mouth, yet it wasn't repugnant. He grunted, his hips jerking and driving his cock with short, erratic digs. Then, he shifted his head and bit her in return. A quick slice of pain followed by a roaring pleasure where everything in her world righted itself, bands of connection clicking into place. The heavy fog of desire lifted and splintered into incredible pleasure as she came for a second time. Ellard drove deep, withdrew and thrust.

He shouted out, his growl partially smothered by her shoulder. His cock jerked inside her, and she felt the wetness of his semen.

She lifted her head, instinct telling her to lick the wound clean. She did so with delicate licks and heard the contented purr of her feline echoing through her mind.

Ellard cleaned her shoulder with quick licks, and each lave of his textured tongue sent a shudder through her.

Ellard, she thought, drowning in the pleasure.

Yes, kitten?

Ellard?

He smiled. *I can hear you.*

"But not all the time. I know how to block," Gweneth said.

"I don't."

"Mogens taught me. He will help you, or I can tell you how to do it. Ry and Camryn have strict rules. They keep some things private."

"I can see the wisdom in that," Ellard said. "I might want to surprise you with a present."

Gweneth reached up to stroke his face. "I like presents."

"Are you pleased?"

"Very pleased," Gweneth said. "During my younger rotations I dreamed about a kind mate, one who loved me. One who would keep me secure yet give me freedom to express myself too. You are that man."

"Grata, kitten. You unman me. I can feel the connection. I know you mean every word you say."

"I love you, Ellard Tetsu, and you should never doubt this. Let's rest until this eve." A mischievous smile earned one from him in return as well as a nod of approval. "And this eve, we can join everyone for the blacklight meal. We can tell them the good news—that we're officially mates and are expecting a child."

"The perfect plan, kitten." Ellard separated their bodies and drew her against his chest with a purr of satisfaction. "I love you, and I've never been this happy."

"Good." A wealth of satisfaction filled her, and she remained silent for a time. Then an imp of mischief sprang to life and she couldn't resist. "We'll have lots of adventures together."

Ellard groaned and kissed her forehead, holding her secure in his embrace. "That, kitten, is what I'm afraid of."

"Just small adventures," she promised and halted his protest with a little wriggle and a passionate kiss. Best cycle ever, and she could hardly wait for the rest of their cycles together to unfold.

Thank you for reading **Hunted & Seduced**. If you enjoyed this book, I hope you'll consider leaving a review and joining my newsletter. The perks? You'll get previews of new stories and see my covers first. You'll also receive access to the many short stories and other goodies available only for newsletter subscribers. Sign up today! https://shelleymunro.com/newsletter/

What's next in the House of the Cat world? It's Christmastime, and Camryn is missing her family... Learn what happens next in **Festive & Seduced**. Turn the page to read an excerpt.

Excerpt – Festive & Seduced

"Ry Coppersmith is impossible." Camryn O'Sullivan, a former jockey from Earth, glowered at the retreating back of her feline shifter mate. His black hair, currently loose, lifted in the gentle breeze as he dodged locals shopping at the market stalls and socializing with friends in the cobblestone market square. She lowered her gaze to his perfect backside and watched until he disappeared under the archway into the honey-colored stone castle.

The castle, hereditary seat to the House of the Cat and home to the king of Viros, perched on top of the hill like a benevolent dragon guarding the residents of Viros, the only city on the planet of the same name. Buildings spilled down the terraced hillside until the city reached the protective walls below—a legacy of the on-again, off-again, currently off-war with the neighboring House of Cawdor, inhabitants on the planet of Gramite. Luxurious houses and the businesses to cater to them stood on the first terrace below the castle, the accommodation and stores becoming smaller and less illustrious with each successive and larger terrace. A central staircase leading from the bottom terrace, just near the city gates, allowed citizens and visitors access to the various streets and ended at the public square outside the castle.

"What's wrong?" Jannike asked, her frown fierce as she rubbed her swollen belly.

"Ry is driving me crazy with his overprotective careful-you-might-break-a-nail behavior." Camryn threw her hands up in a theatrical gesture, raising her gaze from the sea of dwellings and businesses, past the sliver of forest visible beyond the wall to the perfectly clear blue skies of Viros.

A snicker came from one of her friends and she whirled to nail them with an evil eye, but the culprit had turned poker-faced. She suspected Kaya—the only unmated one of her friends. Kaya's bright blue eyes, the exact color of her chin-length, straight blue hair, held explosive humor, and Camryn wanted to yank on her pointy ears in retaliation.

The truth—the blue-haired minx didn't know any better.

Camryn folded her arms across her chest in a silent dare for Kaya to laugh again. Just wait until Kaya found a mate. Camryn would make popcorn, sit back, and observe the show.

"It's not funny," Camryn said. "I can't leave the room without him panicking, and if one of the twins starts to cry, he loses every scrap of color. Quick, let's go to the refreshment shop on the corner of the square before he changes his mind about letting me go out for a few cycle marks."

A flymo zapped overhead, the snub-nose utility vehicle with its chubby, gray rounded body was popular with the locals for shifting cargo and people around the city. It darted around the square and landed out of sight somewhere on First Upper Street. The pilot knew better than to fly over the public no-fly area, currently full of the locals promenading under the shady trees. At night, those trees sparkled with tiny lights. More restaurants and market stalls sprang up and impromptu entertainers thrilled the evening spectators, bringing the square to vibrant life.

Camryn fell into step with Jannike Hondros, Kaya Ignatius, and Gweneth Swithin, all of whom arrived on the planet of Viros with Camryn and Ry on their ship, the *Indefatigable*. Somehow, the planet, inhabited by mainly black leopard shifters, had become home.

Jannike, a tall, statuesque blonde from the planet of Manx Two, had settled into her position as the mate of both the king of Viros, Lynx Leandros, and his best friend, Shiloh Tetsu. Gweneth, a half-feline with long, straight black hair and laughing green eyes, had found a mate in Shiloh's older brother, Ellard. And Kaya...well, according to Kaya, she kept busy conducting mate auditions. Her mantra—fun, fun, fun with a side of hot sex.

Kaya held open the door, and they filed into the cool and rustic depths of an estaminet—a small cafe to any Earthling. The Royal didn't attract the wealthy since the owner subscribed to the plain furnishings and no-frills school. Instead, he placed his energies into the food and beverage part of his business. A winning combination. Most feline ladies didn't patronize this estaminet, preferring the one farther along the square with outdoor dining. A place they could see and be seen.

Camryn and her friends enjoyed this one because the other customers didn't point and gossip. Here, they could have relative privacy and be themselves instead of the mates of important felines.

"You complain about Ry." Jannike rubbed her swollen belly and sank onto a straight-back chair with a groan. "Try being the queen of Viros with two mates, then you might have something to whine about. Lynx and Shiloh insist on me having a security guard."

Camryn gave her a royal salute, one finger extended with no

regard to Jannike's royal status. "I'm still shocked Ry let me leave the castle for refreshments. He's hovered like a bad mood since the twins' birth." And something else was going on with Ry. Not that she intended to confess their lack of bedroom rumbles to her friends...

Purchase Festive & Seduced today
https://shelleymunro.com/books/festive-seduced/

About Shelley

USA Today bestselling author Shelley Munro lives in Auckland, the City of Sails, with her husband and a cheeky Jack Russell/mystery breed dog.

Typical New Zealanders, Shelley and her husband left home for their big OE soon after they married (translation of New Zealand speak - big overseas experience). A twelve-month-long adventure lengthened to six years of roaming the world. Enduring memories include being almost sat on by a mountain gorilla in Rwanda, lazing on white sandy beaches in India, whale watching in Alaska, searching for leprechauns in Ireland, and dealing with ghosts in an English pub.

While travel is still a big attraction, these days Shelley is most likely found in front of her computer following another love - that of writing stories of contemporary and paranormal romance and adventure. Other interests include watching rugby (strictly for research purposes), cycling, playing croquet and the ukelele, and curling up with an enjoyable book.

Visit Shelley at her Website
https://shelleymunro.com

Join Shelley's Newsletter
https://shelleymunro.com/newsletter

ALSO BY SHELLEY

Middlemarch Shifters
My Scarlet Woman
My Younger Lover
My Peeping Tom
My Assassin
My Estranged Lover
My Feline Protector
My Determined Suitor
My Cat Burglar
My Stray Cat
My Second Chance
My Plan B
My Cat Nap
My Romantic Tangle
My Blue Lady
My Twin Trouble
My Precious Gift
My Grumpy Wolf

Middlemarch Gathering
My Highland Mate
My Highland Fling
My Elusive Mate
My Valiant Princess
My Highland Wedding
My Highland Billionaire

House of the Cat
Captured & Seduced
Claimed & Seduced
Merry & Seduced
Stranded & Seduced
Seized & Seduced
Hunted & Seduced
Festive & Seduced
Betrayed & Seduced
Enticed & Seduced

Dragon Investigators
Blue Moon Dragon
Blood Moon Dragon
Black Moon Dragon
Snow Moon Dragon

Dragon Isles
Liza
Cherry
Rena
Sasha

.